Homeward I Lurched

a Gay Zombie confessional

Jim Couper (with notes from Mortimer Smithers)

)kedits@hotmail.com

opyright 2018 Jim Couper, all rights reserved

Dedicated

to Florence and Archie Couper who passed on the love of good grammar, good diction and good fiction.

Acknowledgements

Bulent Hasan for cover art

My wife Lian for reading, editing and proofing something that is as far from her field of interest as an aardvark is from zydeco.

Dylan Couper for making good plot suggestions and technical improvements.

Sara Couper for keeping authors humble.

Rosalie and Tone Neville for unconditional support.

The people of White Rock, a Canadian town, for involuntarily giving literary license to distort their community for the sake of better fiction.

No animals were hurt in the writing of this book.

Any resemblance of living or dead people to the characters in the novel is just weird.

Rated R18. Those under the age of 18 may not purchase this book unless accompanied by an adult: contains coarse language, extreme violence and brief nudity.

Neither a chemical spill nor a mishap at a nuclear plant started it. Neither did global warming, a meteor shower, an ancient curse, a pact with the devil or a research experiment gone wrong. Doctors, geneticists, military scientists and even lawyers were innocent.

1

    I was born for the second time on a sinister autumn night. Through a mass of knotted fishing line, rotted seaweed and decayed fish I slid into life. My head pushed through salty liquid and I slid to a soft landing on foam-covered kelp. It was peaceful, my birth: no screaming, no doctors, no commotion.

    I stood, and that surprised me. Standing should have been many months away for a newborn. Then I took a first step. Looking down I saw a pair of feet that shouldn't have been so far away. Instead of appearing chubby and naked, a pair of hiking boots covered them. My pink socks needed washing. On unsteady legs I took cautious steps in the broken moonlight. Slippery rocks caused me to fall and hit my head. The pain was no more than if I had stubbed my toe on a heavy pillow. That didn't make sense. Walking didn't make sense.

    Through a fog-mire of mental mud I searched like a baby groping for a lost toy and could find neither memory nor recognition. I didn't know my name, where I lived or where I came from. Tears of frustration tried to well up in my eyes: I wanted to scream at the moon.

    "Mmmmmmmmm," was all that came from my tight lips as I tried to spit out my name. Maybe it was too soon to start talking. I needed to be cuddled in loving arms and fed mother's milk.

    "Mmmmammth
    "Mmmnamith
    "Mynamith
    "My namith
    "My name ith ..."

Like static from a broken radio, my mumbled words reached my own ears and I searched to see who had spoken. Rocks, water and two large wet feet that seemed to belong to me produced no sounds. A mob of humming mosquitoes sampled me then flew away.

No name rested near the tip of my tongue. Concentrating created a chainsaw headache, but I needed to know who I was.

"My name ith Mithter …" Nothing came to complete the sentence.

"My name ith Mithter Rogers." The rumble started inside and as words slurred from my mouth I knew I had spoken falsely: they lacked the familiar ring one's name should bring.

"My name ith Mithter Smith."

"My name ith Missus Smith." I hissed like a snake.

A downward glance for sexual recognition found tattered, dripping pants that gave no clue. Protruding breasts did not block the view of stumbling feet enclosed in soggy hiking boots. My putrid rags looked like the attire of a mister. Peeing while standing made sense although I felt no urge.

Like bloated fish floating up from the depths of a polluted pond new names surfaced.

"My name ith Mal … Milth … Mark … Mick … Morth." The last rang with familiarity and I latched onto it.

"My name ith Morth."

I expanded. "My name ith Morthimer." The words clanged painfully as if my head were the clapper in a cheap church bell from which rust fell. Knowing my name brought a little relief, but no explanation for why I was standing on a wet seashore, in the dark, with no idea of who *Morthimer* was or where he lived.

Roiling seas had pushed me, like flotsam from a distant disaster, into a rocky crevice. Why? Why was I swimming at night with my boots on? Where was my mother?

An array of distant lights called to me, but walking towards them proved difficult. One foot landed atop the other, rather than beside, causing trips. No pain resulted when head, hands and chest whacked rocks. I rose, trundled on and falls diminished to embarrassing stumbles.

An image of a woman and two children flashed subliminally. It felt important. My mother and siblings? No. Could I, just born, have a wife and family? So soon? A handsome man stood behind them. Was it my brother?

I had to get home to my children.

Lights grew nearer and their intensity increased as I bumbled forward. More hurt throbbed inside my head. The pain did not prevent me from skimming the surface of thought and trying to remember where I came from, why I had this strange numb life and how long it would last. I felt like death warmed over.

Plodding along a dark suburban lane, with neither destination nor purpose, a feeling of eerie familiarity swept over me: déjà vu rested on the tip of my tongue. I had visited the convenience store on the corner. If I walked through the closed door I could locate newspapers, candy bars, lifesavers and yes, cigarettes. What a joy to stagger in, buy a pack of smokes, light up and savour the delicious aroma. But the clerk wouldn't understand my thick-tongued talk. Instead of a pack of cigarettes she would hand me a bag of briquettes. I might be too young to smoke?

My hands looked thick, puffy and mottled with some sort of disease. I rubbed them through the top of my head and they found thick knotted hair that seemed to grow without rhyme or reason. The smooth round bean of a baby wasn't there.

Putting a rock through the window and helping myself seemed necessary. Hair gel, talcum and skin care products would be a good start in getting rid of the unkempt looks that resulted from my immersion in salt water. Deodorant was likely a need and maybe insecticide would ward off worrisome wet worms that dropped from beneath my cuffs onto my feet.

I picked up a chunk of granite, fondled it and dropped it. The last thing I needed was a criminal record. What I needed was to go home. Where did I live? If the images of a woman and children were real I would find them if I had to lurch down every street.

I started my quest and within a few blocks a restored car, a Mustang I had seen before, sat in a drive and surely the house next door with the crooked garage and weedy lawn had been my home. I wanted to rush to the front door and ring the bell, but thought better of it. Thinking was good. I had made a decision and decision-making was good. Things were looking up.

Like an expectant father I paced back and forth and then decided I would walk around the block and prepare my approach to the woman and children who lived within. Would a warm hug be appropriate or should I say, "Sorry to disturb you. I was in the neighborhood…"

An elderly woman neared me as she hobbled along the sidewalk and interrupted my thoughts.

2

Mort's awakening on the Pacific shore and similar risings in the nearby cemetery were so unprecedented, isolated and convoluted that few experts grasped what had gone on or why it happened.

A meteor shower coincided with one of the biggest sun flares of the century causing Samsung phones to dial randomly and idling BMWs to suddenly reverse. If someone was stowing golf clubs in the trunk and the driver didn't call *fore,* broken bones resulted. Sanyo blow dryers set hair on fire and high-end toasters sent flaming bread across the kitchen. Had the owners of such devices known what was to come they would not have irately called customer help lines. Those who dwelled in basement suites felt a surge of energy, which was a good thing because their cement walls turned powdery and to keep them from caving in they had to work ceaselessly.

These minor mishaps had only the slightest connection to the dead being given a second life as, for the vast majority on planet Earth, Thursday, October 4, 2018 passed uneventfully. No green Martians landed in Topeka, Godzilla did not attack Tokyo and Toronto's air did not become toxic.

Those who suffered most made their home in White Rock, a hamlet on the Pacific shore in the south of the province of British Columbia, in western Canada, just a few miles north of Washington State, U.S.A.

Mountainous topography, uranium deposits, salt water ponds and the aforementioned phenomena combined with lightning strikes to form unique conditions that magnified radio waves created in space by the unique alignment of planets, moon and sun.

The International Radio Astrophysical Observatory, where giant antennae collected radio waves emitted by stars, put the final nail in the coffin that caused the dead to live and the alive to die. The enormous disc antennae, secreted in mountains not far from White Rock, can detect a phone ringing on Mars, it is claimed. Having the capacity to collect radio waves also creates the hitherto unknown capacity to redirect those waves, in the form of electromagnetic radiation, into the earth.

These phenomenal waves, between visible light and X-rays in length, surged into the soil, found a fault and followed it. Some trees lost leaves, mice became hyperactive and crows fell from perches on wires. When the waves hit the buried dead stranger things happened.

Save for a woman who had been hit on the head by a golf ball, declared dead and recovered, no one in White Rock had any experience with afterlife. Of all the fears a person walking in the dark might have, getting a liver ripped out by a ragged creature of the night and getting whacked by a golf ball, resided at the bottom of the list, just ahead of getting crushed by a safe falling from a window.

3

The elderly lady walking with a cane saw me staggering towards her and bolted to the other side of the street. I lurched over to her sidewalk. A shot of recognition hit like a baseball bat: it was Auntie Mary and I knew her as the nasty woman who used to babysit me. She spanked my bare bottom if I misbehaved. She did it when I was too old to be spanked, but somehow, as a teen, I liked it.

"Dreary me," she mumbled when we were feet apart, "What do you want?" She appeared not to know me. I had grown up, but had not cleaned up. My odor may have confused her: it suggested I had vomited on myself on a hot afternoon while losing control of bowels and bladder. She forgot her question and so did I.

I reached out to Auntie Mary. She turned her back to me and shuffled away. I lurched after her. She wasn't fast. Neither was I. Her lame legs, plus the cane, made it a close race. Her hobbling feet matched my constant, slow, lurch. The sound of her staccato cane thumping hard on the sidewalk kept time.

I could hear air sucking into Mary's rusty lungs as the gap between us dwindled. My hand landed atop her shoulder and spun her. Auntie Mary rapped her cane sharply between my legs and whacked what dangled there. I couldn't understand her aggression. No danger lurked for a woman walking alone at night in my quiet town.

"Numbnuts!" she shouted and whacked me a second time. My steely left hand clamped her in place while my right tore away her white-haired scalp. She thrust her cane into my torso and it sank mushily. A malodorous blast hissed outward, then I pushed her to the sidewalk and fell atop.

"No dirty business." Mary screamed as she squeezed her knees together with a determination that could crush coconuts. My teeth slid across her cranium, but her heavy skull protected the most vital part of her anatomy the way the proverbial walnut shell protects its meat.

Without taking a moment to appreciate the guardianship of her brain, Mary commenced an hysterical scream that lasted but a single syllable. A rock ended it. Her aged cranium cracked and I tore off shards of bone from which sprouted tightly-curled, blue-tinged hair that matched brain color. I slurped up the warm pudding that held her memories, her relationships and the strategies that won her card games.

Leaving her cranium as clean as a soup bowl in a charity kitchen my fingers moved lower. I couldn't stop myself and didn't want to. Without thought I dug out dripping spleen, bleeding liver, quivering kidneys and a bubbling bladder that sprayed the other organs with a delicious vinaigrette. I devoured all.

The fabulous feast produced an oral orgasm: my dangling uvula, previously rigid in delight, sagged in satisfaction.

Sated and energized I shambled along chewing the ragged end of Mary's intestine: her body dragged behind. A block later, gnawing rubbery duodenum and squeezing brown effluent into my mouth like toothpaste, I tired of pulling the carcass. It amplified my guilt. I swung intestine and attached body like an athlete throwing the hammer. I forgot to let go and Mary rebounded like a bungee, spilling fluids onto my shoulders and soiling me.

I wanted to say "Sorry Auntie Mary" and tell her I didn't know what had come over me, but in the middle of my ecstasy clear thought was impossible. Now it was too late, she couldn't hear. Auntie Mary went over a hedge and rolled to the back steps of a hillside home.

Slowly I slogged back to my shoreline birthplace and wedged myself among rocks. Cold air, jagged edges, wet clothes and worries about my new lease on life did not keep me awake: I didn't know sleep. Waves splashed my boots, flies buzzed and I thought about the meal that forced my stomach to protrude. Guilt should have forced me to roll into the ocean and drown myself, but I was doing what came naturally. Someone once advised, *be true to yourself.*

"My name ith Morthimer," I said proudly.

An image of a woman and two children again sped through my brain. I had to go home.

The word *brains* barged into my head and I spewed it out, again and again: I didn't know why I did that. I felt stupid with my limited vocabulary.

I abandoned the shoreline and instead of returning home I instinctively shuffled to the local cemetery. From between my teeth, I dislodged bits of the woman who had spanked me. I tried to understand what I had done. It was incomprehensible. Thoughts came with great difficulty. Guilt didn't come at all.

From a distance I saw a raven-haired woman, dressed in black, hover over the body of Auntie Mary at the bottom of a hill. She bared long white teeth and bent to the body I had dined on.

4

On Friday morning, just before the sun fully pushed itself above the horizon, Jack Weston confidently walked outdoors, as he did every weekday morning, to drive to his job at a supermarket, a 10-minute walk distant. His ankle twisted and his head bumped a couple of times as he slid on a slope in his yard. Neither frost nor snow would cause him to lose his footing in late summer and his kids had been whacked on the head often enough that never again would they leave a ball or toy on the steps or in the yard.

In his rapid descent down the incline something dampened his back and caused him to drop like he was on a slide. At the bottom he carefully got up, looked back and thought coyotes had dragged the body of a deer into his yard. But why would a deer wear a pink dress? Beneath grey and red matted hair he recognized a human face.

Weston called 911.

The initialism RCMP represents Royal Canadian Mounted Police, commonly called The Mounties or the cops. Despite the force's horse-riding heritage Corporal Jesse Nesterinko arrived at the crime scene on the passenger seat of a blue and white police cruiser. His senior partner, Sergeant Jane Dougherty, who, much to her dislike, was called either Jane Dough or Plain Jane, handled the wheel and enjoyed control.

An emergency call to their community police office had them arrive with lights flashing and siren shrieking because the panicked caller shouted about a mutilated body and a murder. Decades had passed since a citizen of sleepy White Rock had been counted as a homicide. Jane

Dougherty found satisfaction in continuing that admirable record under her watch.

Jack Weston led sergeant and corporal around the side of his house and pointed to bloody legs, arms, some pink cloth and a bit of a face atop a thin neck. A length of intestine dangled across the grass from the torso. They didn't call an ambulance: a body beyond repair was not hard to recognize.

Sgt. Dougherty phoned for a crime scene photographer, a forensic specialist and a coroner. With yellow police tape streaming from her hand she brushed past her pale partner who leaned against a fence and struggled not to part with his morning meal.

Another call went to the chief of police in the bigger city of Surrey. She phoned a conservation officer with extensive knowledge of wild animals and he started pedaling over on his single-speed sidewalk cruiser – a strange bike for a hillside town. On arrival he asserted that coyotes didn't break open the skull and neither did a cougar. He theorized the victim had fallen off a building or a cliff, shattered her skull and a passing female bear chewed out her brain and abdomen and then dragged her to the back steps of the suburban home.

Through house to house questioning Sgt. Dougherty learned the victim was Mary Cotsworth, a senior citizen, who had been at a bridge party and was not in the habit of falling from buildings or walking on cliffs.

The sergeant traced splashes of blood uphill to what appeared to be the scene of the murder. The walkway bled with red. Small bits of fat and gristle lay about although some of Mary had undoubtedly gone to a bulldog that rested on a porch licking its numerous jowls.

It could be little but murder, thought Dougherty: a murder so odious only a psychopath from a mental hospital could have committed it. She followed bloody footprints until the last faint impression vanished and then she phoned for tracking dogs.

At her office Sergeant Jane did a database search and Corporal Jesse made phone calls. No psychopaths had escaped from mental hospitals or prisons. The duo returned to the crime scene and met a man with a pair of sniffing, snarling canines. The bloodhounds took long whiffs of entrails, orts and bloodstains and one lurched in the direction the footprints led and the other strained the leash in the opposite direction. The handler followed one yelping dog and then the other, but ultimately each circled back to where they had started, snarled at each other then bit the hand that led them.

While police constables searched underbrush and back yards Jane and Jesse knocked on more doors. Not a single person had heard screams, shrieks, howls or outcries of any sort. Did Mary know the killer and not fear him? Did he attack from behind? The trail went icy cold: no clues, no motives, no logic. Sore losers at cards made statements about how Mary played bridge, but none seemed capable of killing her over $1.75 in questionable gains. She had no enemies, didn't deal drugs and didn't belong to a motorcycle gang. Her estate didn't amount to enough to cause anyone to look forward to her death.

Three crime scene specialists arrived in early evening and two hours after taking samples of body parts they reached an inconclusive consensus about what didn't kill Mary. To Jane their leader said, "Never seen anything like this. Looks like an animal, maybe a cougar ... haven't seen cougar this year. Not near here. No feline bites, no scratches. Might be a bear, maybe a crazed grizzly. No grizzlies seen here. No claw marks. Not coyotes or wolves. Some kind of mad animal maybe, but not sure what. Doesn't look human caused."

After the CSI trio departed they faxed Jane a brief report.

"It's all shit," she told her corporal. "They speculate that everything from racoons to the abominable snowman might have done it."

"A snowman with a big belly in October?" Jesse questioned.

"Abominable, like an abomination, nothing to do with bellies."

"Yea, I was kidding. As if a big snowman came out of the woods, tore an old lady apart and then melted."

"Report says a similar case happened two years ago near Kamloops and people saw Bigfoot running from the body."

"Wouldn't it have to hop?"

Jane started laughing then caught herself. This was serious business. She had worked with Jesse for more than a year and still he caught her off-guard. Often she wondered if she was laughing at his intended joke or his stupidity.

She had only two years on the handsome underling and worked in the same office: remaining aloof had challenges. While he bounced from one woman to the next Jane stayed home, tended her garden and put in volunteer hours warning high school kids about drugs, sex and driving. She had extensive experience in one of the three. Fortunately the students enquired about her adventures behind the wheel and showed no interest in whether she took illegal drugs or practiced safe sex.

Jesse summed up. "So we got a snowman with a big belly and a big foot that rips an old lady apart and then hops away with some of her body parts and melts."

"It's not a snowman. Natives called it Sasquatch. In Nepal it's yeti, a big, hairy, secretive cryptid that survives in the wild. Most people think it's a myth, but every once in a while someone catches a glimpse of one. The sightings come from reliable, serious people, but no one ever gets a photo – just a footprint or a tuft of white fur. Sort of like glimpses of the Loch Ness monster or Ogopogo. Some think this yeti creature descends from *gigantopithecus*. I looked that up."

"It stands to reason a big abdominal snowman would take a gigantic piss-icus."

"So that's where we stand," summarized Sgt. Jane, again declining to smile. "One of the most violent murders in British Columbia and the only suspect is Bigfoot. This is the first murder in this town since the days of gold miners and gunslingers. It's on our watch and we have to solve it."

"I don't get how the report can dare to suggest Hopalong the snowman did it?"

"Just gives measurements and analysis that add up to nothing. Just mentions Bigfoot. Mrs. Cotsworth was dead when she hit the yard. They found human hair on her cane and her body. Man's hair, hair that hadn't grown for a couple of months. From someone about age 30. She had no men in her life. The ones at the bridge party were all over 60. Her purse was found in shrubbery with nothing missing so it wasn't robbery. Wasn't rape. Scratches on her body match human fingernails. Animals have claws. Sasquatch would have fingernails, I guess."

"I'd go with the monster theory," the corporal said. "No person here or anywhere around here is gonna do that. So we have to track down this big foot creature."

"Feet weren't that big. The bloody prints are bigger than average, but not enormous. Wore an outdoor boot. Being tested for make and who sells them."

"Is Hannibal Lecher still in jail?"

Relentlessly Jane knocked on doors, searched yards, measured distances and examined video from surveillance cameras aimed at parks in which nothing untoward happened. She felt guilty her force had not protected Mary.

5

At first suggestion of dawn's early light, Ramon Reynolds, proud proprietor of a profitable White Rock hair parlor, whistled a happy tune as he loped across the dewy grass of the town's hilltop cemetery. He appreciated the view of a snaking river that slithered out of the broad delta below. A path that his hiking shoes had helped trample meandered between tombstones and served as a shortcut to his father's house.

The eerie silence and isolated setting sometimes caused him to imagine weak voices calling out from below and beyond, but to save 10 minutes he endured the fertility of his imagination. With the first bite of breakfast at his father's table he would laugh at his superstitions and enjoy the best of times as he amazed his dad with details of his hairdressing business and how clients lined up to sit in his chairs.

A tune from The Sound of Music … The Hills are Alive … whistled between his dry lips as he thought about the hot Colombian brew that waited. His feet met the ground in the usual manner as he passed tombstones, but unexpectedly the hairdresser's right leg plunged downward and his whistling suddenly sounded like an asthmatic Scotsman inflating a tattered bagpipe. Ramon Reynolds scrambled to get his leg out of the knee-deep hole but more ground collapsed beneath him. His ankle couldn't break free.

The thin hair stylist expected to see his foot wedged between rocks, but instead a fear worse than brain cancer became reality as, in the dim morning, five pale snaky fingers wound around his tarsus and a bony head broke through loose dirt. Its rotting jaw, dripping maggots, lunged forward and crooked teeth sank into his leg. A stench of foul putrescence followed. He looked forward to waking from his nightmare.

Reality hit with pain and panic. He writhed, screamed, squirmed and his adrenaline-infused muscles ripped his bleeding leg from the steely grip. With hands atop the hole into which he had fallen Ramon hoisted himself to freedom and fresh, fragrant air. The hand grabbed his shoe and he regretted his obsession with tying laces neatly and tightly. It pulled him back into the black to shoulder depth.

In different circumstances, with time for contemplation, Ramon might have used his mental dexterity to imagine the predator's teeth whitened, clumps of missing hair replaced, sallow eyes brightened and blush applied to rotted skin. Had he done so he would have recognized the living corpse as a dead ringer for his childhood sweetheart Barbra O'Day. Two years ago he wore a black suit and watched her descend into the earth. With wet eyes he had thought about how his skinny schoolmate had taken steroids, bulked up, strutted a stage and became Miss Abfest at Crabfest. Were it not for a burst aneurism she would have moved on to the regional finals.

Even if he said, "Hi Barb, remember me; we took French in Madame Lapage's class," the monster would not have backed off.

Ramon groped for a rock, branch, shard of tombstone – any weapon with which to knock the teeth out of Barbra's stinking face. Sand, dirt and grass filtered through desperate fingers. A flurry of one-legged kicks and jabs at the miserable visage did nothing to discourage the thing that chewed on his leg like it was a kabob.

Prime pieces of lower limb vanished into the mealy, ravenous mouth and his blood dribbled down her weak chin. Loss of blood would bring death, Ramon realized as a gusher erupted from his calf. He whipped out his belt and applied it as a tourniquet just below the knee where the creature noshed. The belt stopped the eruption of blood and although he felt lightheaded Ramon knew that death no longer lingered at his doorstep: he had a chance. He grabbed dirt by the handfuls and threw them down on Barbra. Clumps of sod, loose gravel and anything he could grasp, including wilted flowers in a plastic pot, hit the reeking head.

Ramon used his good leg to gain leverage and push himself upwards. Head and shoulders of the ghoul lunged like a striking cobra and Reynolds jerked the limb back.

Like a dog obsessed with a bone the monster went back at the captive leg and her next bite, higher up, included a bit of the belt. Loss of his tourniquet equalled the loss of life so, with a gush of red, he slid it to a new position above his knee. The foul thing attacked the knee, pulling loose skin and baring the patella.

Kicks and punches had no effect and the tug-o-war with the leg was a dead heat: Reynolds retained bone and the monster got meat. He battled more furiously than one would expect from a pale, middle-age hairdresser whose only strength resided in fingers and arms that clipped and styled all day.

The monster rose, head almost above ground, and in a single bite, through denim jeans, removed Reynolds' underused reproductive organs. A horrendous high-pitched scream, sufficient to wake the dead, followed. The monster swallowed.

Geysers of sweat soaked Ramon's shirt and he vomited before seeing bright lights. Aware of his impending state of shock, the hairdresser steadied himself and countered by thrusting forward and pushing his thumbs into the soggy eye sockets of his assailant. He smelled sun-baked road-kill as yellow eye-snot filled his palms. No sounds of protest came from the beast: it did not beg for mercy.

Both parties pulled back as if to re-evaluate their battle plans. Ramon's hand found what it had been grasping for – a rock, smaller than he wanted, barely palm sized. It crashed against the vile skull and nothing happened. He did it again and thick black fluid dribbled from Barbra's cracked skull. Her mouth still bit randomly. On the last hit the sandstone rock crumbled, but the head snapped sideways on its pustular neck and the thing toppled backwards into its grave.

The joy of survival diminished as Ramon contemplated hobbling around his hair salon on one leg and never being able to give pleasure to a bedmate. His elbows found purchase on the surface.

A leg in a pond of piranha would have had more substance than his: he didn't know if it would support him. The cockeyed head ended his contemplation as its teeth removed toes from the dangling foot of his good leg. Undeterred, Ramon reached farther, found a weightier rock and pounded the hands that pushed against dirt to rise out of the grave. The crack of breaking fingers inspired him: both left and right became useless pancakes. He scrambled from the grave and rolled to safety.

Blood fled from his foot so he ripped the lace from the shoe with the missing toe and tied it around his ankle. Then he yanked off his Grateful Dead T-shirt and stuffed it into the gaping red hole in the crotch of his pants.

Crawling commando-style, Ramon scrabbled towards a steep slope, praying he could get to the road that wound along the bottom of the hillside before death made its call. At the top of an embankment consciousness vanished. His last effort of supreme will was to push himself down the hill. On the descent his head hit a rock, knocking out his front teeth and breaking his nose. Unconsciousness spared him pain. He came to rest on the pavement of a quiet road.

An ambulance, speeding to hospital with a woman about to give birth, saw him, braked and skidded towards his head. The deep tread of new radials clung to the dewy pavement and halted the heavy vehicle before it crushed Ramon's skull. The front right tire slid onto his arm and broke bones. The driver backed up, crushed fingers and loaded Ramon into the back.

6

The raven-haired woman in the dark business suit who had stooped to sample blood from Mary's corpse sat down for dinner soon after at one of White Rock's upscale restaurants. As the waiter presented the wine list she retched a reeking concoction of yoghurt, cabbage and coagulated blood onto the floor. Patrons lost their appetites as a stench worse than an August outhouse overwhelmed their crab cakes, coffee and croissants.

The woman, who had used Mary to top up a diminishing blood supply, as often she did from fresh bodies, didn't know what had come over her, but suspected Mary had passed her best-before date. The taste had been a little off and Mary looked far worse than the usual car crash cadavers and heart attack victims.

A symbiotic relationship between two tribes of the dark had enormous potential, but dissolved because bodies that had their brains and innards eaten left little of the running red for vamps. What remained was somewhat off and follow-up vamps sucked choking red dust into their mouths.

On the other hand, organ-eaters found that guts that had been drained of blood did not have the same appeal as pre-vampire organs. Dry innards, after the long-tooths had helped themselves, smacked zombie gullets like mouldy peanut butter without lubrication from jam or milk. Body parts bunched in the maw and initiated coughing spasms that caused revenants to projectile vomit parts of their own bodies.

A food co-op did not blossom.

7

For hours, in the dark, I lurched along suburban streets until, before me again, like a church with a saintly aura, stood the house I knew and loved. The bright blue trim I had painted myself and the single-car garage with a slight lean could not be confused with any other. The weedy lawn needed cut and an old refrigerator decorated the porch. That wasn't the way I left it. In the drive sat a white Dodge Caravan with no wheels ... I used to drive it to school. I taught grades five and six. I specialized in math. I could count past 10 and knew algebra and geometry. *The square of a right angle rectum equals the radius of a pie.*

Schoolchildren loved me and I loved them. After class I coached soccer and on weekends I took the team to matches against other schools and once we won. Sometimes other teachers said I shouldn't be alone with children. For some reason they didn't like me. Specially the gym teacher.

My wife came to a few of the games. She had a name ... Melon or Melanoma. And I had kids and knew their names: little Calculus who moved to music and might dance on a stage someday. And Abacus, who dreamed of being a co-pilot.

Perhaps I could get a peek, just one glimpse of my cherished family before stumbling off to a destiny I didn't know. I was dressed in sopping, blood stained rags and couldn't just knock on the door and expect an invitation to step in. Tight drapes prevented peeping through the front window. As I stumbled to another window the front door opened and little Abacus ran out. Behind him a lilting voice sang, "Get back inside you little shit."

The lad, upon seeing me, stopped dead in his tracks. "It's Daddy! Daddy's home." He sprinted forward and hugged my leg. "Daddy smells like a big fart."

In an excited voice he asked, "Where have you been? What did you bring me?" My son tugged my pant leg and pulled me towards the door. I wanted to sob with joy at being reunited with loved ones, but tears did not come. I wanted to hoist Abacus in the air, hug him and never let him go but a piece of grey skin slid from under my sleeve and fell atop a dandelion. The hug could wait.

Abacus pulled me to the door. A woman, my wife, lit from behind with a halo of luminescence, stood motionless on the stoop: an apparition too beautiful for eyes. "Mort?" she whispered.

I nodded: that was my name. She grabbed the railing for support, "I gotta sit down." She backed into the house.

Without invitation I followed and saw beautiful Calculus crawling across the living room's deep shag carpet towards me. She climbed onto my foot and played with a worm. I looked at my laughing daughter and thought about dinner. I wanted to slap some sense into my head, but feared for my waterlogged ears.

My wife's name, musical, Metallica, Meatloaf...Melody. She had fainted into a plush chair. Slowly she raised her head and stared, bright-eyed, "Oh my god Mort. You don't look good. Have you been to hospital? I don't feel good."

Melody started to sway onto the arm of the chair, but was startled by the opening of the bedroom door from which a large tattooed man in a bath-robe emerged. "Who the hell are you?" he demanded as he stared me down.

Abacus gleefully supplied introductions, "That's my Daddy. This is new Uncle Albert."

I said nothing, realizing they wouldn't understand. A thick sticky substance formed behind my lips. I wanted to spit, but only dribbled.

"You look and smell like shit," said the man in the robe. He looked angry. "Why the hell don't you get back to where you come from? You look like them zomboid fag things on TV. There's gotta be a reward." With that Uncle Albert landed a roundhouse right on my chin and knocked off some lower lip. The flesh, along with purple dribble, flew across the room, hit the window and dropped next to a marmalade cat that scooted away.

The blow didn't hurt. Pain had departed. A second blow hit my stomach and Uncle Albert looked at his fist cloaked in cobweb mucus: it dripped maggots. I had concerns the blow might handicap my ability to retain a meal.

Albert reared back for another punch, but I grabbed his arm and bit off his thumb. Like a girly pig he squealed and turned to the fireplace with eyes on a brass poker. Unsure of what to do with the thumb in my mouth, I swallowed. The taste didn't make me want more thumb, but I wanted more something. I jumped onto his back and tore into his neck. Before Albert could say *uncle* I knocked him to the floor, flipped him over and used my hard nails to un-zip his stomach. A pancreas, or something like it, came out and slid into my mouth. While Albert squirmed and cried like a child I went euphoric.

With strength that surprised me I pinned him and dug for liver. Albert grabbed a decorative copper plate with Elvis engraved on it and pushed it protectively over his abdomen. I did not want to taste *The King* so shoved the plate up and over Albert's face and devoured his large liver. It had been pickled by alcohol and its flavor went beyond anything I could have imagined.

I pried the poker from Uncle Albert's oversize fingers and used it to open his oversize head. As I slurped up irresistible dessert, tremors of pleasure rolled through my body like storms of ocean waves and then there was calm. Melody had given me such pleasure a few times, but never had it lasted so long.

"No dessert until you finish your dinner." I could hear my long-gone mother's warning. I had disobeyed her rule by cracking the cranium and digging in. I returned to the torso's cornucopia of organs. Another old rule: *Don't bite off more than you can chew*. I wondered what kind of bowel movement I would have?

My children were silent. Then Abacus announced, "Daddy ate Uncle Albert."

I got the courage to speak and suggested, "Ssssigarette." It sounded like my mouth was stuffed with tobacco, but Melody, the wide-eyed wife of my life, understood. She weakly raised a thin finger and pointed to a side table. From between two dirty beer mugs I picked up an open pack alongside my favorite lighter. I remembered smoking was not allowed in the house.

As best I could, with little remaining in the way of a lower lip, I kissed Melody on her pale cheek. Albert's enzymes overflowed and dribbled down her neck and onto the little breasts I fondly remembered fondling. She looked stunned.

Seeking the outside door so I could go out and light up, I wandered into the bedroom, saw a closet of fresh clothes and knew a change was required. My filthy, frayed shirt, thick with blood, thumped to the floor. Shoes and pants followed then I caught a sideways glimpse of a figure coming at me. From a dark corner a horrid, filthy personification of evil sprang forward. I raised my arms in defence: the ogre raised its arms to attack. I backed away, tripped over my pants and fell behind the bed. The attacker vanished.

Oh my god, what has become of me, I thought as I stared at the mirrored doors where the attack originated. I wondered how my thin, frail limbs had the strength to best Uncle Albert. The face that stared back could have belonged to a moth-eaten doll. Between my legs hung a purple, puffy legume and a black sac that undoubtedly housed pathetic peas.

Downcast eyes fell to toenails and then moved to fingernails that seemed longer than normal. I had heard they keep growing after death. All the better to open organs. Hair supposedly kept growing too, but my light brown topping looked no longer than normal. Except for bald patches where bits of scalp went missing, it appeared neat and orderly. A red tuft in front looked trendy.

Was I alive or dead? Such thoughts initiated a hatchet migraine that halted any philosophizing. Perhaps it would sort itself out. I grabbed what my hands fell upon: a pair of pink, plaid golf pants with an elastic waist and a purple Vancouver Canucks hockey sweater. Given how clumsily my hands moved these were good choices. I stuffed my feet back into damp boots, but didn't dare tie the laces lest I knot them together. My family stared at me lurching past. A bloody body lay on the floor. Who was that? Was I responsible? Whatever happened wasn't quite clear in my head, but I felt connected. I should right the situation.

I dragged Uncle Albert a few feet across the mushy red carpet and propped him against the fireplace. After I pulled his clothes together and pushed in his stomach he looked like he was waiting for a glass of wine.

A little voice recognized my need for neatness and said "Daddy's home!" I went outside with my smokes.

The lighter flared and turned my thumb black before it ignited the white stick. Watching cigarette smoke curl in front of my face brought back memories of failed efforts to quit. Now I felt no fear of cancer from the smouldering smoke that wafted through my body and gave no pleasure whatsoever. New life was just one big disappointment after another. Quitting wouldn't be a problem this time.

I shuffled across the lawn towards the road, wiping Albert's bile from my chin and being careful not to let drool drop onto the Canucks' hockey sweater. Every step put me farther from Melody, Calculus and Abacus. Instead of dealing with the upsurging repeat of Uncle Albert I should have been saying goodnight to my children, reading them a story and then slipping into bed with my wife and impregnating her with the third child we dreamed of. She would offer forgiveness; she would understand that dining on Albert, whoever he was, couldn't be avoided: it was just nature.

I made a U-turn to beg forgiveness and heard a distant siren. Surely she wouldn't turn me in. She had vowed to stick with me for better or worse, in sickness and in health, till death do ... This was just a rough patch.

As Auntie Mary and Uncle Albert were digested, instinct directed me uphill to Memorial Cemetery. There I encountered a female creature with flat hands, broken neck and punctured, dribbling eyes. The thing had come from a tombstone with the name Barbra and wandered in circles, tripped over rocks and staggered to a cliff over which she fell. It didn't concern me.

A disturbance in the soil in front of a gravestone got my attention. Without thought I dropped to knees and scooped dirt like a dog uncovering a precious old bone. The population of filthy, homeless creatures that trod the upper deck increased as a corpse rose from its grave. I didn't understand that at all. The newly arisen pitched in and helped uncover more living corpses that emerged from the earth like worms in spring. With the lightening of morning sky, the recently resurrected retreated to the deepest, darkest parts of the forest and left me standing beside a hole in the ground. I looked down at my legs and feet and wondered if I was one of them. No dirt cloaked my clothes: that was a relief. Then I remembered what I saw in the mirror in my bedroom. Could it be possible? I dared not think, let alone say out loud, the Z word.

* * *

For two nights bodies rose from the soft earth. Many long-departed had lost eyes, muscles and tendons and their mildewed bones clattered as they searched for food. One wandered onto the road, got hit by a speeding car and the bones scattered so far and wide the driver believed she had hit a ghost. Another wandered uphill into coyote country where a pack seized him and enjoyed the bony bounty. The longest-dead, naked and white boned, could not be helped and they could not fulfill their destiny of a second life. Eventually they blindly wandered over cliffs and fell apart in the ocean.

Extractions of more recent vintage lumbered downhill towards town and on the way stopped at a trailer park. Friendly residents opened doors and were greeted by decomposing ghouls who, without introduction, knocked them over, tore out their guts, smashed their skulls and ate their brains: all without a word of gratitude, a nod of appreciation or a bouquet of flowers. Those who thought it unwise to swing wide their portals to strangers received no reward for their prudence as the night army smashed windows, crashed doors and devoured those who resisted within. Nourished and energized, the tattered tribe stumbled quietly through the woods and followed the scent of emerging new life in the distant Catholic graveyard. Even those without noses knew where to go to help fellow ghouls get a foot up and out of the ground.

8

Following a rare late night Jane Dougherty slept deeply as beeps from her phone unconsciously annoyed her. The caller left a message. A second call caused her to roll over and pull her pillow over her ears. A third stirred her into irritated answering action.

"Wadda ya want?"

"Sorry to disturb you Sarge, but if I didn't call you'd be mad."

"I am mad; make it worthwhile."

"Get over to Cream Bay trailer park. More murder. You won't believe it."

Sgt. Dougherty did not call second in command, Jesse Nesterinko and wake him as she had been wakened. It seemed like mere minutes had passed since her head found her fluffy pillow in the deep a.m. Jesse had been up as late as she and he valued sleep more than most. Investigating Mary's murder and filing reports had put both of them into double overtime although only he thought of claiming such.

The situation at the trailer park must be an especially nasty marital dispute, Jane thought, otherwise the call would not have come to her in the early hours. On her way to the park she vaguely recalled hearing the caller mumble something about *more murder* as she shrugged off sleep, but he might have asked for *more money* or commented that the park's terrain was *mostly muddy*. Probably someone had waved a knife or threatened to jump out a window although the most one could expect from a mobile would be a sprained ankle. The idea of a second homicide on her watch was inconceivable. The first one blanketed her in disbelief, self-doubt and determination to catch the culprit.

Assorted lights scratched the dull sky as Jane numbly steered her way through a mass of police cars, fire trucks, ambulances and unmarked vehicles that belonged to various levels of authority. Realizing that one's worst fears are artifacts of a nightmare has a reassuring appeal and for a moment Jane believed Mary's murder and the scene at the mobile park would vanish when she opened her eyes. Only in a bad dream would a mutilated victim appear in the backyard of a stranger's house. She pinched her arm. It hurt and she didn't wake.

The cluster of cars made parking difficult. Jane didn't want to stumble about in semi-darkness as she didn't know what kind of psychopath might lurk behind a big maple or red cedar. Impatiently she drove onto a wooden fence, already mostly down, and parked on the front yard of a neat double-wide.

"Normally I'd warn you about disturbing evidence," said a serious plain-clothes officer, "but I don't think it matters." She vaguely knew him, but he obviously didn't recognize her in the multi-function jumpsuit she slept in. She ducked under yellow tape, stepped over a splintered door and entered a well-appointed living room that had every appearance of normalcy.

"What's up," she said to a plain-clothes she also did not know.

"You Jane Dough?" he asked tersely.

"Jane Dougherty, yes."

"OK, step in here and give us your opinion of how this relates to the woman recently killed."

He led Jane to a modern bedroom with unmade bed and a side table laden with TV remotes and the remains of a meal. A good-looking young man and woman lay on the floor, eviscerated, with heads smashed. She gasped at the horror of the moment and at the realization that Mary's death was not just a weird, one-of-a-kind atrocity committed by someone who had gone off the rails.

"The other rooms are worse," the plain-clothes warned, pointing to an open door. "Two kids: teen boy and girl. Their dog too. Do you want to see?"

"Not now. Don't have to," Jane gasped. "Same as the other. My God, this is beyond …" For a moment words wouldn't come. "…beyond anything, beyond belief. Who, what, could do this? Why?"

"It's not just this house," the detective droned. "Whole damn park has been decimated. Bodies pulled apart, heads smashed. A trail of footprints leads deep into the woods. Dogs refuse to follow. I've sent a team after them."

"Who are you?" Jane asked quietly.

"Detective Peyman Richards, from Richmond, easy to remember. Part of a tactical unit that's come to help. Got here in less than 20 minutes."

"This is unbelievable. Get Jesse down here."

"I don't know Jesse. I'm not under your orders."

"This is my town and I'm in charge," Jane shot back. "I'll call him myself. Meanwhile let's quit standing around and get after the killers."

9

Amidst a splinter group of newly-born skull crackers I randomly lurched along back lanes, private yards and public parks. Incapable of forming a plan, mapping out a path or even conceptualizing a purpose, my leadership qualities exceeded only those of a garden slug. Where did they all come from I wondered and had a vague recollection of a graveyard. The Z-word emerged like sewage from a stinkhole and I dismissed it. Ragtag numbskulls surrounded me as if I was Messiah.

The shuffling mob took advantage of opportunities to overwhelm and consume pedestrians who enjoyed a stroll and remained, to their last breath, oblivious to news bulletins, sirens and rumors. Joggers survived since, after only a dozen steps in pursuit, corpses abandoned a hopeless chase. Laboring lumberers could not catch the plumpest, pot-bellied pacer who suffered shin splints.

Auntie Mary and Uncle Albert weighed heavy on stomach and conscience, if that's what I had, but still I craved more. When misshapen teeth of fellow night walkers pulled purple sinew I felt compelled to stick my face into the fray and dine. No one backed off to accommodate me and I could not push through to warm liver.

An overweight man driving a battery-powered scooter crossed our path. Scabby arms pulled him from his mount and 50 filthy fingernails attacked: he didn't survive the group grope. Again I could not get to the meat of the matter and watched as yellow fat spread across the sidewalk like melted butter. I dragged my grey tongue along the greasy surface without satisfaction, without shame. The taste gave a notion of caterpillars in a blender. I wondered how low I could go and, in mid-thought, forgot what I wondered about.

The disabled driver displayed a bigger than normal brain after a rock from a thin hand did its duty. There looked to be enough to go around, but that opinion belonged only to me. Others knelt, shoulder to shoulder and pushed to get the biggest share. Long bony fingers poked into eye holes and festering tongues lapped seepage. My finger managed to scoop a bit of the victim's intelligence paste and it stuck to my palate. It needed to be washed down with aqueous humour, mucus, urine, blood or bile, none of which I could reach. As my comrades dined, the paraplegic's legs spasmodically twitched and jerked as they had refused to do in life.

A lurcher wearing a gold tile necklace spelling *Suzie* lumbered beside me. An accident appeared to have crushed her to death and her legs bent backwards at the knees like a stork's, which made walking, even slow lumbering, difficult. She clambered onto the scooter and motored ahead of the others until the road curved and she didn't. Suzie puttered through a wooden fence into a community garden that had no wheelchair access. The machine felled tomatoes, cabbages and sunflowers before plunging into a compost heap and covering its driver in garden waste.

Suzie twisted the throttle and the little machine burrowed deeper into the damp, rotting vegetation that silenced it. After minutes of immobility the driver accepted that her ride had ended. She jammed a ripe tomato into her mouth, spat it out and awkwardly hobbled back to the main group with decomposing cabbage adorning head and shoulders. Fellow lurchers found no amusement as their sense of humor had gone south when their bodies went under.

I offered no smile of acknowledgement when Suzie awkwardly shuffled beside me and rested her heavy hand on my shoulder for support. I could not have cared less, as caring held a position at the bottom of my emotional totem pole, which had been laid horizontal by rot. My labored thinking tried to focus on the end of life. Thoughts oozed from the overcast interior in stop motion that slowed to a crawl. I didn't know where I was going or what I was doing.

Had I turned off the stove? Did I cancel newspaper delivery? Did I cancel a secret appointment with my friend the dentist? What was that about?

Only one thing had a comforting ring: *My name ith Morthimer Smithers.* Suzie heard and appeared not to care. She didn't introduce herself.

I gnawed on the five words as I walked, repeating them often and alternating them with *brains*. The utterances reassured me although I didn't know reassurance. I walked on; comfortably dumb, comfortably numb.

To escape the eternal blackness and to continue walking the glorious surface I had to eat organs and brains. That was my instinct: I didn't learn it from reading *Zombies for Idiots* or by watching late-night infomercials. Never had I tasted anything as euphorically delicious as Auntie Mary. Every organ shot unique rivulets of flavour into my mouth: cherry-bombs of taste exploded on my palate. Dark red liver, with its store of earthy iron, could not be improved if a Cordon Bleu chef prepared it with exotic spices on a buttered, cast iron skillet. Her bladder sprinkled an under-taste onto her salad of organs like an exotic vinaigrette. Glands full of energizing enzymes complemented intestines full of fetid organic matter. The taste sensations exceeded anything ever put on a plate for the living. And the brain! Dessert. Each bite a multi-orgasmic feast that trembled through my wretched body and made me jut my bloated tongue into every cranny in search of another jolt of pleasure. I cared nothing about halitosis. I craved a cigarette.

A fellow reanimate, walking nearby, puffed casually and again it looked enticing. Delicious grey smoke wafted from both the walker's nose and from maggot-holed lungs that hung like black, dripping drapes after a fire. The smoker had surely succumbed to cancer, but now enjoyed his poison like never before, free of anxiety caused by warnings on the package. I had to give it another try. With two fingers I made smoking motions, but the walker didn't offer to share. I reached for a puff of the long white cigarette that had lots of burning left in it. He hunched his shoulders and turned his head to protect his treasure. Generosity didn't come with the new territory. I grabbed the steaming stick from his fingers. It broke and fell. He picked up the burning section and took a long drag. Before I could retrieve the other half he stepped on it and twisted his foot. His cheeks quivered: he may have tried to smile.

I harbored no concept of being hunted and knew nothing of my vulnerability. Nevertheless, when I sighted flashlight beams dancing in the treetops I knew danger. Unless those who pursued could be stopped my kinsmen and I would return to the black.

Using hand signals and urgent pushes I designated several tribesmen to lurch back and lurk behind thick cedar trees. I wasn't certain why, but lurking and lurching seemed the best things to do; the only things to do. My thoughts arrived from a mental conveyor belt that creaked at quarter-speed and required oil. That was an improvement over the moment I first wobbled on weak legs and didn't know my name. Still, I couldn't get a grasp on my second walk on the bright side. A blurred notion of a woman, two miniature people and a house danced just beyond lucidity. I might have visited them, but memory wasn't what it used to be. Where did I work, when was my Costco membership due, who won the Stanley Cup? And when did I celebrate my birthday? A pocket search uncovered no soggy wallet with credit card or ID. Age 30 felt right: a married man with two kids living in a small town. That seemed boring. Maybe I was in witness protection after testifying against the Hells Angels. Perhaps I worked as a lumberjack or a game hunter although I didn't feel particularly muscular or athletic. My upper arms puffed, but the puffiness came not from strong bulging pipes, but from some strange skin condition that turned my epidermal layer grey and made it swell. I might be an explorer who died of an exotic disease. Or I might have a secret buried so deeply that I couldn't reach it.

10

The secretive coastal clan never killed intentionally, but occasionally crossed the fine line separating need from greed. That same line divided recovery from death for the blood source. Overindulging – siphoning to the last drop, or even second or third last drop – was the pitfall of the rookie vampire imbiber. Euphoria could so overwhelm that stopping before the last slurp from a carotid took a high degree of self-discipline.

When leeches dipped into a living vat, the victim became unconscious and when he or she awakened, an hour or two later, no memory of the minutes before the bite remained. If the withdrawal was made by a self-regulating straw the reservoir would live to give again.

Out of boredom, rather than need, vamps slept for much of the day and passed their nights hanging around dangerous intersections made more dangerous by cloaks hanging over stop signs. Drinking deeply from a screaming car crash victim, immobilized with broken legs, had little risk and a few pints sustained years of dormancy in crypt or cave if that was the life-style choice. Integrating into society and watching everyone except themselves grow old remained the other dreary option.

Several dozen vamps lived patiently in the town of White Rock, passing their time with computers, movies and electronic games. All knew their destiny, which was to have no destiny at all.

Vamps didn't sing, dance or take drugs and were not lively party people. Laughing and finding joy in living through eternity did not come easily.

After sun the flares, electrical storms and radio-wave-reversals hit somnolent bodies and gave a jolt never before known, that attitude changed. No longer could they sleep away a lazy afternoon.

The emergence of dormant vampires from crypts and caves, because of the charge funnelled into the earth, required an unanticipated infusion of new blood. The zombie invasion made that simple task difficult. After flesh-eaters had torn apart a body, the remaining blood had all the attraction of sun-ripened pig piss.

The tedium of time dulled the vamps mental acuity and as a result they possessed diminished deductive reasoning. They paid mechanics, lawyers and electricians to solve problems. When the shocks of October 4, 2018 woke and energized them, many vamps believed the apocalypse had arrived: an apocalypse their kind had been awaiting for millennia. Although most had turned atheist, given up on change and abandoned all spirituality, the new energy provided hope that a future with meaning and promise waited, just around time's only corner.

A small group of bloodsuckers crept from basements, crypts, graveyards and other places of seclusion and joined regular resident-vamps who marched to the centre of town without fully knowing why. Their nostrils recognized blood-nectar and they followed the scent.

Mary's body, spread on back steps, had proved disastrous. Ghastly mutilation spilled her valuables: only a few tarnished drops remained for the lady in black who had stooped over her.

Blood-thin vampires moved painfully and could not devise a plan to get blood, other than to fall upon someone recently deceased, or severely injured, and slurp enough drops, spilled or otherwise, to infuse sufficient energy to track down a full tank. Sucking a healthy human, when running on fumes, could be extremely dangerous. Healthy temps did not react favorably to their necks being groped. A punch in the face, kick in the gut or knife in the heart could result. Thus the vamp motto: Drink before you get thirsty.

Arisen vamps, electrically infused and ready to go, gathered at a forested park near the waterfront. Blood had to be obtained in order to maintain their energetic state. Licking the entrails of those felled by the zombie attack at the trailer park had humiliated them. Humiliation fit better than thirst so they cleaned up dribbles and splatters before police arrived. Like degenerate dogs, they licked from window panes, kitchen floors and cupboard doors. But without confidence, courage or juicy carcasses the new suckers' energy declined and with it their inclination to satisfy needs.

When the flashlights of zombie-chasing police darted through trees the time for action had come. A pudgy cop – a doughnut eater – waddled behind while his mates jogged forward. Sweaty, panting and aching, the laggard managed a stalwart defence when five straws fell upon him. He knocked several aside, but with all the arms dragging at him and all the fangs sinking into him, his hands could not reach weaponry.

The handsome vamp leader, Victor, more than a millennium old, wet his canines first and drew from the right jugular while others pushed and pulled to share the left. Some bit at wrists and some drained ankles. Victor took only a demitasse since desperate times called for diminished measures. He nodded to his pal Vanessa, ravishing in black leather with tsunamis of quivering cleavage, and she took over. Vanessa drank a little then allowed others to puncture with hollow teeth and suck for a few seconds. Even those getting a slow stream from veins on chubby blue legs felt better.

The cop dropped like a wrinkled white sheet and would not recover. Guidelines had been violated.

When the fat one's absence was noticed a young policewoman volunteered to go back and look for him. The commander ordered a second officer to accompany her.

Dry vamps, admiring the ruddy complexion and energetic pace of Victor and Vanessa, grew desperate and reckless; characteristics seldom seen in vamps. Sighting the two police who had backtracked to find their missing partner, they prepared to gang-drape and siphon. The male cop drew his gun while the female aimed her Taser.

"Stop right there," they nervously shouted, almost in harmony.

Ignoring the order, the leeches surged, the ones behind pushing without concern for the safety of those in front.

"We'll shoot," the cops sang, like a barbershop duet, but their words had no meaning.

"Final warning," came as a falsetto from the baritone male. The surge continued and the policeman fired, his bullet going through the abdomen of the closest assailant. The target pulled his dark blue shirt from the tight belt of his navy pants and saw a hole from which sepia syrup slowly seeped. He pushed his finger into the hole and when he took it out the high-viscosity leakage ceased and he continued forward.

More gunshots spoiled the quiet as bullets went through arms, legs and abdomens without effect. The female fired her Taser X3 and the bolt of electricity hit a leech's chest and radiated through his body. He convulsed wildly while remaining on his feet. The next vamp, a woman in a tight black dress, also started a weird satanic dance when struck in the neck by the Taser. Like a puppet controlled by electric stings she leapt in the air to some unheard beat, legs flailing. More bullets passed through bodies and within a minute every vampire, save Victor and Vanessa, who skulked in the background, had been hit by gun, stun gun or Taser.

After learning their main weapons didn't repel the attackers, the two police reached for night sticks, but this reaction of last resort came too late as bodies and bicuspids swarmed until they fell to the forest floor as pale sacks of skin and bones.

While others imbibed, Victor picked up a stun gun, looked it over and fired a charge at Vanessa who was shocked, but commenced a demonic highland fling with a smile on her face. Vamps who had previously been tasered demanded another hit and soon all were twirling and laughing as if the guns had been loaded with amphctamines and nitrous oxide. Victor decided he should take a hit, but the depleted weapons had fired their last and he didn't sample shock therapy.

11

Along with my band of shambling cannibals I came upon a small cemetery to which we had been instinctively drawn. It was nothing more than a tiny native burial ground with some token totems, mostly broken. It had not found recent use.

I didn't want to go to another cemetery: I wanted to go home. I wanted to make up to my wife and play with my kids, but somehow I had lost my way, both in spirit and direction. I wanted to meet with my friend the dentist. Maybe we would play dominos or checkers.

We pushed rocks and scraped sacred soil as our stout fingers dug towards a source of slight vibration. Skeletal remains, held together by slim sinews, clambered to the dim light. They clattered, stumbled and stared, dumb as bricks; dumb as us. They were several steps short of a credible lurch. An arthritic centenarian pushing a walker could have moved faster. Jaws snapped in a quest for flesh. I knew the feeling. We backed away: out of sight.

Five RCMP members reached the First Nation's burial plot and saw, standing in the moonlight, three partly fleshed skeletons. Cops' mouths hung open as the resurrected Natives' mouths chomped on air. From behind rocks, on the opposite side of the cemetery, a darkly-dressed cabal of blood suckers watched us, watched the Natives and watched the cops. The good, the bad and the ugly faced off while the indeterminate stood in the middle.

The skeletons, with arms horizontal, staggered towards the police. The first reborn Native lost his delicate balance and clattered to the grass after just six beginner steps. Those behind tripped over him and became a heap of shaking, rattling bones. Stupefied police, cautiously stepping towards the reeking pile, tried to sort out this practical joke. One grabbed his radio, reported the location and relayed what he saw. They laughed at the seething mound before them, bragging they had tracked down the murderers and corralled them.

With pointing, pushing and gesturing I directed my mates to use trees and rocks for cover. Hiding was not in our DNA. We drooled at the sight of our darkly-dressed competition, rich with rouge from recently siphoned blood. Yet they didn't smell right or look edible.

Laughing cops caught a wave of stench then turned and spotted my poorly-hidden gaggle. Six vampires, licking lips and baring white fangs, stepped into the clearing and approached police from the side opposite us. Before reaching the constables and the mound of groaning bones they stopped and pulled away a stone slab. From deep within an ancient cavity wobbled forth a sorry creature wearing pink feathers, chartreuse leggings and a light blue vest of bone and shell: the first gay vampire Indian chief. His pain found my sympathy gland. A transfusion would have done him a world of good.

The dark ones moved quickly and I couldn't figure them out. It didn't help that a woman launched fangs into the farthest cop and the uniform screamed like a slaughterhouse pig. Police put dozens of bullets through the shady denizen. The vamp hung from the neck of the stout policewoman like an eel in a swamp until both went down and only one came up. The cop lost blood so fast she never knew what bit her. Remaining constables fled as if departing a deli with salmonella. We lumbered after them with no hope of catching unless a cop suffered cardiac arrest within 10 yards.

The dark ones had not only speed, but stealth. As the cops raced blindly downhill, zigging and zagging to avoid pursuers, the suckers took a circuitous route and intercepted them at the seaside. Bullets did nothing so the three police unholstered Tasers and fired. With palpable relief the charges stopped leeches in their tracks and got them bounding into the air with heels kicking. A police boat, siren wailing, came to their call from the opposite side of the bay. Before its prow touched sand, Tasers ran out of energy and the boat crew could do little but haul aboard three ashen bodies that weighed less than expected. A hospital prepared for their arrival.

12

Claustrophobia clutched at Sgt. Jane Dougherty as she wedged her way from the front door of the community policing station towards her office in back. Blocking her way were RCMP officers from Surrey, Vancouver and Richmond who had set up stations behind whatever desk or box they could procure. Someone had let media reps in and, with that door open, they came and went as they pleased and half the police officers had camera or microphone in their face. A mumbling gypsy-like woman stuffed herself into a corner and a well-dressed gent yelled into two phones, one at each ear. Tracking dogs yelped and every cop who arrived or departed felt the need to do so with lights blazing and sirens blaring.

    The Sergeant didn't know the count for the world's biggest mass murder, but feared White Rock would get a top 10 listing on her watch. She had something monstrous on her hands. As the highest ranking member in the tiny detachment, she had to exert control and halt the murderers before any more carnage took place. She couldn't come to grips with the idea of a band of renegade men, or women even, raiding a mobile park and eviscerating the occupants. The whole thing stretched beyond bizarre, beyond horrendous.

    In Peace Arch Hospital a man, missing most of a leg and genitals, moaned about zombies eating him. Six officers were MIA and the last call from one of them targeted dancing, blood sucking vampires and Native skeletons.

    Why would anyone murder an elderly woman walking home from a bridge game? Why would someone try to eat a hairdresser taking a morning walk through a cemetery? No matter how often the question plowed through her mine she couldn't find an answer.

Jane whacked her nightstick on the wooden counter of the police station's entry room. Nothing happened so she did it harder. The buzzing chamber quieted.

"Listen up," she shouted above murmurs, phone rings and barks. "I need your attention and I want your help. All RCMP members go to the right side of this room, everyone else to the left."

After confused movement Jane shouted louder, "I said everyone else move left. That's your left, not mine. Look where I'm pointing." The horde reshuffled.

"OK, everyone look to your right, that's my left. Those are the people in charge, the ones doing the investigation, the ones with authority: they are the police. This station is now closed to media, lawyers, hangers-on, do-gooders and anyone who isn't a cop. If you've got a camera, recorder, pencil, notepad whatever, it's time to go. No alarmist stories please, everything you know is alarming enough. Tell people to keep inside and barricade their doors and windows. We'll let you know when we have news. And don't tie up our phone lines with calls. Out you go. Thanks for cooperating."

As she scanned the emptying room Jane noticed a fit young man with light hair who wore a beige suit that matched both his complexion and the color of the wall behind him to such a chameleon-like degree that she previously hadn't seen him.

"And you?"

"I'm a senior officer with CSIS; Canadian secret service, more or less. My division investigates alien sightings, UFOs, that sort of thing. Before you kick me out, I think I can help. This is not the first time brains and abdominal parts have been removed from bodies. There have been cases in Germany, Norway and of course, California. I'm waiting for calls and if you don't mind, I'll keep in the background, out of the way. I'll let you know as soon I get additional info. But I need access to all that you know."

Jane nodded an OK. She liked his demeanour: no pretensions, strong and fit. He could be an asset if he could procure whatever information he talked about.

To the remaining police she said, "We've got work to do. When you talk outside this room, when you're on the phone, when you talk to your spouses or partners there are words you don't use: zombies, vampires, ghouls, bigfoot, undead, Dracula, Nosferatu. These come from fiction, not from factual reports. Hysterical people imagine all sorts of things and then start doing strange things including hurting each other. Our first duty is to locate our missing officers. Three, in serious condition, have been rescued and taken to hospital. Three are still missing. Two men on an ATV are tracking them from the Cream Bay Park and another two are backtracking on foot from the beach towards the park. Let's get them some help. Wilson, set up a patrol from Centennial Park. Take some officers from out of town."

While Wilson selected his helpers Jane directed comments to familiar faces, "Let's be realistic here. We're out of our depth. Parking tickets and domestic disputes are our line. More help is coming. A unit from the capital is on its way and so is help from Vancouver. Experts are flying in from all over the place. I want spot checks and searches of every vehicle leaving town and entering town on the main roads. Officer Amelia, set that up. And be forewarned, you'll make people mad. Add traffic tie-ups to their tensions and you won't see many happy faces out there. Jesse, set up guards at vulnerable trailer parks and ungated communities."

The sergeant abruptly turned towards her office and a young man in a police uniform started applauding. Jane turned her stare into a glare and snapped, "This isn't a performance, you idiot."

She took four steps along a hall she knew as well as the four steps across her living room and then closed her office door: the quiet surprised her. Alone, she could think clearly and avoid confusing interruptions. With desk phone in hand she started a mental list of those who must be contacted, taking not a moment to savor the satisfaction of restoring order to the front of her station.

First came forensics, which added little to her knowledge other than to say a strange dry mucus had been found on chewed parts of Mary's body. Tooth marks were human, so no marauding coyotes, cougars or bears had done it. She wondered about the dental structure of Sasquatch, but dared not inquire.

Crime scene investigators unearthed no new clues and offered no opinions. Tracking dogs still refused to track and their keeper had left a phone message complaining of a gypsy woman hanging around who kept repeating, "I hear dead people." Jane regretted connecting the necromancer with the dog handlers.

The officers on the ATV had not reported and neither had the foot patrol. She wanted to go find them herself, but felt she could do more good on the phone. She shouted down the hall to Jesse and told him to find a few officers and get them on the case by taking a fourth route to find the missing police. He suggested a helicopter would help.

With black phone in hand she called headquarters in Regina and quickly got the commander. He knew the situation, but didn't know about additional missing officers.

"This constitutes a national emergency," he said. "The premier and prime minister must be informed. I'll do that. A plane with 20 Emergency Response officers takes off from here within minutes. A motorized unit has left Victoria and another has left Kelowna. They'll reach you in four or five hours. Who's in command there right now?"

Jane didn't have the answer to his simple question. So many people came and went that her police station resembled a mall at Christmas. Some were chief of this and head of that, but no one had come right out and said they were taking over.

"I'm sergeant, highest ranking officer in White Rock. No one has relieved me. We need a helicopter."

"OK, fine." The voice on the phone sounded frustrated. "This is probably beyond you, beyond anyone local. You sound bright enough. I'm sure it's not your fault the villain hasn't been captured."

"Villains," she corrected. "This is not the work of one person."

"Right. Perps, villains, whatever. You know the lay of the land so keep co-ordinating until I find the right person. If we don't figure this out in the next day or so the prime minister will call in the army and we Mounties will vanish into the background. It's our job to capture the bad guys, not the army's, so let's get on with it. Questions?"

"A helicopter?"

"Search and Rescue has one. I'll try to get it."

"More questions?"

The commander interpreted Jane's pause as she formulated her next query as a lack of questions and the call ended with an electronic click.

From Jane's perspective, bringing in the army would not be a slap to the face of the RCMP. She would mobilize them in an instant if the decision were hers.

She shouted down the hall for the secret service man. At least he had a different approach. If aliens were eating her people she couldn't be blamed for not tracking them down and putting them behind bars. She fingered an autopsy report on her desk and when she looked up the agent stood before her.

"I'm Donald Sinclair. Senior agent I guess, although we generally don't use ranks."

"I'm Jane Dougherty, sergeant. Tell me what you know."

Agent Sinclair sat, rolled his chair up to the desk and told the sergeant he still didn't know a lot, but similarities to cases he had referred to were more than chance.

"For instance," he said, "a massacre in Norway. A dozen citizens in a small town get disembowelled and have their brains removed. No suspects, no clues: just a mess in the woods and at a cemetery. Winter comes, the place freezes over, never happens again. Locals say an abominable snowman attacked. Some saw big footprints in the snow. If yetis did it why don't they do it again? Just one attack in other places too. So, think about aliens? Strange electrical charges were known to happen. People reported lights in the sky and aurora borealis exploded with rare colors. In each case, Germany, Norway, Lithuania, Iceland, Scotland, people reported lights in the sky and strange electrical happenings. My department, two people really, has investigated alien landings for several years. We believe the aliens pick an area, dig up the dead for study and collect the brains and organs of living people. They put them together. The cases are all pretty similar: small towns, maximum 50 dead."

The man Sgt. Dougherty had perceived as articulate, athletic and sincere started to look mentally challenged as he babbled about aliens and yetis. A bit of drool decorated the corner of his mouth, his ears stuck out and his bulging eyes looked to each other for support. She wondered if he had a midriff spare tire like her own or if it was her old chair that forced him to hunch forward so he looked like he packed extra pounds.

"There's one more thing in common."

"What's that?"

"Thin bloodless, dead pets, hardly more than skin covering bones."

Jane's laughter erupted so spontaneously that if her mouth had contained coffee or masticated muffin Sinclair would have been shotgunned.

"A lot of people think it's funny," Sinclair declared, deadpan. "You think it's funny until you hold the little lifeless creatures in your arms."

"And your explanation for that is...?" Dougherty questioned, swallowing her guffaws, but not her sarcastic tone. Reports of dead cats and dogs had filtered in.

"We believe aliens try to inhabit an earthly form, like a dog, so they can get close and study us in secret. They don't get the blood or the shape right and they die, but they get close."

Jane scratched her head. "Let me recap, if possible. Every few years aliens come to a small town and dig up some dead. They take the brains and organs from the living and maybe do something with them. They reincarnate themselves as cats and dogs to spy on us, but die because they get the blood wrong."

"That's basically what we're working on," the agent answered. "Do you have a better explanation?"

"Every explanation is better. Hell, I can't think of a worse explanation. A motorcycle gang harvesting body parts to sell on the black market is a better explanation and it's what I'm working on. Maybe something in the water has driven people mad. Werewolves are on the loose. We've also had reports of dancing vampires and zombies. Those explanations are better. Is this your full time job? I didn't know we had a department of alien affairs."

Since the agent seemed to have all the time in the world to formulate his answer Jane stood and announced, "We're in the middle of a crisis. I don't have time for more talk."

"The crisis is over. They stop as quickly as they start. I go out and bury the bodies of pets then a clean-up team comes and makes most of the weird evidence go away. The strangest mass murder in Canadian history never gets solved."

"Thanks for the clarification," Sgt. Dougherty said as she edged the g-man to the door. "Bring me blood-drained pets and you'll have my attention."

"I'll do that," Agent Sinclair closed the door without a click.

Before he got to the end of the hallway Jane's phone rang with a frantic call from a woman who said her cat was missing.

13

Rumors about an Arizona motorcycle gang involved in the red-market body-part trade roared through town louder and faster than a Harley chopper, but for three nights no deaths occurred.

Both flesh-eaters and blood-drinkers busied themselves with nocturnal movement on the fringes of town. Vibes, less powerful than previously, emanated from a cemetery in neighboring South Surrey, but a wide tidal river separated White Rock from the new suburb. A long bridge joined the two, but traffic moved slowly as police inspected every car before allowing passage.

A resurrected athlete, who had been buried in her gym suit, tried swimming the gap. She thrashed with strong arms before her heavy bones dragged her down. Salmon nibbled as she drifted to the bottom where she walked for a few minutes before settling into sediment. A second athlete, a volunteer lifeguard and slow learner, followed suit and got in eight strokes before sinking. A third, no quicker on the uptake, grabbed a log, pushed off and rolled off.

A sidewalk ran the length of the bridge, but even the dimmest knew they would be captured or thrown off the bridge if they dared walk along it. No foolproof route led to the echoes of the helpless dead on the other side.

Ten of the most courageous carnivorous cadavers spent the night like spiders on the grid-work beneath the bridge, painstakingly making their way across. One lost her footing and joined the salmon. Another's lost his grip on a rusty girder and dropped like a dead balloon.

Following their strenuous crossing the eight huddled under the far end of the span, wrapped themselves in newspapers and blended with a gaggle of homeless. One of the street people became a meal. The others fled and never reported the death of their fellow hobo.

* * *

While my companions crawled beneath the bridge like confused monkeys I felt a compulsion to keep my feet planted on solid ground. A flesh-eater named Mona stood beside me, swaying and moaning. I found her few remaining tufts of blonde hair attractive although her rotted blouse and flat chest, over which various insects crawled, could not be construed as a turn-on had I been capable of being turned on.

Adding to Mona's lack of allure was her habit of sticking out her tongue and catching the end of a stalactite of purple snot, the tip of which held descending maggots. She drew the white morsels into her mouth, chewed laboriously, then swallowed with a pronounced gulp. Mona rubbed her grey shoulder against me and tried some sweet talk. Grunts and squawks dribbled from her lipless slit and carried no recognizable word. The mumbles that limped from my own little lips could not have been understood by me either, had I not formed them first in my muddled mind.

I harbored a feeling of betrothal to someone whose name I couldn't remember. I didn't want to be untrue to whoever that was so Mona held limited appeal as a playmate for a playdate. Instead I eyed a well-muscled gentleman in a mottled gym suit and visually undressed him, which was not difficult as his private parts swung through rotted gaps. He caught me staring and when I smiled he quickly shuffled ahead.

Within my cranial fog dwelled a once-sapient, sensitive mind I could no longer find. To recover my thinking I would gladly have shed my love of brains and organs, although consuming those delicacies seemed the only purpose to my re-being. Hunger struck as I ruminated about my bad habits. Steak and kidney pie came to mind as did liverwurst, blood pudding, rib-eye steak, rump roast, tongue, artichoke heart, chicken fingers and ground Chuck.

* * *

The dark menace detected the same emanations from the South Surrey cemetery as did the ragged moaning roamers. Neat, orderly, well-groomed and well-dressed, they moved carefully and orderly with no sense of desperation.

On reaching the bridge the vamp band gave no thought to paddling, swimming or swinging. Not one of them frequented public beaches: intemperate water with unpredictable waves had no attraction. A bubbling, multi-jetted Jacuzzi, set to the perfect degree, waited at home.

Vanessa loaded six suckers into her minivan. She showed convincing ID to police, explained they were going to a Rotary Club meeting and got a quick okay to cross the bridge.

Victor opened the marina gate with his key card and started the twin diesels of his cruiser. Vampires climbed aboard, sped up the river and docked near the cemetery which they located with a combination of instinct and GPS. They arrived well before lumbering, lurching flesh eaters and had plenty of time before sunrise to open crumbling concrete crypts and help comrades who gave off signals of energy, animation and thirst. Some had been in seclusion for mere months and were being released prematurely while others, despite the new electrical charge, looked wan and wasted as they approached best-before dates.

Under normal circumstances vampires ended their dormancy by working their way free and heading downtown for a drink or two at the bar they owned. Vanessa slowly explained to each newly arisen that due to the zombie plague, blood was in short supply and the bar could spare only a short sip. Getting a fresh supply required more guile than ever.

Painful sun began streaking the sky and they retreated to the woodland surrounding the cemetery. They pulled dark jackets over their heads and rested for the day. A woodsman would not find them among rocks, leaves and fallen trees.

At dusk the eaters arrived and the cemetery sounded like the tune-up for a kindergarten band as moans, groans and creaking bones spoiled the tranquil air. Moaning zombs dug their way out of graves and crawled along the ground to help others break out of their earthy prison. Thirsty vamps groaned about the bad news and the unfair competition.

The vampires would have stayed aloof except one revenant lurched towards a straw who, with ripe red lips and rosy cheeks, proved too tempting. The zomb sensed blood rushing through the vamp's organs and wanted her, all of her. The target may very well have stood there and been chewed to bits had Vanessa not rushed over with a weighty rock and planted it in the zomb's face. The rock's recipient, a recently-risen undernourished weakling, didn't care about the rock one way or the other. It stumbled forward and got a hand on the innocent vamp. Vanessa assaulted its face until nose and teeth disappeared. That proved fortunate because the zombie gummed the surprised vamp's shoulder and would have torn off a sizeable chunk had its incisors been in its mouth instead of down its throat. Even so, a layer of skin vanished from the vamp and bright red blood spouted onto Vanessa's dark blouse. She whacked a few more times and even when the head looked like a crunched paper bag the thing kept trying to bite. The weakling fell forward onto what remained of its mashed turnip of a face. From a prone position it grabbed an ankle, gummed it and peeled off more skin.

    Victor staggered forward with a chunk of granite tombstone so weighty he could barely keep it off the ground. When it landed the head flattened and its owner blindly crawled until it fell into the grave from which it had come. The tombstone again landed on top of it and held it in place while polished shoes kicked in dirt.

    Vanessa knew a policy of laissez-faire would not work. She scanned for more weaponry and her eyes alit on what she most feared. Behind a stone slab a pair of shapely, shaking legs, wearing red leather pumps, jutted out and a filthy head sprayed red as it bobbed up and down. Every time it rose a crimson tide followed and the air filled with an eruption of unwanted parts. The zomb searched for the nirvanesque ecstasy that accompanied eating. Organs that went down its gullet instantly came up again. The horrid taste of fresh vamp had no relationship to the haute cuisine found in regular Grade A humans. Foul parts flew into the air like clay targets at a skeet shoot.

    Within an hour newly-risen flesh-eaters had chased away every vamp. Two MIA were the red-shoed victim and a resurrected vamp who wandered from crypt directly into the arms of a zomb who tore him apart and upchucked the pieces. The few misguided vamps who sank canines into zombies' necks projectile vomited.

    Victor, worried about changed circumstances, unpocketed his phone and speed-dialled hookers. "Meet me behind Second Sip," he told them and gave precise times separated by 15-minute intervals. He strolled to a dark spot behind the nearby coffee shop and waited.

"I guess you're Demona," he said to a blonde wearing a short skirt and sweater. "I specified you wear a low, revealing blouse."

"Yea, I'm Demona. But I got little titties and it's cool at night. I was scared you'd be turned off. Where you wanna go?"

Victor opened his wallet and counted out five 20s. "I'll pay you first, if you don't mind."

"No problem," she said and grabbed the money. "What will it be?"

"Come into the trees and I'll show you." Victor suggestively glanced down and then backed towards a thick oak.

"I'm not going into the dark with you. No way, that sucks."

"But I like nature. I'll add another 50." Victor pulled out his wallet and waved a bill.

"Well, maybe, but nothing kinky." Demona snapped the bill from his fingers then added, "Kinky costs more than 50 bucks."

She no sooner stepped into the shadow of the overhanging tree than Victor wrapped one hand around her mouth and hauled her out of sight.

"Now we'll see what sucks," he said as he pulled her sweater below her shoulders to the tune of ripping seams. Her breasts, large or small, held no interest for him. Body parts, Victor presented her bare upper body first to the skinny native who clattered from the woods. The gay chief moaned in shameless ecstasy as he had his way with the blonde. The powerful red drug surged from her neck into his veins giving tumescence to his scabby wrinkled body. The other side of her neck went to a semi-dormant woman wearing a charcoal sari who only got a small portion of the potion due to the chief's potent thirst.

Thus went the night as hooker after hooker went for the money and succumbed to a sucking. Straws drove the whores' bodies to distant dumping places where the women would wake without recent memory and with $100 or more in their clasp.

"This isn't a sustainable resource," Victor warned when drinkers lost control. "We have to think of our future. A dry hooker is a dead hooker and a dead hooker can never bleed for us again."

After every prostitute and call girl on the contact list had arrived for dates, demand still exceeded supply. Newly animated bodies had prodigious appetites and Victor didn't know where he would find more blood. Very few people cared about missing and relocated hookers, but if vamps started slurping from regular humans who didn't have shady night jobs, what would they do with the spent bodies? Dozens of memory-deprived business people waking up in wooded parks would alert police. Detectives would compare notes and know something wasn't on the level. Victims would be sent to doctors, blood tests would be done and when it became known that all had the same anaemic condition thousands of years of secrecy would be in jeopardy. It could be worse than Salem.

14

As head of the local RCMP detachment Jane Dougherty could elect to work weekdays 9 to 5, however she took her share of weekend and graveyard shifts. With terror and turmoil raging through her town she caught a few winks only when her head involuntarily drooped onto her chest and then slowly edged downward onto her desk. There it stayed until the phone rang or someone rapped on her door, usually minutes later. The analog clock on the wall did not designate a.m. or p.m. and hints of daylight only filtered in from afar.

No thoughts went towards eating, calculating overtime or taking a 15-minute break to enjoy the donuts that had added an inch or two to her waist and helped her grow into her nickname, *Jane Dough*. Age and weight seemed to have found a fixed ratio. As a 20-year-old she hit the scales at a perfect 120. Ten years later she weighed 10 pounds more. A month ago, on her 35th birthday, the scales told her what she expected – 135. She envisioned herself at age 50: 150 pounds with a silver Brillo pad atop a double-chinned head that presently sprouted curly light-brown hair enhanced with an auburn tint she applied herself.

Already her knees were troublesome and at age 50 she'd walk with a limp and the chairman of the board would ask, as he had asked a dozen times before, "Do you think you can meet the physical demands of your position?" The chauvinist referred to her inability to wrestle in the mud with suspects and to physically subdue gangsters in alleys.

The chairman couldn't comprehend that when she politely asked perps, "Would you please put your hands behind your back so I can cuff you?" there had not been a single refusal; not one charge of resisting arrest. If she encountered one of the murderers she would employ that basic strategy.

Before involuntary sleep again dropped her head to the desk and robbed her of discouraging thoughts, Jane decided her department was being too reactive and too passive in this time of crisis. Rumors that the army would take over circulated freely, but until that happened the local police ruled. She scribbled some notes and then phoned newspapers and TV stations to tell them a curfew had been put in place and anyone on the streets between sunset and sunrise risked being arrested or killed by predators that came out at night. A reward was offered for the capture of the killers. Jane's budget had no funds for rewards, but she would find money if necessary and hoped it would be necessary. She gave Constable Smith, chatting aggressively with a woman in the front office, the job of creating curfew notices, printing them and posting them around town. How traditional she thought: sepia posters nailed to trees. Wanted Dead or Alive: Reward.

An assessment of the station's armament took 15 minutes as did sending out notification that all squad cars must carry tear gas, two shotguns, two spotlights and extra ammunition. Bullet-proof vests must be worn at all times, said the bold type, and riot shields must be in the back seats of cars and carried during any confrontation with any force of evil. She liked that phrasing.

At the rocky shore where her officer made the call about dancing Draculas the tranquility of rhythmic waves contradicted the horror. One officer had died of blood loss, according to the hospital, and the other two were receiving transfusions in intensive care. Their prospects looked good. The loss of an excellent police officer and a good family man pained Jane and brought shudders of sorrow whenever she thought of his children playing at the police picnic. She had visited the hospital and spoken to the two pale surviving police who had no recollection of what happened to them. Even when she recreated the scene they remembered nothing of fighting on the beach or going to hospital.

There wasn't much about local life Jane didn't know. No cults, gangs or weird sects made their homes in town or in surrounding hills. Yet, on a quiet autumn day, came some monsters that killed citizens and officers by ripping out guts and brains and by draining blood. In White Rock, of all places! In one of the quietest, most crime-free towns in North

America. Everyone in town talked about zombies, aliens, evil spirits and vampires, but she wasn't going to be sucked into that line of senseless thought.

Jane found it hard to accept that much of her detachment had been destroyed and many citizens had been bizarrely murdered. The shock and trauma were relentless and the carnage went beyond anything she had ever read about or heard about. If her professional position had not made so many demands on her actions and thoughts, she could have been swept away by despair and hopelessness.

Lights from distant roadblocks flashed constantly while two helicopters destroyed peaceful thought and broke up a perfect sunset. One belonged to a news service and the other looked like Search and Rescue. Apparently headquarters had got a bird in the air, but hadn't bothered to share the good news. Behind her a dozen army men in full combat gear started to unload a truck and set up a command post. Did that make it official, she wondered. Had the army taken command? No one had sent confirmation. Communication was the first casualty in a crisis. Damn it, she thought, nap for a few minutes and it's a whole new ball game when you wake up.

With all the protection around her, with 10 men with grenades and Colt carbine rifles waiting for something to blast, she still felt on edge, frightened. Every snapped twig and every kicked stone brought a rush of adrenalin and she expected Jack the Ripper or a skeleton from a horror movie to pounce. A voice from behind startled her. She spun, withdrew her sidearm and crouched on the gravel.

"Hey, don't shoot. It's just me," agent Sinclair blurted. "I've got what you wanted."

Where did he come from, Jane asked herself. Her eyes and ears had taken in everything. The combat unit questioned every person it encountered yet Donald Sinclair, in plain clothes, walked up behind her as if she was lined up to buy a coffee and Boston cream.

"Scared the shit outta me," Jane declared. "Why didn't you say something?"

"I did. I said 'don't shoot.' Anyway, I've got the goods." Sinclair stuck out his left hand and what looked like an old English saddle from a miniature horse dangled from his muscular forearm.

"You're going riding? Kinda rocky around here."

"Look more closely." She took two steps towards him and lifted what was draped over his arm and then quickly stepped back.

"My God. It can't be."

"Got him a few hours ago."

Jane poked at the thing dangling lifelessly. "It's so cute with its little legs and head. It isn't real is it? You're not a joker? That isn't a prop?"

"No ma'am. I've never found humor in a dead dog. Specially all drained and flat like that. Don't forget, you're actually looking at an alien."

Jane lifted a spindly leg covered in brown fur. "I just never believed. How is it possible?"

"We rarely see this, but it happens. Pets go missing all the time. Aliens abduct them. Aliens do things we can't understand. See things we can't."

Jane lifted the chin of the Bassett hound to look at its shrunken, leathery face and the body slipped off the agent's arm and landed on a rock. "Oh I'm so sorry. I didn't mean to hurt him."

"He's dead."

"I know, but I damaged him. He's so helpless. How could anyone do that to him? Look at his lifeless paws."

"Actually I don't think anyone did. The aliens' project has gone wrong. They intended to duplicate the creatures so that they, themselves, can live among us and study us. But they didn't make them right. Their blood and other fluids leaked out. They went flat."

"How come my men on the beach suffered the same? Hardly any blood left in them. It's either that or they got disembowelled and lost their brains. You say that's the work of aliens?"

"The explanation for that is more complex. It has to do with aliens seeing their prototype creatures go flat and they believe Earthlings killed them. Earthlings killed the baby creatures they made. So they avenge the murders."

"That's ridiculous; convoluted beyond plausibility. You mean aliens drain blood from my officers and tear them apart because they think the police hurt the dogs that the aliens got into as disguises? Here we go again with another pointless recap." Jane picked up the fallen creature. Bits of tufted skin remained on the ground when she hoisted the light body and placed the little fellow back on Sinclair's arm. Sinclair didn't answer so she added, "Your hypothesis has a few flaws."

The silent stalemate became awkward then he spoke, "I'm open to other interpretations. This isn't the first time I've held these in my arms. My partner and I are the only people in the world who research these kinds of massacres. No one else connects the dots."

"Ok, sorry about not understanding. Had only had a few hours sleep. I've lost count of the number of officers down. There's a guy in hospital with a chewed-off leg mumbling about zombies. We got a call from an officer who saw dancing vampires. A report suggested Bigfoot did it. You have a flat dog over your arm and you say it's an alien. We've passed madness. This wasn't covered in training."

Jane continued to walk along the beach looking for evidence the CSI team missed, that her investigators missed and the special team from Surrey missed. She kicked stones and turned over twigs hoping to find a signed note from a drug dealer ordering the extinction of all his imagined enemies in the cruelest way possible. Sinclair drifted behind reminding her of a ghost. That's the only thing missing, she thought, a ghost. Maybe Sinclair will rush forward with Casper in a bag. He said it's over; stops as quickly as it began, better be right.

Jane turned to shout to the agent and found him just two yards behind. Before she could address him he quietly said, "I told you it was over, didn't I? That it ends as fast as it starts."

"You did, and I wanted to ask about that. What happens next?"

"Tha"s the easy part. My partner Joey arrives and we clean up. We get rid of all the things that people don't understand, including this." He raised his laden arm slightly to show what had to be cleaned up and the slippery dog took another tumble.

"Anyway the human bodies get picked up, cremated if possible and a long, slow investigation eventually files a report, in a year or two, saying that some sort of botulism from home-pickled beets caused stomachs to explode and skulls to break. That's what people want to hear. They want to believe that as long as they don't eat Aunt Maud's pickled beets they remain safe. Sure, the people who witnessed it don't believe a word, but that's OK because people don't believe them."

15

Funerals in which the living paid tribute to those who died horribly took place over several days. Bodies not cremated found interment in one of White Rock's two cemeteries. A government-sponsored memorial service for fallen police officers overflowed a South Surrey hockey arena.

The mess left by zombies in the cemeteries had disgusted the vamps and they made an effort at restoring order by pushing dirt back into graves and smoothing out the ground to cover puddles of drool and various viscera. A heavy rainfall helped.

Before first light on the day after mass cremations and burials zombies stumbled to both cemeteries like filings drawn to a magnet. A bounty of newly-buried had been recharged and reanimated during their brief 12-hour stay in the dark. Dead police officers, in particular, needed help getting out of luxury coffins because the public coffers had sprung for the finest cherry and mahogany secured with stainless steel screws. The electric charge in the ground prevented cement from hardening, so little resistance came from that containment.

Considerably less had been spent on underground housing for trailer park victims and their econo-coffins came apart easily, although digging out from under a ton of soil could never be described as easy. Dirt in the eyes constituted just one of many problems. Lack of light made it difficult to know up from down, although zombies-to-be intuited they had been laid to rest on their backs and thus dug upwards. Gravity caused loose soil to fall on them, but confirmed they were headed in the right direction. A Cream Bay man who had installed flooring for 50 years and loved every minute of it requested in his will that he be placed face-down in a custom coffin so that, for eternity, he would stare at its inlaid mosaic floor. Never did he clue-in to gravity as he clawed downwards and the light of day never again shone upon him.

The town's two graveyards became hives of activity as zombs, on bony hands and knees, scooped dirt and aided the emergence of fresh, lifelike bodies. In the end, the exercise produced somewhat disappointing. The majority of unearthed bodies, sent to their deaths by hungry zombs, had neither innards nor brains. Lack of a brain did not immediately separate them from mentally-challenged comrades who helped them dig out, but the lack of innards made it difficult for them to stand and walk without knuckles dragging the dirt. This ape-like posture did not put them on a lower rung on the undead social ladder since discrimination did not raise its ugly head.

The vamp wearing red pumps, who had been chewed to death at the cemetery, had been laid to rest. Vampire deaths came rarely and when they did, their bodies had to be dealt with in the traditional human way. Still shod in red shoes, the woman rose as the first zompire, a species with a desire for a red drink to accompany a meal of meat. Her fangs sank into the neck of the zombie who helped her out of her grave. She first wanted blood, but learned she was in the wrong department when damp dust, suitable for the surface of Mars, caught in her throat. She redirected her pearly incisors to the midriff of the same zombie and pulled a mouthful that had all the attraction of a dog turd on a hot sidewalk.

As a zompire she found no satisfaction in eating or drinking what was at hand and wandered into the woods to give wildlife a try. A bite of a bear's behind tasted good, but the zompire's brief life ended as the big, brown beast turned and chewed relentlessly on the foul flesh.

16

Mona, myself and a few other shamblers made our way, in the black night, to the Catholic cemetery and found several newly-buried extricating themselves. Owls and other birdlife flocked to trees to watch the unfolding of events, their happy hoots drowned out by moans and groans. Disembowelled body after body took first bent steps, fell and got up. Without innards to hold them straight and without brains to provide rudimentary instinct they stumbled in empty circles.

My fog-enshrouded thoughts concluded these pathetic creatures needed food and they would not be able to get it themselves. I picked up a rock and went hunting, but no moving target presented itself. I practised throwing, but wasn't able to hit the broad side of a birch tree with a small stone. My left knee got most hits and it wasn't a target. Eventually I came upon a grey, scabby cat that purred around my ankles enjoying my unique aroma. I gently picked up the purring pussy, intending to take it back to the needy, but my face snapped into the soft underbelly. Its legs kicked and claws dug, leaving thin bloodless trenches in my putrid cheeks. The cat's little head cracked against a rock. I finished dessert although the morsel of brain did not match the rainbow of flavors found in humans.

Again I felt an urge for a cigarette. I tried to conceptualize the dangers of smoking while a hint of emotions struggled to emerge: shame for what I had done to the cat, regret that I had so little control over carnivorous cravings and embarrassment for not sharing the pet with the more needy. My emotional morass would have registered one on a scale on which 10 was remorse for forgetting to bring in the garbage can.

Dropping the bloody, matted fur, I made a vague vow that I would behave better in the future and lumbered off. I could now see a future, a minute or two ahead, but beyond that my picture needed adjustment.

At a quiet intersection a brown delivery truck stopped for a red light and I lunged forward and smashed its window with a rock. The startled driver stomped on the gas and protesting tires launched his truck into the intersection where a small convertible T-boned it. Air bags exploded, metal bent, rust fell and an eerie silence prevailed until a pretty blonde passenger in the car uttered a plaintive cry. Blood seeped from a split in her forehead. This time I did not let temptation get the better of me despite the fact I imagined the taste of her brain mixed with her blood.

I led her to the curb where she sat, dazed, shocked and sobbing. My hand touched her head and I licked my fingers, hoping for remnants of brain drain. Both male drivers bled profusely, but lived. I pulled them from their smoking vehicles and dragged them to the edge of the road beside the woman. Before another car arrived my right hand grasped the pant leg of the car driver plus the ankle of the sobbing woman and my left fastened onto the ankle of the delivery truck driver. Dragging my semi-conscious trio like a triumphant hunter, I shuffled back to the cemetery.

Only token resistance came from the male drivers, dazed and in shock, as my friends feasted. In contrast, the woman, who had writhed and screamed the entire way to the hillside cemetery, doubled her resistance when she saw what happened to the men. I dumped her on the dirt in front of five ravenous eaters and she bounced to her feet and took strides towards freedom. Mona's steely fingers latched onto her long, flowing locks. The escapee screamed and squirmed, but the mouldy hand didn't let go.

A resurrected shell of a policeman, buried in uniform, grasped a furiously kicking leg and stilled the woman by twisting her ankle into a notch in an overhanging tree branch. She hung, screaming, with skirt hanging over her distorted face. Hungry zombs found her position accommodating: like lamb on a spit, Greek style. Instead of enjoying cooked outside layers, they focused on chewy insides.

I didn't understand the woman's commotion, nor did those enjoying her. We did not recollect pain and no longer feared death. We did not recall or know much of anything. Many did not remember they no longer had capacity for food storage. No sooner had they jammed spleen or kidney into mouth, chewed and swallowed, than the items dropped out of a big hole where a digestive system used to be. Other zombs picked up these fallen organs, pushed them into pie holes and found them at their feet. One liver fed many, but satisfied few.

    A zomb who had met her maker from natural causes cracked the inverted woman's skull with a shard of shale and contents dribbled to the dirt. Onlookers fell to their knees as if someone had shouted *52-pickup*. They scrambled for dirty brain bits and benefitted from the onrush of neural synaptic energy.

    I wondered what to do about hollows who got no benefit from body surfing yet did it compulsively. Then I wondered about my wondering. The fog had lifted a little. My name: Mort. I opened my mouth and said Morrth. The name oozed out, lopsided, like I had a starboard lisp.

    My name is Mortimer Smithers. I clearly heard each properly pronounced word in my head, but after the syllables drooled across my tongue and seeped from swollen labia my ears were assaulted with, *My aim ith more slivers.*

17

Where Ramon Reynolds' left leg should have been, a hospital blanket sagged. His right, encased in white from the knee down, lay atop the covers as did the rest of his body including two arms clad in blue plaster casts. Bandages swaddled his crotch so he resembled a child with an overflowing diaper. More bandages girded his head: a large blue bulge in the nasal area indicated severe damage.

Ramon's curly red hair dangled over the edges of white wrap. Stitches held together his black, swollen lips. When he smiled, more empty spaces than teeth expressed happiness.

Officials at Peace Arch Hospital, after days of delays, allowed Jane Dougherty and Jesse Nesterinko to talk to Ramon. When the two police walked in his sedation had worn off and a doctor had just explained that his right toes were missing, his reproductive organs were gone, his nose would never be straight and his arm would remain crooked. The good news was that his missing toes would not cause a limp as he had just one leg.

Ramon was furious: nurses had trashed his bloody Grateful Dead t-shirt. "It was an original," he shouted through thick lips and broken teeth. "Do you know what that's worth on eBay?"

A tall nurse carrying a wad of soiled bandages received his vitriol with a benign smile. The nurse hurried off without hazarding a guess as to what the shirt would fetch on an internet auction.

Following quick introductions Jesse hesitantly asked, "Could you tell us what happened?"

"A zombie ate my fuckin' leg, that's what happened. And after that he swallowed my favorite organs. My best T-shirt got a spot of blood on it and the nurse destroyed it. I'm so goddam mad."

"How do you know it was a zombie?" asked Jane.

Unexpectedly Ramon smiled, unashamed of the huge gaps between his teeth. "First, she was in a grave. Second, her flesh was rotting. Third, she ate part of me and wanted more. That defines a zombie in my book. She also stank like a shit hole."

"You were found at the side of the road. Where was the grave?"

"At the cemetery, up the hill, where else? In Wal-Mart? I crawled away." A trace of smile displaced anger.

"Have you ever seen a zombie before?" Jesse took a turn with a question as Jane backed towards the room's only chair and sank into its seat, stunned by eye-witness evidence that her town really was under attack by a dead, dark force. Ramon silently shook his head.

"Is this your first zombie encounter?" Jesse insisted, hoping Ramon would turn out to be a member of a weird, dead-worshiping cult and his observations would be worthless.

"I've walked through that cemetery for years. Never seen or heard a peep. I admit I've been scared sometimes. I've seen zombies in movies. The art people do a good job. Just like the real thing." Ramon paused for a brief giggle, then added, "They need to work on the skin. Add maggots, worms and slugs."

Jane leaned forward and told Ramon she had visited crime and accident victims in hospitals and rarely seen one smile.

"Hell, why wouldn't I smile? I'm alive. I can't believe it. That thing had me and I got away. But not before I got her. And that ambulance could have run over my head instead of saving me."

"Did you say you killed it?"

"Not sure. She wasn't looking too good last I saw. Her head was practically backwards and her hands looked like clown's gloves. I pounded her with rocks. I lost my T-shirt. Did I mention that? Makes me so mad."

"You can get another," Jesse placated. "But are you sure it wasn't some robber hiding in the cemetery waiting for someone to pass?"

"You think someone's gonna dig a grave, hide in it all night and wait for someone to fall in? It was a goddam zombie. I'm not crazy."

Jane called her station and ordered two men to head to the cemetery to investigate. With voice recorder and notebook in hand she asked Ramon if he would tell his story from the beginning, giving details.

At the end of his lengthy account a voice from the doorway asked Ramon if he had seen any bright lights. Jane looked around and Donald Sinclair, in beige suite, stood at the entry.

"How long have you been here?" Jane asked.

Sinclair said he heard the story from the beginning. "It explains a lot. The aliens are reanimating the dead. That's a perfect way to study us with minimum harm. That explains the gutted bodies, not just here, but in other places."

"That's so nice about minimum harm," Jesse said with a sarcastic nod towards Ramon, who sported a smile that made him look like a field pumpkin carved by a spastic hand.

"Not what I meant," Sinclair countered. "I mean the aliens don't want to hurt us. If they wanted to it would be easy for them to wipe out the whole town. How could they know that when the dead are resurrected they start eating flesh and brain? Let's consider …"

"You said it would stop. You would clean it up and blame it on canned beets."

"This is new territory. It's exciting. I mean where is it leading? Has it stopped? I don't know. Are aliens going to abduct us? I'm out there every day offering myself. I want to be first to go. I've got an antenna rigged up and I'm ready to talk." From the floor he picked up a box with rabbit-ear antenna sticking out and plugged it into a battery pack around his waist. "I should have been listening. I'm tuned to a frequency no one monitors."

"You're telling me," Jesse quipped.

"Am I in any sort of trouble?" the hairdresser asked.

"What for?" Jesse countered.

"For assault. I bashed a gal's head in and turned her hands into dinner plates."

"Looks like self-defence," Jane said. "The rules have changed. You killed the dead, or the undead, or something that's not covered in the criminal code."

"Except she probably isn't dead," Ramon continued. "She might be wandering around the woods, blind with her head on backwards, her jaw snapping and hands like a basketball player. Her rotting flesh stinks like dog shit and she looks like something the cat vomited. It's her fault I don't have my T-shirt. I saw on TV what happened to those poor trailer park stiffs. What a mess. I'm so lucky. And to answer that other question sir, yes, I saw a bright light. The morning sun just touched the horizon."

"Bright lights are a common phenomenon of near death experiences," Sinclair offered as a nurse entered the room and announced it was time to go.

"Someone's been eating too much fruit cake and it isn't Ramon," Jesse muttered on his way to the door.

18

The colonel from Ottawa offered Jane Dougherty not a word of thanks for her ceaseless work when his hard heels clacked into her station and he told her he was taking charge. Four days of nothing but here and there naps had depleted her of the will to resist and the desire to see written orders.

The 50-year-old colonel sported a black, two-toothbrush, moustache that a dictator could have worn with pride. Every item of his clothing appeared to have come from the dry cleaners an hour earlier. A brass band and red carpet might well have preceded his military march into the station a few minutes before midnight. Three well-dressed soldiers accompanied him and stood at attention in the background.

Jesse, grumpy and bearing a grudge, told the military man that although he might now be in charge, he should be aware of an after dark curfew and anyone wandering around, including colonels, had a good chance of being jailed, shot or eaten alive. Jesse added that if he didn't get his car out of the no-stopping zone it would be ticketed and towed.

The colonel shouted an order at a private and then, with a slight clicking of heels, turned, faced Jane Dougherty and said loudly, "I've been briefed of the situation here. Who are the insurgent killers and where do we track them?"

"If it was that easy it would be done and you wouldn't be here. My name is Jane Dougherty and that's Jesse Nesterinko. You haven't introduced yourself."

"I offer apologies. Colonel Mayhew-Shostakovich."

"Bless you," said Jesse quietly.

"I beg your pardon."

"I thought you had sneezed."

"Are you attempting humor with my name?"

"Excuse him," Jane interjected, "Junior here hasn't learned when to rein in. May we just call you May?"

"No, you may not."

Nesterinko butted in, "You may call me Jesse and she's known as Dough although she doesn't like it, so Jane would be better."

"I wasn't addressing you. Step back."

Jess took a large step away from Jane.

"Mayhew-Shostakovich combines ..."

"Gesundheit," Jesse whispered.

"... Russian heritage with English reform. Do you have a problem with that, Private Nesterstinko?"

"No problem colonel. Just sounds like a snotty sneeze."

"Now, fill me in with details Sergeant, I'll listen."

Jane took a deep breath and began her recitation. "It started with a senior woman being murdered and a man walking in a cemetery being attacked and badly bitten. Close to the same time there was a slaughter at a mobile home park. Next some of my men went down. A car and a truck crashed, but no victims, no bodies. Half the hookers here and in South Surrey claim to have been date raped. They are anaemic and amnesiastic. That's a mouthful: weak and remembering nothing of the hours after the attack. The guy in hospital says a zombie ate his leg. And a woman, suffering some sort of post traumatic disorder, says her dead husband ate her boyfriend right in front of her kids."

"Much appreciated sergeant but I've studied the reports and you've added little that's new except about the prostitutes. Elaborate."

"About 18 hookers, strippers and addicts have wakened in the woods, at widely ranging spots. They don't know how they got there. A few recall getting a phone call to meet a guy at Second Sip coffee shop and next thing they know they wake up in the woods. They have $100 or more new cash in their purses. The women suffer headaches, neck wounds and weakness: can barely walk and talk. Doctors say low blood pressure, slight puncture wounds, nothing more. We've had similar complaints before, but never so many in one night."

"And how do you assess that situation sergeant?" The colonel barked the question.

"I don't. Could be a motorcycle gang at work or ..."

Jesse interrupted, "We know someone you might want to talk to. It could be alien abductions."

"Don't talk nonsense, boy," the colonel retorted. "Stick to the facts. Take another step back." Nesterinko took a step back and spoke again, "You probably won't be able to hear me tell about the dead pets from back here."

"You've got animals on your mind as well as aliens?"

Jane interceded. "A special agent from CSIS showed me the dried out body of a blood-drained dog."

"What the bucking smell," the colonel shot out and then quickly muttered, "Excuse my language."

"You didn't actually say it," Jesse quipped with a wry smile.

"I thought it, that's enough."

"Whatever," Jesse whispered. "We got things to do. There's a community needs saving and talking ain't doin' it." He strode to his shared office in the back.

"Tell me about the dog," Colonel Mayhew-Shostakovich ordered and Jane explained about missing pets, Agent Sinclair and his theories.

"Tell me more about the alien theory," he again ordered, and Jane tried to decipher Sinclair's theory, but ended in a tangle of contradictions.

"Tell me about the zombie theory," he ordered.

"You may be in charge of military operations Mr. Mayhew, but to me you're just another complication so I'd appreciate if you didn't order me."

"Oh spit, have I been doing that? Sorry about the language. OK, please tell me all you know about the man in hospital."

Jane gave a synopsis.

"I've no more questions," the colonel stated abruptly. "If you'll excuse me I have to engage the enemy. We'll maintain the curfew. Anyone out after dark dies. I'll have combat troops on every corner."

The Colonel yelled unintelligible orders to his three soldiers and proceeded towards the door. Before he got outside Jane shouted, "I don't want you killing my people just because someone not too bright goes for an evening walk. A warning or arrest would be sufficient."

The colonel turned, puffed out his chest and replied, "Your point is taken sergeant."

19

In the darkest shadows, beneath branches that overhung lanes and alleys I lurched. My ponderous plodding irritated me. Why couldn't I stand tall and walk like a regular guy? Why did I schlep along like I carried bags of bowling balls? Leather hiking boots covered my feet, not fluffy slippers with bunny ears, yet I stumbled forward like a challenged sloth with bad knees. I needed to get in shape so I could heft my feet, swing my arms and walk like a man, even a girly man.

My hands sensed none of the cool dew as I put them below my chest and pushed away from the ground. I could do push-ups all day, albeit in slow motion. Strength wasn't the issue.

I tried jumping jacks but, despite the strength in my legs, my heavy feet wouldn't leave the ground. Like firefighter's hoses filled with stagnant water, my arms swung hopelessly, refusing to fly above shoulders. I needed a personal trainer but I might eat him.

Blurred recollections drifted into semi-awareness as I fretted about my state. Fretting was good. Was I dead? Did the dead fret? What brought about my demise? An auto accident had not been my undoing and I had not bled to death from an open wound. A heart attack had not struck me down in my prime. It had to do with water. When my band crossed under the bridge I had turned back. Now I knew I feared water. I was an aquatic scaredy-cat.

A weak moon cast helpful shadows between scattered clouds as I walked and thought. A semblance of memory pleased me and now I knew I possessed an IQ higher than a domino tile. A boat floated into memory. A small craft, a kayak: one I had painted pink. I loved to paddle. I had set out on a dead-calm day after lifeguards had ended their season. A squall came up and whipped mist from waves and spread it like fog across the water.

Towards home I paddled, being cautious because deadheads, residues of lumbering, floated inches below the surface. A motor roared and a fool with more horsepower than brains blasted across the bay. Mist amplified the roar then something hit my craft and bits of bow splintered across the water. Shards of Kevlar slowly sank, but only the first few inches of my kayak had been shattered.

Cleverly I leaned back so the trickle of water that entered flowed to the stern and the remains of the stem rose out of the ocean: I could continue paddling. Occasionally bailing and stroking towards shore, my future looked promising and I took it as a good omen when a salmon jumped through the open bow and into my boat. The two-pound fish, with beautiful iridescent silver and green flanks, flipped about, slowly dying. I didn't want trouble for fishing without a license so I reached to throw it back into the sea. The bow dipped and gallons of water set the fish free and sank my boat.

Desperately I reached for the life jacket as my slender craft settled into the cool liquid. I had tied a lifeline to the uninflated jacket so the wind wouldn't blow it away and it went down with the ship. Camera and binoculars hung from my neck, secured with a knot so that I wouldn't lose them. Pockets held coins, a multi-tool and rock specimens picked up on shore. Hiking boots that carried me around rocky parkland clung to my feet like bricks and pulled me to a watery grave.

Eventually, I imagined, camera bag and binoculars fell from my drooping neck and rocks slipped from decayed pockets. My body floated upwards and wind pushed it to shore where it lodged, like a pile of rags, among rocks that no one clambered upon in October. The vague feeling that I differed from the other afterlife that surrounded me found confirmation. Never had I been displayed in a casket, never had I known a mortician and never had I clawed my way out of a grave. Cold Pacific salt water had cradled my brain. Then a strange force recharged me and allowed me to think ponderously, if not profoundly or profusely.

"Yeth," I said as the 15-watt lightbulb of thought brightened. I understood why I was waterlogged and wished I could wring myself out. It all made sense, if sense could be made from a second coming. Were there others like me? What about people who starved in the woods, died under an avalanche or drowned in a bathtub? A Craig's List posting might bring together a support group.

Did you drown, starve or suffocate?
Feel alienated, alone?
Join Zombies Without Friends.
Meet Tuesday, 6 p.m., at Second Sip.

20

Despite Donald Sinclair's absurd predictions, weird antenna and bizarre theories Jane Dougherty took a mild liking to him. A gentle manner, self-assurance and quiet, low-key demeanour were qualities she appreciated and seldom saw in men, especially the men she dealt with. Talking to him was like finding a tranquil oasis in a desert storm. How unfortunate his theories could not lead to a satisfying end. As much as she would like to believe in his little green men and alien abductions, an earthy rubber cell would likely serve as his future home.

Jane could accept that humans did not live alone in the universe, but Sinclair believed, without a shred of proof, that aliens were here now. Would he walk in with a Martian tucked under his arm? Would she then believe? The inconceivable challenged the implausible. Had she not received so many reports identifying zombies she would have laughed at the idea. People were being eaten alive. That was the truth.

Every few minutes Jane eyed her wall clock: she had agreed to meet Sinclair at 10 a.m. A few minutes after 10 the longest legs she had ever seen on a woman approached her office. They stemmed from a bimbo body of the first order: frizzy blonde hair, lips afire, mascara applied with a paint roller and a severely unbuttoned blouse revealing two dolphins coming up for air. A heavy knock shook her door then Sinclair stepped in and announced, "I'd like you to meet my partner, Joey. She just got in this morning."

"Good morning Joey," Jane muttered in a gobsmacked way and stuck out her calloused hand with broken fingernails. The buxom blonde shook with arm-wrestler ferocity and whispered a return greeting. Jane pushed back unruly brown curls and licked dry lips, "Anything new?"

"This is it," Sinclair answered and Jane assumed his pronoun referred to his partner. Before she could respond to the banal announcement he continued excitedly, "This is where and when it happens. I'm out there waiting for …"

A voice that sounded like firecrackers exploding in a locker interrupted, "He's loony," Joey cackled, "Out of his tree. He's had this alien thing up his ass for a year now."

"Hold on," Sinclair countered, apparently habituated to the voice. "You know as well as anyone that things aren't always what they seem. Sometimes …"

"No, they ain't," Joey interrupted again with a double negative that made sense. "We've got a horde of goddam zombies eating people and you see aliens. Get over it. These ain't no zombie aliens. Things are just as they seem and that ain't no goddam good."

"My theory may seem challenged at the moment, but there's still time. Imagine …"

"Imagine yourself in a strait jacket being fed with a spoon." The edgy voice spoke louder than necessary and accentuated what Jane was thinking.

"We don't have time for bickering," Jane declared. "Do you have anything new to tell me?"

"Back off Joey," Sinclair ordered. "Yes. There's an outer space research antenna not far from here. I believe it receives interstellar communications and collaterally directs them into the ground. That's what reanimates the un-living. Other places where similar slaughters have occurred have the same type of antennae. We're onto something here, something we should have seen long ago. This supports the alien theory."

"My ass!" Joey's oral fingernails scratched across a vocal blackboard. "A nearby antenna does not support an alien invasion. Yes, the antenna could be directing some sort of energy into the ground, but there sure as hell ain't no reason to believe it's directed by Martians. You got little green men in your pants."

As Sinclair's lips formed the beginning of his retort Jane again intercepted, "Who's in charge?"

"I have seniority," Sinclair replied. "I've been here longest. I hired her."

"And I've got the smarts and I'm gonna be advanced out of this department to do something worthwhile."

"I've always found saving lives worthwhile," Jane said. "What do you know about zombies? How is it possible? Here in White Rock. Can such things exist?"

Sinclair pushed his chair so its wooden legs scraped the floor and silenced Joey. Unimpeded, he continued, "Here's something interesting. Vampires, and most other man-made monsters and aliens, all have a base in literature with seminal works such as Dracula, War of the Worlds and Frankenstein forming the backbone of beliefs. Zombies, on the other hand, stem from an oral tradition. That gives credibility. They have a history of hundreds of years starting with the Bokor ..."

"Don't dig into that pile of shit," Joey said. "Zombies are right here in this town today. That's the whole story. That's all we need to know."

"Have you two reported to Colonel Mayhew?" Jane asked, again halting the verbal duel.

Sinclair responded, "Yes we've checked in. Mayhew scoffed at the theory, but told us to give him a written report that he promised to read carefully. We have a four day deadline."

Joey hissed slightly more quietly, "That guy's another nutbar. If he'd stop being sorry for swearing, or not swearing, or whatever, and get on with his fuckin' job he might get something done."

"Have you visited the Dominion Radio Observatory?" Jane asked, "That's the one with the big antenna you're talking about."

"Would go, but we have to work on that report for the Colonel," said Sinclair.

"It should be in your report. Check it out and let me know what you find."

After they departed Jane called the morgue and learned nothing unusual had happened with bodies. None had sat up and talked or gone for a walk. In the morgue's cold storage you stayed dead; at least during the day. No one volunteered to work the night shift to see if the dead banged on steel drawers.

A return call came from the chief health inspector and Jane wanted to know what it would take to get an order requiring that all dead be cremated. She learned it was unprecedented territory. Religious beliefs were guaranteed in the Bill of Rights and Freedoms and death rites usually had religious overtones.

"What about encasing them in cement?" Jane asked.

"Cement isn't holding for some reason. We've had basements collapse."

"OK, can you make steel coffins and weld them shut?"

"If the surviving family agrees, we could. Who'd pay for it?"

"Who cares who pays? This is an emergency. A national emergency The army's in charge. Will you do it?"

"Sounds reasonable. It will take a few days to put it all together, but it can be done."

21

Vampires had been waiting thousands of years for the apocalypse, or, as they called it, the third coming.

Reaching a consensus and forming a plan of any kind had never been their style, but now discussion came as naturally as sun in summer. Dozens of comrads, awakened prematurely, needed blood. Too often a newly awakened dragged a local into the bushes and sucked to the last drop: not acceptable. Resources had to be managed and a body drained could not be recycled.

The proliferation of flesh eaters made human resource management difficult and made normal vampire life impossible. It was ironic that vampires experienced their much anticipated third coming at a time zombies were having their second coming. The undead depleted resources at a horrendous rate giving no thought to ecology, global warming or endangering the species they depended on. Because of them people no longer walked the streets or went out at night. Hookers and call girls stopped responding to phone calls.

When the anthropophagites struck, viable bodies went to waste. With so many soldiers on the streets the vamps couldn't get a sip in edgewise and soldiers didn't serve well as donors. They stuck together like stingy members of a Sunday church with no offerings.

Night prowling became the *modus operandi* of thirsty leeches and it proved difficult and unproductive. Many vamps broke into houses and found them empty: owners had fled to cottages, to homes of distant friends or to vacation spots. Looting held no interest.

Inhabited houses were now so well secured that a bank would be easier to get into, had money been the need. A blood bank made a much better target and vamps worked at getting one of their kind a job as a security guard at Red Cross.

Vamps didn't enjoy working and when they did take employment they proved lazy and irresponsible. Good references were difficult to come by, thus their resumes short and job prospects bleak. Fortunately living for eternity produced excellent retirement opportunities. Long term investments nearly always paid off as did the prudent collecting of art and coins. When they worked it was part-time and done to relive monotony rather than poverty.

Living beyond suspicion for century after century required the constant reinvention of identities, thus vamps had expertise in obtaining false birth certificates, social insurance numbers and drivers' licences. Some would accuse them of fraud and forgery while others would appreciate they had little choice if they didn't want to be celebrated as oldest war vet, oldest car operator or oldest pensioner. A driver's licence awarded the same year as the invention of the car and a birth certificate dated 1726 were sure giveaways. Vampires enjoyed publicity as mice enjoyed cats.

Shotguns, handguns, machineguns and even potato guns presented no danger to the vamps whose self-repairing superblood could mend all but a broken heart. With a stoic reserve, garnered over centuries, their hearts seldom broke. More serious cardiac penetration from wooden stakes, metal stakes or even plastic stakes spilled far too much blood and the impaled vamp vanished for all time. Garlic, silver bullets, mirrors and crosses annoyed them to no end, but did not kill or repel.

The big danger, when vamps prowled for blood, came from home-made zombie traps that, almost overnight, became the in thing in backyard decor. They consisted of six-foot-deep holes in the ground camouflaged with tarps. Theoretically zombie steps on tarp and goes into hole. Springs pull edges of tarp into air, zombie hangs in tarp, alarm sounds and homeowner goes out with hatchet and dispatches enemy.

Unfortunately homeowners often forgot that zombies rarely traveled alone and homeowners got eaten.

Vampires carried Swiss Army-multi-tools and when they fell into a zombie trap they cut through and ran. Males had a steel plate sewn into their jackets to deflect bullets and blows from sharp weapons and ladies' bras had carbon-fibre cups that extended beyond breasts.

Although they did not like to socialize, and long-term interests were best served by not meeting as a group, vampires called an emergency assembly at Vladimir's Bar. Several showed up.

The zombie infestation created so many problems that those at the meeting didn't know where to look for solutions. They had no ideas on how to deal with the additional vamps that had suddenly come to life and had to be fed. Curfews, cannibalism and mass hysteria made it next to impossible to get a red drink unless cranberry or tomato. Those beverages had the same appeal as curdled milk.

A few irritated vampires got to their feet at the meeting and demanded a posse be formed to hunt and kill zombies. An equally determined group replied that none of them owned guns, none of them knew karate and none of them had any knowledge of how to kill a zombie. If police and army couldn't do it how could they?

"Knock off their heads with a cricket bat," a meek insurance consultant suggested. "We downed one at the cemetery." She appeared ready to swallow her words as listeners quietly stated that none of them were good athletes and their hand-eye coordination would lead to hitting a fellow vamp instead of an undead head.

"I couldn't get near one for the stink," a part-time psychology professor concluded.

"Wear an oxygen mask when you step up to the plate with your cricket bat," the insurance consultant responded.

"Poor analogy, it's a wicket," corrected a woman. "Besides, wielding bats would set us apart. We don't even support a sports team."

"We've passed the point of caring about mixed metaphors and about being seen as different. There are already questions about why we don't have children, why we don't age, why we don't bowl. At a time when zombies drink our breakfast juice before we get to the table, the least of our worries is people wondering why we have cricket bats. We're in our greatest crisis since witch hunts."

A young woman, a part-time dental hygienist, walked to the front and stood behind a pile of stacked chairs that served as a lectern. "We've been through worse," she said. "We've seen world wars. We lost members to mustard gas and gas ovens. We've been through drought, famine and gay lynching. We've survived polio, yellow fever, small pox, Spanish flu and more pandemics than I can name. Here we are –

survivors. This is just a rough patch. No need for alarm. Go home, watch TV and this too will pass."

Half the audience applauded mildly and when it quieted another woman who also worked in a dental office stood up. "That's easy for you and me because of where we work. When a patient is under and the dentist steps into the outer office we can take a sip. At the end of the day we can upload a pint at home. But it doesn't go far. It doesn't feed a community. I've been working extra hours and taking longer sips. Patients have been waking up weak and sick and not knowing where they are or how they got there. This only happens when I'm on duty. Sorry friends, but I have to stop. I have to stop when I'm needed most. For us in medical it's easy to say be patient and say this will pass. Ditto hair dressers, manicurists, psychologists, masseuses and anyone who can get a customer to sit alone in a chair. We can no longer stand by. We must fight the plague that steals our blood."

A normally reticent vampire, who kept up appearances by pruning trees, stood up and announced, "I saw them drown. They can't swim. They don't even know they can't swim. They just walk into the water, flap their arms and go under. Pretty funny."

The speaker paused for laughter, but none came. "Here's my plan. At night a few of us plump ones stand at the end of a dock as bait and lure zombies. When they get near, we jump into the water and swim away. Zombies jump after us and drown. Easy to execute, no downside."

A high-pitched voice shot out, "None of us are plump."

"Insignificant point," the slightly portly pruner replied. "I've put on a few pounds eating peaches and plums. I'll do it. I'll stand at the end of the dock. Anyone with me?"

The second dental assistant answered quietly, but loud enough for all to hear, "I'm with you. Everyone go home before curfew except us two. At 2 a.m. we make our way through alleys, avoiding patrols and catching sight of zombies who chase us to the dock."

The plan could hardly be rejected. Quietly heading home made everyone a part of the plot: they felt good about participating and were in no danger.

Two hours past midnight the dental assistant and orchardist cautiously exited the tavern's back door and skulked across the parking lot to a laneway. The army patrolled with a barrage of illumination, the purpose of which was to announce their coming so other patrols didn't shoot them. They also announced their coming to those they hoped to capture or kill.

Zombie stink, and accompanying flies and mosquitoes, permeated the air to such a degree that the vamp duo could not determine if the enemy hid around the corner or had passed an hour ago. The pair skittered from alley to alley, slowly heading towards the ocean. They heard noises and the stench got stronger. "Brains" reached their ears and they become afraid, extremely afraid. A slouching figure launched itself slowly from a doorway. The vamps quickly reversed and found two drooling bodies behind them, blocking their retreat. Jaws snapped audibly while they hummed "brains" as if a TV jingle couldn't escape their heads.

For the first time in their long lives the vampires feared their end was nigh. Regeneration of broken limbs and infected lungs happened systematically, but when brains and innards went hither and yon there would be no recuperation.

The spry vamps deked left and, as dumb zombies lunged for them, darted right. Fingers grasped and the straws gasped, but the twain did not meet. When more revenants stumbled out of doorways the duo mockingly patted their stomachs, pointed to their brains and shouted, "Come and get us, dinner's ready!"

Taunting continued as they headed to the shoreline and gingerly backed down the town's long pier. As per plan, zombies followed, then searchlights, flashlights and flares lit the sky. A gunshot sizzled through the air, whizzed through a zombie body and hit a houseboat's pontoon. Along the wooden walkway, a few yards above salt water, an undead horde shuffled, mumbled and stumbled. Army gunfire put light to the night. Bullets found their marks and flesh flew. A motor on the back of a boat caught a bullet and caught fire. Flames illuminated the eerie mob and those who embraced darkness covered their eyes or looked away.

Bullets didn't stop the ghouls from continuing their stagger along the dock, closing in on their pale prey. They didn't notice the blizzard of flesh – their flesh. Even when pieces of heads blew into the air, feet kept going and the hum continued like an atonal men's choir in need of direction.

At dock's end the vamps met a sturdy wooden guardrail, something they hadn't anticipated. A low plank had been removed to facilitate lifting of crab traps and the duo furiously kicked at the board above. A dozen desperate blows sent it sailing into the sea. Now nothing would deter the lemmings from marching out of their depth to their death.

Black Gucci shoes and matching Dernier jackets came off in preparation for a dip then a bullet thudded into the tree pruner's shoulder and knocked him to the wood deck. Another bullet slid through the hygienist's hip and she fell beside the pruner. Zombies quickened their lugubrious pace. The pruner recovered and got to his feet but couldn't stop a tuxedoed flesh-eater, more fleet of foot than the others, from lurching at him. It bit into his arm and both lost balance and tumbled into the salty brine.

The zomb made no attempt at swimming while the vamp did a desperate breaststroke, dragging attached carnivore. A downward pull, as if from a battleship anchor, came from the zombie who would sooner sink with meat in its teeth than remove its bite and grab hold of a piling.

The hygienist got up on her good leg and pondered how close she should allow the rest of the zombies to come before taking the plunge. A bullet holed her stomach and made the decision for her as it knocked her off the dock and into the black bay. She landed on the back of the heavyweight that bit into her comrade. The force knocked them apart and the attacker vanished into the deep. One zombie down, according to plan, she proudly thought and waited for the next.

"Thanks," gasped the pruner as both swam beneath the dock and looked back for the cascade of stinking flesh.

For memory-challenged zombies, bodies out of sight were out of mind. The long walk on the dock turned into an abbreviated stroll. Uniformed men crouching behind blazing machine guns presented a bigger feast than the disappeared duo that hadn't even smelled right. Skin, hair, bone and muscle filled the air like debris in a hurricane as tattered revenants marched fearlessly forward, into the firestorm.

"Hold your positions," the army sergeant ordered. Swiss-cheesed zombies reached the men and hand-to-hand combat ensued. Bayonets and rifle butts harmed the zombies as kids curious fingers harmed bowls of jelly. With five soldiers brainless and gutted on the ground, the remaining men disobeyed orders from their commander who stood back from the carnage. Terrified, they retreated and lived to fight another battle. The sergeant followed.

The undead despaired of the chase, dispersed in many directions and found refuge in sheds and dumpsters as sunlight touched the tops of trees on distant mountains. Several buried themselves in sandy soil so that not even an eye showed. Others burrowed into gravel and rocks where they felt the comfort of home.

In cold water beneath the dock the vamp pair waited for the inhuman waterfall. After 10 minutes they realized their mission had been a bust and were it not for a bit of good luck one of them would be at the bottom of the sea. The swimmers knew their clothes on the dock would lead to their discovery so the pretty dental worker volunteered to emerge and confront troops who had returned to gather their dead. She dog-paddled to shore then waded out of the ocean with hands held high.

"Please don't shoot," she yelled before stepping onto sand.

"Hold your fire," the sergeant ordered. "Hands on top of your head lady."

"Zombies were chasing us; we saved ourselves by jumping into the water."

"Where's your friend?"

"He decided to swim home. We live across the bay in Crescent Beach. He's a champion swimmer. Probably in bed by now."

"You can lower your hands. You've been wounded."

"It's nothing really. I'm OK. I'll be on my way if you don't mind."

"You're not OK. You've got a hole through your stomach and a chunk of your hip is missing. You're in shock. You need help." He turned to his troops. "Someone bring a blanket. Get a medic and ambulance up front, now."

The hygienist quickly replied in a soft voice, "Really, I think you're overreacting. It's just a little hole. Missed the vitals. I'll be fine. I should be getting home, there's laundry to finish."

"I can't let you go lady. You're delirious. You've got a hole in one side and out the other. I can shine my flashlight through it. You need medical attention."

Before the hygienist could further refuse treatment a blanket arrived and so did a medic. He gaped at the hole in her middle and swore he had never seen anything like it: it wasn't bleeding. Four privates lifted her onto a stretcher and into an ambulance.

Halfway to hospital the hygienist beckoned the attendant to come closer, as if she was going to confess she loved him. She got a perfect hit into his left jugular. A half-mile later she begged the driver to stop as she had to urinate. He told her to pee in the potty in back, but she replied that she might miss with the ambulance bouncing around and she didn't want to embarrass herself. He pulled over and as he stretched to provide toilet tissue she scored squarely with both eye teeth. She had blood to spare and share.

The hygienist stepped out of the ambulance with its two unconscious occupants and wondered what to do, where to go. Emerging daylight made her head feel like someone was trepanning with a dull drill. If she wore dark sunglasses she could tolerate the discomfort, but she hadn't thought about bringing glasses on a night mission.

Zombies had no use for the wide sandy beach, she presumed, so she made her way to the shore, sat in deep shade beneath a willow and examined her superficial wounds: healing had started. The sky brightened: her head throbbed. Despite taking a dunking her high-end phone still worked so she called Vanessa to pick her up. Twenty messages on the wet cell asked about the mission. She answered only the tree pruner who deserved to know how she escaped. From his land line he said he had laid low under the dock and then tried to call for a ride but his phone was waterlogged. He hailed a taxi that demanded extra tipping to make up for the dripping.

A black Mercedes with dark tinting, driven by a dark woman with large ebony sunglasses, took the hygienist home. In her dim kitchen she spurted excess blood into a one-litre jar she put into her refrigerator. Then, feeling sorry for herself and her race, she went to bed and rested soundly while her wounds healed. Fresh blood helped the process.

22

Donald Sinclair returned from the Dominion Astrophysical Observatory and its array of antennae like a man who had found salvation. His partner Joey returned like she had failed her audition for *Sex Kittens from Planet X*.

With hands flying to express excitement Sinclair danced around Jane Dougherty's office loudly explaining that the huge antenna had the capability to capture signals from space and direct them into the ground.

"You should see the suckers," he shouted as gleefully as a child discovering chocolate, "They're bigger than a house. They're humungous funnels sucking life and energy from the sky and shoving it into the earth. If …"

"I know them," Jane interrupted. "You don't have to describe them."

"But I never knew their size, never realized that aliens could channel themselves as radio waves, beam themselves to antennae and travel through the earth. As they pass through they energize the dead. It's all making sense."

Joey's hands covered her ears. Her face sucked lemons. Jane asked, "What's your opinion?"

The wire brush voice scraped rusty steel and Joey tapped forward on heels that needlessly exaggerated her height, most of which came from legs, "I'm so embarrassed. Not just for myself, but for the department. My partner sees a maple tree and it's a hideout for aliens. He sees a car and it gets energy from little green men. It never ends. You win Donny boy. I've had it. I quit. You're now the entire department."

"Good," he replied without hesitation. "You've been a hindrance since you joined. Now I can progress."

"Sit down," Jane ordered harshly. "We need both your reasoning. You can quit, but not in the midst of my town's crisis. Mayhew needs the report. He needs to know about the antennae. How close are you?

Joey bent her legs and eternity passed before her posterior, bound by a tight red skirt, found the chair. "A dozen pages. I tried to talk to him but he's too busy. OK, this might not be the time to quit. I'll wait before I make it official."

"Sorry to hear that," Sinclair interjected and Jane spoke like a schoolteacher.

"Cut it out, both of you. Joey, what's your take on the antennae?"

"They're key elements, for sure. In other towns where dead may possibly have risen, radio antennae point to space. We spoke to the chief astronomer and he said last week's conditions could be repeated: exceptional sun flares, lightning storms, radio waves and shit like that and they somehow interact with the protective mountains, an ocean and maybe uranium deposits. All other outbreak places have similar topography. Something has to be done with those antennae. Sun flares are active right now."

"How do you see it, Donald?" Jane questioned quietly and Sinclair answered softly.

"Remember your high school biology and physics? A guy named Luigi Galvani made frog's legs twitch by applying electricity. Less known is what Jean Laborde did with heads fresh from the guillotine in France in the 1880s. He used needles and current to get the eyes to wink and the mouths to move as an indication that the heads were aware of their surroundings.

"That's what it's about. Electricity in the form of radio waves and magnetic waves. They make the dead come to life. The antennae suck waves from space and force them into the earth. The antennae are the problem: we agree on that."

Before Jane could ask another question Sinclair continued. "This department's focus is aliens. If we don't look for aliens then what use are we? I've got a kid to support. I can't have the department close its doors. I'll lose my job if I can't find aliens."

"Is your wife looking after your child?" Jane asked, slightly disappointed that he was spoken for. Occasionally she glimpsed

Sinclair's thoughtful underside and it made her forget the fruitcake that came in thick slices with a bounty of nuts.

"No, my daughter's with my sister in Ottawa. My wife died. We were camping in Quebec and she went for a walk. Her body was never found. Bears, alien abduction, Sasquatch ... I'll never know ..." Sinclair covered his face with both hands apparently ready to break down then sat upright and concluded his thoughts. "You see, our focus is aliens, not motorcycle gangs or disease."

Jane felt a twinge of relief that his wife had exited the picture and then felt guilty about the thought. At least she now had some understanding of why such a good-looking, quiet-spoken guy had jumped out of his plane without a parachute. Perhaps losing a life-partner did that. Especially losing one who went for a walk in the woods and was never seen again.

"I never imagined you worried about your job," Joey cackled with the subtlest hint of sarcasm.

"Have you got a partner?" Jane asked, to avoid more acrimony. She used the word partner cautiously because she had a slight suspicion Joey might walk on both sides of the street.

"No, I'm alone. Probably gonna stay that way. Haven't had much man luck. They come and go. How about you?"

"Well, at least, for you, they come," Jane chuckled, unsure about Joey's depth. "White Rock can be lonely when you're the female top cop. It's not easy going to a nightclub with a guy who knows you're counting drinks and assessing his ability to drive. A goodnight kiss in lock-up isn't romantic."

"You're better off that way. I never know what men are after and if it's the wrong thing then I'm screwed." Joey laughed as a horse would laugh if it had a sense of humor.

Sinclair had nothing to contribute to the line of conversation so brought it back with, "What about the antennae?"

Jane and Joey turned to him, frowning. The chitchat had provided a moment of relief from the tensions that dogged them.

Sinclair and Joey listened while Jane called the radio observatory. They clapped when the head astronomer agreed to point the antennae east, the direction of least interstellar activity. They would be tilted as close to the ground as possible. All electronics would be off within the hour.

That's real Canadian efficiency, Jane thought as Donald and Joey departed. No red tape, no reports to be filed, no permissions requested. A call to Colonel Mayhew went unanswered so she left a message about the big dishes being turned off.

She then called Jesse, whom she hadn't seen for a day. Usually their paths overlapped several times during routine work hours, but regular schedules had become a fond memory. In times of extra stress, Jane had noted, Jesse enjoyed extra sleep. She called his cell and his landline. When the message service clicked in she left her standard, "Me Jane, you call."

A sleepy voice called 20 minutes later and Jesse said he would be late getting in as he had an appointment with his dental hygienist.

"Here we are," Jane responded, "in the midst of a national crisis and the most important thing in your life is getting your teeth cleaned. At least you'll look good with perfect pearls glistening from your coffin."

She could hardly believe she had a thing for him a few years back despite his being her junior by three years and being under her command. Mentally he was her junior by a decade. Fortunately he didn't pick up on her subtle advances and nothing ensued.

Jane's occasional forays into the dating field gave a spark to men in their late 40s and 50s, but after an evening of talking about medical plans and government bonds nothing stoked her fire. In sleepy White Rock, a haven for retirees, the average age reached the stratosphere and discussions at coffee shops centred on who did the best colonoscopy, who cheated at lawn bowling and what retirement homes served the best meals. The only spark she thought about fanning belonged to a married man with kids. Such a relationship had the promise of a campfire in a monsoon so she invested her time in corralling speeders and jaywalkers.

Desperately Jane wanted information about Mayhew and his battle against the forces of evil, or whatever they were. The radio scanner had burbled with hints of a battle, but she had ordered her men off the streets so she received no first-hand reports. None of her RCMP members had been injured since the arrival of the army and that gave relief.

Civilians found less than they hoped for in the way of protection from the army. Those of limited IQ – and there were many – insisted on trying to take video of enemy action so they could be first to post zombie clips on YouTube and Facebook. Instead web sites flourished with last words such as *Oh my God* and *Oh Shit!* Cell phones and cameras, found beside corpses, contained images of blue sky and body fluid rainbows.

Jane drove to the King George interchange at the edge of town and stopped where a dozen army men and women, in full combat gear, hunched behind a barricade of sandbags. Machine gun barrels, mortars, flamethrowers and bazookas stuck out. Traffic passed unchecked at the rate of just a few cars per minute. Despite her flashing blue and red lights and the announcement *Police* over her speaker, a young soldier trained his machine gun on her head. She got out, glued her hands to her head and shouted that she wanted to know how things went last night. The soldier slowly lowered his armament and replied that he didn't have clearance to disclose anything.

Jane answered, "The enemy know what went on. The only people kept in the dark are those that can help."

He replied, "Yes ma'am."

The post's ranking officer responded to her request for information with, "Yes ma'am."

In situations such as this Jesse's skill exceeded hers by a wide margin: he could make a mute mule talk.

A brief siren blip announced her arrival at his house. The front door swung open and he appeared awake, alert and in uniform. As they drove along North Bluff Ave. Jesse made a call to cancel an appointment with his hair stylist. Every two weeks many dollars were spent creating the impression he didn't care about his black curls: the wind-blown look was a natural after-effect of a day on the yacht. The dark curls emphasised the gleaming whiteness of his perfectly aligned teeth. Jane assumed he had kept his appointment to have them cleaned, but chose not to mention it.

At the first army post Jesse found a uniformed sergeant and easily convinced him the police should be in the loop. The sergeant dramatically told of a fight on a dock against monsters that wouldn't die. He spared no details about biting ghouls and mysterious swimmers. "You guys might want to talk to a woman who was taken to hospital in an ambulance. She had a hole in her gut like nothing I've ever seen and she wanted to walk away and go home. Her buddy supposedly swam home across the bay like it was a community pool."

A trip to the hospital revealed the ambulance with the wounded woman never arrived and both driver and medic had been found at roadside, unconscious without their patient. Both had puncture wounds in their necks and suffered serious blood loss although there was no sign of bleeding.

With all the new info whirling in her head Jane headed back to the station, stopping once to write a ticket for a driver who didn't signal a left turn. The driver protested, "Here we are at the crossroads of civilization and all you do is worry about a stupid turn signal?" Jane walked to her car without comment. Normally she hated the business of stopping drivers, even if it might someday save a life.

"Why ticket him?" Jesse insisted before she buckled up.

"I just wanted to do something normal for a change, something routine. I know, it doesn't make a lot of sense."

"I sorta understand. My hairdresser appointment would have been something normal. Although, come to think of it, last time I had a trim the routine went out the window. I fell asleep in the chair and woke up with a headache like Elephant Man. For days I was weak and had sores on my neck. Must have caught some kinda bug. Not going back to that place."

"Right," agreed Jane, not caring. "Now recap."

"Okay. In the middle of the night two civvies go for a walk on a dock after curfew, in plain sight. Why? Rhetorical question. Suicidal? As a duo? A tribe of monsters attacks them. Army blows zomb-things to bits, but they don't die. Army accidentally shoots both civvies. They don't die. Zomb things attack army. Army guys get guts and brains eaten then run away and then the rest come back. One civvy falls in water and supposedly swims miles to home. In mid-October. Both leave shoes and jackets behind. Did they plan a swim? Rhetorical. Civvy woman, full of gaping bullet holes, says she feels fine and wants to go home. Army puts her in ambulance. Ambulance driver and medic wake up with holes in their necks and civvy is gone. Typical day in White Rock?"

Jane's bland, tanned face still sported a look of amazement as she pulled into the police station parking lot slowly shaking her head to clear disbelief. "The whole thing's incredible. It's hard to believe, but we're under attack by flesh-eating zombies and blood-sucking vampires. Right off the silver screen."

"So zompires and vambies have control of our town," Jesse stated excitedly. "They own the night. It's them, completely unarmed, against the RCMP and the army. Guess which side is winning?"

Jesse rolled down his window, sniffed the air and wrinkled his face, "Man, if there's one thing I hate it's the smell of zombies in the morning. And in the evening. And at night." He stepped out of the car first. After nearly bumping into Jane at the front bumper he continued, "We should evacuate every living person, contain the enemy within a 10-foot electric fence and then blow them apart with grenades and bombs. Who cares about houses and cars? Level this place."

Jane slumped onto a bench in front of the station where she had discussed justice with many miscreants. "We have to convince Colonel May to order an evacuation. His headquarters are secret and he hasn't returned calls. Can you find him?"

"How much do we have in petty cash?"

"Close to $80 I think. Why?"

"I'll need beer."

"What for?"

"Beer and boobs – that's what get men talking."

"Then go for beer. I don't want to have to explain to the board that I used petty cash to buy a bra to squeeze out cleavage so soldiers would talk."

After Jesse's eyes rose from Jane's slight chest bulges he left with $40 and said he would be back with co-ordinates of the secret location. In 25 minutes he returned. "Just cost four beer. I'll take the rest home since we can't keep 'em here. You'll never believe where that big brass bastard is headquartered."

"On a luxury houseboat?"

"Better than that: Missing Hill Winery."

"Of course. Luxury hotel rooms, restaurant, fine wines, great views. Should have figured that out. Let's go."

The winery, looking like a Moorish castle perched halfway up a mountain, appeared impenetrable. Thick gates that normally opened to a flood of tourists were tight as a wine cask and guarded by six soldiers: a sure indication that more than wine wanted protection.

"We're here to see Colonel Mayhew Snottsabitch," Jesse snarled through a half open window. "Tell him it's RCMP Sergeant Jane Dougherty and her able assistant." The soldier on guard duty didn't rush off to get his boss. "I cannot state if there is or is not a Colonel Shostakovich at this location at this time."

"If he wasn't here I don't think he would have told us to come see him," Jesse quickly snapped.

"I can't respond to that, sir. However enquiries can be made on your behalf. That will take several minutes. Please move your vehicle to visitor parking."

Jesse wheeled into a huge parking lot that contained randomly positioned Jeeps, troop carriers and tanks. They walked next to a row of vines and plucked sour grapes until the guard called them. "Follow me. Colonel Mayhew-Shostakovich will see you in 17 minutes."

A small door within the thick oaken gate allowed the two police to enter one at a time. They walked under a stone archway and in the middle of a lush green lawn sat six military trailers. The guard pointed to a stone bench and ordered them to wait.

With a wooden walkway erected around the top of the walls and dozens of ladders reaching it, the winery looked like The Alamo as represented in movies. Machine guns had been fitted. Searchlights, bright enough to allow televising of night football, glared against daylight. A bell tower sprouted additional spotlights plus a lookout post. Gun barrels of varying sizes pointed towards the ocean in readiness for an armada attack.

"I wonder if they have boiling oil to pour on the insurgents?" Jane snapped. "They sure keep the big brass protected."

"There's a lesson here," Jesse said. "Our office needs steel doors, electric fencing and security cameras. Keeping us safe should be priority one. To hell with the people we're paid to protect."

After a few minutes of shifting on the cold seat Jesse asked the guard, "What kind of reading material do you have?"

"Military code-of-conduct book," the guard shot back. "You want one or two copies?"

"I was thinking Hustler. One copy: we can share."

Jane and Jesse discussed the zombie-proofness of the winery until Colonel Mayhew-Shostakovich exited a trailer, walked over and stuck out his hand.

"What the muck, how did you find us? Sorry for the language."

"Your men told us where to find you," Jesse shot out as the Colonel led them to director's chairs in the sunny courtyard.

"So what's your business?" the Colonel asked, showing no interest in the security leak.

"White Rock must be evacuated," Jane demanded. "The number of people dying escalates every day. Last night a dozen probably died, but since the army now deals with 911 calls I'm out of the loop so there could have been more."

The Colonel told her that her estimate of the overnight death count was close, but there were signs it should decrease in the future.

Quickly Jane retorted, "The entire south coast doesn't get that many murders in six months. Evacuation is the only logical answer."

The Colonel calmly replied that shipping out 30,000 citizens was not something to be taken lightly. He said many would refuse to go. Alternative actions had been taken and seniors' homes now had doors reinforced and windows barred. Soldiers stood guard 24 hours a day. Extended care patients had been moved to Vancouver as had the inmates of a nursing home. That was as far as it was going to go. The army would step up protection with reinforcements that would arrive in four hours. Every block would have a battalion of combat troops if that's what it took.

"What about schools?" Jane protested.

"We're continuing as normally as possible to minimize panic. Since all attacks happen at night, schools need not be closed. Students go to school only by bus in a protected convoy."

Colonel Mayhew pointed to a picnic table covered with a red and white chequered tablecloth and offered a glass of wine. "The winery has been very good to us."

In tandem Jane and Jesse answered with clarity and volume, "We do not drink on duty."

Jane asked if the army's equipment included infrared sights and night vision binoculars. The Colonel answered that predators' bodies apparently did not give off heat and thus the equipment proved worthless.

He said more tanks and flamethrowers had been ordered and would be deployed to local streets.

The two police departed with the feeling that army action was reactionary and no permanent solution would come from the winery on the hill. Evacuation was not on the menu.

At her desk Jane called the regional health officer to check progress with steel coffins.

"It's a double negative," the doctor replied. "I can't find anyone to build them for less than $7,000 and I can't find a mortician who would stock them. Even if free, no one wants them. They don't want the dearly departed in a cold steel coffin, as if it matters. It's cozy oak or pine with clear grain for the loved ones."

"Can't you order that steel has to be used?" Jane protested. "This is a public health issue: your jurisdiction."

"As I said, religious rights and human rights prevail. I've got a few to agree to steel strapping around the coffin. At least you know they can't be opened. Besides, most now opt for cremation when I paint a picture of loved ones rising from the ground and coming home for dinner. No one likes the idea of mother chewing their brains out. Sorry, that's the best I can do."

Her last call went to forensics in Vancouver where bits of flesh blown off by bullets went under the microscope.

"Same thing again," the chief physician reported. "No blood in the veins. Some sort of low voltage electrical charge travels through stagnant blood. That's all I can report. Never seen anything like it and hope I never see it again. Don't understand it yet. How are you guys doing? I hear it's bad."

Jane conceded that bad was an understatement and the situation had deteriorated. She described the slaughter of army men and when the Vancouver scientist asked why the town had not been evacuated she could only answer that the same suggestion had come from her. Colonel Mayhew equated evacuation with defeat, which rhymed with retreat.

Jane thought about the day's news and stepped across the room to turn on a dusty TV that sat in a corner. The remote had vanished years ago; probably stolen by a kleptomaniac she arrested. Pressing the on/off button brought to life an announcer who verged on hysteria as she updated the situation. Her town, thought Jane, would only fade from national attention when more dramatic news could be deployed with more hype and more fervour. Only an overnight return of the ice age or a Korean train crashing into an overloaded ferry could compete with rampage by the reanimated. She trod across the room and changed channels.

The underfunded local station showed the last seconds of an ad for a zombie survival kit then another ad commenced. The announcer's trembling voice sounded like the dam that held back his tears would break:

"No one wants a loved one to come back and attack. The Zomb-Bomb spares the horror of having to behead a mother or uncle who has risen from the grave. Simply attach the Zomb-Bomb to your loved-one's coffin. When movement is detected it detonates silently, beneath the earth. The recently departed stay departed the way nature intended. Security and protection is yours, thanks to Zomb-Bomb. Available at undertakers and selected retailers. Technology based on proven land mine use in Syria."

Wow, thought Jane, free enterprise may have the answer. Why didn't the coroner come up with that? Her phone rang, but she didn't pick up. Voice mail announced, "You have 50 new messages, your voice box is full." Pressing number seven to delete kept her mind off how helpless she felt.

23

Mona made me want to regurgitate both Mary and Uncle Albert who sloshed around in my lower regions with bits of a cat.

Maggots had chased away worms, spiders and centipedes in a battle for territorial turf on Mona's chest. On her leaky black scalp the last few strands of limp, mildewed hair hung lifelessly. Her fingers ran through them as if she had a comb. Her smell, when she lifted her arms, could fell a horse. Quickly, by my understanding of quickly, I walked ahead: putting a few yards between us, giving my nose relief. Then I heard the unique shuffling of Suzie's feet, propelled by stork-like knees. She smelled better than Mona, but her conversational grunts and groans made no more sense than Mona's moans.

In prior life I had been anything but a chick-magnet. My soft voice and slight build made me attractive to older men who often befriended me. I fought them off because I didn't know any better.

Now two women chased me. As I picked up the pace I wondered what they wanted. I knew what I wanted: it wasn't physical. I needed conversation, an exchange of opinions. I needed to understand what was going on. Was I the equal of the two behind whose combined charm was on a par with flies in an outhouse? Surely not. Surely I was more than a drooling, shuffling, brainless hunk of rotting meat. Surely I wasn't the one who chomped down on Uncle Albert.

My memory wasn't that good, although it seemed to be improving. I knew my name and the name of the planet I lived on. But had I really devoured people?

Compulsively, yet cautiously, I trudged towards a distant cemetery as the sound of explosions introduced fear to my icy heart. From tree to tree I slunk until I found a rocky outcrop overlooking the necropolis. Flak-suited soldiers, banks of flood lights, roaring generators and armored vehicles occupied the greenery below. Gravestones had been blasted to dust. Bazookas and mortars, with twitchy fingers at the ready, pointed at lush grass beneath which citizens had found peace everlasting.

Mona trod forward, oblivious to danger, with arms outstretched to warmly envelop the closest soldier. The soldier, alone with his grenade launcher, focused on the targets ahead of him, oblivious to what approached from behind.

Mona chomped a chunk from his neck and both lost balance. She plunged her hand, up to the elbow, into his abdomen and pulled out plums. When the two hit the grass, his prostate reached her mouth and its seminal juices spilled down her throat. The soldier's scream, high above the general din, attracted attention.

Knowing his buddy was a goner, a young private lobbed a grenade that detonated between Mona's feet and blew off arms, legs, maggots and all that held her together. Mona and the soldier became a downpour of flesh and bones. I moaned in despair. The loss of a fellow walker and the waste of an edible soldier pained me. Near my feet a parched pancreas thudded to the dirt. Waste not, want not. It gagged in my throat and I ejected it as I would mouldy mashed potatoes. It must have belonged to Mona.

"Don't bite off more than you can chew." I heard my mother's scolding voice. Blubbery flesh pushed at the elastic at my waist. I had overeaten and couldn't take in any more yet I felt hungry; starving.

Beside a white grave-marker thin arms reached through dirt. Then a head pushed from the ground like a dandelion slowly emerging in spring. The back of its skull was missing and brains absent. Upwards it pushed. The stout man struggled to his feet and took two stumbling, slouching steps. Soldiers, breathlessly watching the birth of an undead, unloaded their fury. Guns and grenades sent flesh and bones in all directions including upwards. A moment of silence followed, then pieces thumped to the ground and clung to branches.

I cringed at the overkill yet could not understand my revulsion at the destruction of a cannibal with no ability to think or retain nutrition. Was this blasted creature my kin? Had I sunk that low? Did I care how low I could go? My thinking impressed me. I felt I should write it down, create poetry. *Roses are dead, violets are blue, you act like a zombie and look like one too.*

Having learned nothing from seeing bits of Mona fall from the sky Suzie stumbled from the woods with hands forward and within seconds became dust in the wind. Oddly I did not feel a void in having lost two women in my life because a fresh young female in uniform caught my eye. She had retreated behind rocks to disassemble her rifle. She squatted, facing the action, and in a minute I was behind her. My right hand covered her mouth while the other searched beneath her bullet-proof vest and found plump breasts and tight abs that held no interest. Talon-like nails sliced her cavity. Experience taught me where to find kidney and liver – they tasted like they had been sautéed in the finest virgin olive oil and garnished with exotic herbs and spices.

I had eaten Marks & Spencer's steak and kidney pie, but her organs exceeded the British product 1,000 fold. Low in her cavity I unearthed a cluster of tumours that detonated in my mouth like grapes that had ripened to perfection on a French vine. This poor woman had but a few years to live. Surely, had she known, she could have spent her time doing something more worthy than hunting the half-dead. My level of concern impressed me as I tediously thought that maybe she could have done better and given something back to society as a realtor or a Mary Kay rep.

Like a crazed coyote I dug in, favoring tasty morsels that added minimal bulk to my distended belly. My waistline would become a major concern if this eating habit continued and why wouldn't it, given the addicting pleasures? Thoughts of constipation came. A pressing need to sit on a toilet haunted me, but I knew it would not be an emptying experience. I couldn't even fart. A drug store laxative might help, but would it be approved for dead intestines full of human remains? I wondered about complications with other medications I might have been taking before deep water pickled me.

In my travels I had picked up a rucksack and kept a tire iron discarded at roadside. The instrument's sharp end chipped against the soldier's skull and worked its way around her hairline as if cutting into the rind of a grapefruit before peeling it. I gently whacked her head with the lug end then unhinged her lid. My teeth pulled at the meninges and then my face dove inside, sucking and slurping as I shamelessly moaned and groaned. My dark tongue unseated the last mushy dribble then I rested against a tree, shivering, exhilarated, exhausted and wanting to do it again; wanting Ex-Lax.

Her pretty young face gazed skyward and moisture ran from her eyes. Had her last thoughts been of her mother answering the door to find two men in uniform preparing to announce the news most feared? A gold band girded her ring finger. Did her final thoughts go to a husband? Or children: a little boy and girl who would never know the woman who had brought them into the world? Did she think of her family as I thought of Abacus, Calculus and Malady? I wanted to sob over what I had done to a woman who had done nothing to me, but my eyes stayed dry. I concentrated on how she deserved her fate because she had taken up arms against a sea of strangers without trying to understand them. Disease would kill her anyway.

Was there any help for addicted flesh-eaters? An AAA: Anthropophagi Anonymous Association? I didn't want to be addicted. Peer support would go a long way. In front of a group I would say, "I have a problem. I am an addict. I eat people."

For starters I would cut back to one meal a day and no pets. Schools had counsellors: I could see one without charge. I was a teacher.

The slain soldier's skull fit back in place, but toppled to the dirt as I pulled her jacket over her gaping midriff hole. If I could have vomited her brains back into the empty cavity and up-chucked her guts into her torso I would have done so. But then I might eat her again. And her vitals had mixed with my other stomach content, including the cat: I might regurgitate a fur ball into her skull.

After fumbling to undo a bow in her shoelace I yanked off her left boot, removed her sock and stretched it over the top of her head so it held her skull together. She looked good, like a cool rapper.

When I hoisted her onto my shoulder and started walking she felt like dead weight with all her military equipment adding unexpected poundage. Perhaps I had lost strength. I dropped her and picked up a fallen branch. My hands snapped it easily. I pushed up the bloody sleeve of my stained hockey sweater and flexed a bicep. A muscle the size of a household water conduit popped up and I wondered how such an unimpressive bulge could snap deadwood the thickness of a model's thigh.

With the soldier bouncing on my shoulder, I walked uphill through moonlit evergreens until I found a quiet clearing with soft soil. Despite the long trudge my legs didn't tire and I wasn't short of breath. There was no intake of air at all and no movement from my chest. What's with that, I wondered: I could run a marathon if I could just pick up my pace.

Deadfall littered the ground so I grabbed another branch, snapped it over my knee and used the sharp end to scrape out a trench at the edge of a glade. When sufficient soil had been scratched away I dumped the young soldier into the trench. Before piling rocks and dirt over her, I checked her ID: Mandy H. McDonald. Into the soil I etched an overlapping M and M, like a pair of golden arches in need of support.

Sunlight began burning into my eyes: I needed seclusion. Checking into Holiday Inn wouldn't be easy. Would the clerk at reception be suspicious because I had no luggage?

After some wandering I came upon a hollow tree that had its innards blown apart by a lightning strike. It looked comfortable and the price was right so I squeezed in. Sleeping upright should have posed a problem, but discomfort didn't enter the picture. Reclusiveness rather than rest met requirements; any port in a storm would do. Pounding guns from below disturbed me ever so slightly. Dogs barked as they passed as part of a patrol.

Shadows danced on the forest floor and I marvelled at how my mental dots started to connect: A led to B and B caused C. Linear logic returned: the volume of an isosceles rectangle contains a cute angle. A hole is equal to parts of its sum.

24

Vladimir's Bar had been brokering booze in White Rock for as long as anyone could remember, yet few ever stepped inside to enjoy the good prices and understated decor.

Pool tables, dartboards and shuffleboard had never been added let alone video games or an ATM. The dim drinking hole had no music, no strippers and no happy hour. If not for bargain beer and wine, the bar would have few customers. The regulars, mostly doleful men and sorrowful women, drank alone because life offered few other options.

Every week a newcomer or two wandered in, had a drink and never returned. Such visitors felt neither warmth nor hospitality and were not offered an opportunity to join a customer rewards program.

In the darkest corner, oblivious to the zombie invasion, sat an overweight woman, known to the bartender as Farting Fannie. She busied herself picking crusty green pieces from her left nostril. At the bar a young man in a business suit consumed vast quantities of draft beer, as was his routine. The barkeep seldom talked to him and did not call him Norm or any other name. On occasions when the drinker had to be identified he got fingered as Barstool Bob, which became BB, as in "BB needs a refill."

Two athletic young men who looked like agents for an insurance firm held down stools at the end of the bar. They wondered why, of all the taverns in all the towns, they had chosen the one that didn't attract women. The only females in the place, save Farting Fannie, hunched over a table, held hands, talked quietly and paid no attention to anyone else. Those six customers made it a busy afternoon at Vladimir's.

Echoes within the dreary establishment didn't bother the owners because a financial bonanza from a crowd of happy imbibers was the last thing they wanted. A numbered company composed of 18 hollow-fanged citizens constituted joint ownership. Vladimir's Bar had two purposes, the primary one being to launder money, something the owners had in abundance and couldn't get rid of without drawing attention. They loved technology and closely followed the release dates for new gadgetry, but buying the latest in computers, cameras, cars and giant TVs diminished their financial stronghold the way a running tap in Spokane diminishes the reservoir behind Grand Coulee Dam. The owners horded a cache of gold, stamps, coins, jewellery and other precious items collected over hundreds of years. Some treasures had crossed the ocean in oak chests, centuries back. Only during the Great Depression did select rainy-day savings need cashing-in.

 The financial sun always shone, but certain government departments made matters difficult by keeping computerized records and doting on ever-livers with pension plans and old age security. Instead of solving problems these benefits of socialism created dilemmas. Cancelling a pension while alive meant entanglement in miles of bureaucratic red tape and endless questions. Collecting the same pension for more than half a century made matters worse, particularly when picture ID showed someone who didn't look a day over 30.

 Purpose number two of Vladimir's Bar could be ascertained by visiting the basement and carefully looking in the back of large coolers that had cases of beer stacked at the front. Licensing officials attributed surplus stock to bad management, but that problem did not appear on their inspection agenda. Sanitation and health did, and in those categories the bar managed a passing grade. The owners feared that an overzealous inspector might pop open a bottle from the very back of the cooler and fill a glass with a rich red substance that did not taste like an alcoholic beverage. During the best of times gallons of blood resided in recapped bottles of dark ale and fine red wine, but now only two bottles remained for the direst emergency.

 Behind a cooler that could only be moved with the combined strength of four regular men, or six vampires, a heavy, soundproof door opened to reveal The Vault. It served no purpose, but instilled a sense of security as a place to hide if one ever needed to disappear. Of late The Vault had received considerable thought and discussion, but no use.

After *the awakening*, as they called it, the vampires installed an enormous flat-screen TV in Vladimir's drinking room so the workers could keep up with breaking news about flesh-eaters. They did not hang it behind the bar where patrons could enjoy a full view, but put it around the side in a dark spot where vamps tended to huddle when they visited the establishment they owned. Customers craned their necks to view the screen since it constituted the sole entertainment on tap. Placement gave thirsty vamps a view of patrons' pulsing jugulars as they twisted to see the TV. Because of the six-foot screen, more vampires than usual dropped by to talk about recent happenings and discuss future plans. Some even bought a drink although alcohol had little appeal: no bloodsucker ever got drunk.

Leadership could not be listed as a vampire asset alongside faithfulness and patience. An adage about time curing all ills served them well and was oft repeated like a tired mantra mumbled by a gnarled guru.

While customers slurped beer, a coterie of vamps quietly entered and gathered around the flat screen. A stern voice from the surround-sound speakers warned, "What we are about to broadcast is shocking and disturbing. Under no circumstances is it suitable for children. If there are children in the room please have them leave. The images that follow are real and contain extreme violence. To protect privacy we have blurred faces."

Those watching saw a thin teenage boy use a sharp stick to poke at a shadowy figure standing six feet in front of him. A voice from another young male provided commentary that encouraged the boy to attack the dark figure. The thin boy dropped the probe and threw lighted matches at the shadow. Commentary was sarcastic; mocking a newscast from 50 years back:

"And now we will see if our new citizen is flammable. First a little lighter fluid is applied..."

Next came a scream, jumpy camera action and footage of the sky as if the camera had flown into the air and fallen. The camera appeared to come to rest on a hedge and between out-of-focus leaves it showed the youth who had been holding the camera and providing commentary. He screamed horrendously as a mutilated adult fell on top of him, ripped apart his abdomen and stuffed its mouth.

The camera had good focus and sufficient night lighting that details could be seen clearly. The eater looked like something that had walked away from a train wreck.

After 20 seconds of unrelenting horror the TV announcer cut in. "This happened last night. The camera that took these pictures was recovered this morning by one of our employees on her way to work. It has since been handed over to the army. As you can imagine there was heated discussion in this studio about whether we should air this video. We concluded it is in the best interest of the people of White Rock to know what they are up against. It's hard to believe what happened to this young man. Let me assure you that what you just saw is a small portion of what is in the camera. There is no way to explain this delicately, and again, make sure no children are near. Following what you viewed, the young man's head was smashed and his brain consumed by the creature. Now we go to reporter Marlene Ronson who has been trying to get a reaction from army personnel."

The bartender clicked his remote: the screen went black. Barstool Bob vomited a quart of yellow, chunky beer across the counter and onto the floor. Farting Fannie quit working her nose, stood up and announced, "If that's the kind of movie you're gonna show then you won't be seeing me." She knocked over a chair on her way to the door. The two women at the back solaced each other with tight hugs. The two suited agents sat silent, mouths agape.

The vampire contingent removed their eyes from the dark TV and stared at each other. A female broke the silence, "We have to do something."

No one picked up on her lead. Another woman added, "Anyone have ideas?" Quiet continued until the barkeep turned on the television again and it showed a static head-shot of the monster that devoured the teen.

A new voice-over announced, "Colonel Mayhew-Shostakovich, in a news release, says the Canadian Army is offering a $1000 reward for any zombie brought in dead or alive. To be declared dead the zombie must have its head detached and the head must be in a separate container from the body. The army has receiving stations in Totempole Park and Missing Hill Drive. They will be open regular business hours, closed Sunday."

The announcement satisfied the need for something to be done. One vampire commented, "That should help get rid of them."

Heads turned right as a commercial started with the sound of hand clippers trimming a hedge. A zombie mob, from an old black and white movie, surged forward. The voice-over alliteratively announced, "Bullets, burns, bruises and bombs won't stop a zombie, but the Z-D-Capper will."

A man with an oversize tree pruner pushed a pair of scythe-like blades around a small watermelon, pulled a trigger and the fruit fell in two pieces dripping bright red juice. "A Z-D-Capper reloads in seconds with a time-honored cross-bow mechanism. It has enough power to take the head off an alligator. The first time you turn in a beheaded victim the Z-D-Capper pays for itself. Supplies limited."

One of the vamps, a dentist wearing a charcoal trench coat, commented, "If the army's reward doesn't stop them, that decapper thing should. I'm getting one. Might get one for my mate too." Assorted nods and mumbles followed.

Response to the reward came next morning when a rough boy, mid-teens, dragged a tarp along the sidewalk to the army's waterfront payout post. A bloody axe dangled from his belt.

"I've got a live one," he declared, explaining to gathered media that he had dug a hole in his yard and disguised it with a tarpaulin covered in leaves. In the small hours of the morning he heard his alarm cans fall as a zombie tumbled into the hole and the tarp closed. Wisely he didn't venture out until sunrise and then he whacked his prey, winched it out of the hole and dragged it along the sidewalk to the payout station. A crowd gathered as the boy raised his axe and aimed at a bulge in the tarp, already stained red. A corporal stepped in front, stopped the chop and cautiously unravelled the tarp. A bleeding, sweaty, semiconscious body, within a gasp of its last breath staggered forward. The boy stepped backwards in shock at the sight of his father.

The second reward claimant arrived in a dirty old Bentley and said, in an English accent, "I've got a body in the boot."

The onlookers looked baffled until the driver hoisted two duffle bags from the luxury car's trunk and disdainfully dumped them on the sidewalk. The smaller revealed a grey head with scars, scabs, sores, clumps of missing hair and split lips. The corporal in charge called the police. Jane Dougherty and her deputy arrived minutes later. She identified the man claiming the reward as a known drug dealer from nearby Surrey. The head belonged to his motorcycle gang rival.

Jane asked the Englishman to put his hands behind his back so she could cuff him. He cooperated.

Before they drove off with the Englishman in the back seat a farmer roared up in his rusty pick-up and pulled back a tarp to reveal a body covered with enough duct tape to seal the venting of a skyscraper. With roaring chainsaw the farmer prepared to separate head from body, but the corporal stopped him, saying a live captive would be valuable for research. The farmer collected his reward and quietly drove off. Jane noted his plate number so she could hand over additional police reward money when she figured out how to get it.

The army now had a live zombie with a cavity in the back of its head where a brain should be and a hole in its abdomen where a stomach should be. Duct tape circled its head and mouth, but the zombie hummed its theme-song, *brains*.

No one anticipated a captured live zombie so the soldiers rolled it back into the tarp and dragged it to Jane's cruiser. Two privates started to stuff it into the back seat, causing the English prisoner to scream like his clothes were on fire. Jesse popped the trunk and the soldiers folded the body in and slammed the lid on its twitching fingers.

At the police station they put the zombie in a cell next to the Englishman who whined about the stench and demanded a lawyer. Jesse told him the duck-taped guy in the cell next to him was a lawyer. His rates were reasonable. With legs taped together, the zombie banged into bars, fell down, rolled on the floor and mumbled constantly.

The army paid more rewards for severed heads, then delivered two more intact undead to Jane's jail. She booked them as Zombie Doe II and Zombie Doe III and added them to Zombie Doe I's cell, making sure handcuffs snugly secured wrists and ankles. Gender could not be determined without further investigation and Jane didn't want to go there.

The drug lord protested that being in a cell next to three reeking deads was cruel, unusual, unjust and a violation of human rights. Jane told him he was correct, but she didn't care. She didn't have a lot of sympathy for men who recruited teens to sell drugs.

25

Early morning light put a pink tint to gnarled trees that clawed into the mountainside where I trundled, searching for the shallow grave of my slain soldier. Unsure of where I had scraped out the unmarked grave, I wandered all night.

Earliest morn proved to be the best time for freedom of movement: soldiers had packed up after a night of protecting townsfolk and daytime patrols didn't begin until after sunrise. As long as I remained within the dim forest the shadowy light could be tolerated. I toted a rotting rucksack full of odds and ends picked up on walks. My cranium cracking wrench had been jettisoned because the bits of hair and dried blood that stuck to the rusty lug gave bad vibes. I didn't enjoy being a killer, particularly a premeditating murderer who toted the tools of his trade in a backpack.

All traces of the grave had vanished in the night: the Mandy M. double arches must have flattened under the light rain. All the tall trees had similar long-needled branches, one rock looked like another and all footpaths seemed identical. I rounded the same bend on the same path for the fifth time and saw a soldier's arm push through dirt and shove aside rocks and rubble: the very rocks and rubble I had piled.

A helpful pull got the soldier to her feet. She staggered a few steps, bumped against a tree and clung to it like an old friend. Then she shuffled in circles, each a little wider than previous. I had given birth to a beautiful girl, although I felt responsible for the drips at the back of her head and the empty abdomen. Despite the disfigurement, I loved her as I loved Abacus and Calculus and the one whose name was on the tip of my black tongue.

Now she had life: reborn into the new order. She should thank me and call me Daddy.

While my baby practiced her circular walk I lumbered back to the outskirts of the cemetery frustrated at my inability to move with speed. At best I could ploddingly place one foot six inches in front of the other. At least I no longer placed one atop the other. My hiking boots, swollen from time under water, dragged in the dirt, bumped against rocks, snagged on fallen branches and pointed at each other. My knees had seen better days and my hips creaked. I felt like a bumbling dread rather than a walking dead, if that's what I was.

The graveyard looked like an abandoned battlefield with trenches, mortar holes and a mess of bones and body bits. I craved the orgiastic feast that gnawed at my innards, begging for repetition. I was a junkie. How low can I go? The question formed like a flickering candle in the back of my dark cranial cave. Eating another's leftovers was lower than dumpster diving behind a food bank. I scooped brains and bits into my pack and waddled to my slain soldier.

The young lady's walking circle had widened and it took half a worried hour to relocate her. I again studied her ID tag and wondered about the middle initial *H*. Heady would be her newborn name. With hands steadying her shoulders I looked into her snotty, bloodless eyes.

"Me Morth; you Heathy."

Heady didn't flinch when I pulled the soggy sock from her head, but my hands reacted too slowly to prevent the back of her skull from hitting the dirt. From my pack I scooped gooey gobs of grey brain and stuffed her cranium as I would a thanksgiving turkey. The dirt-encrusted skull fitted back in place like a lost jigsaw piece and her sock slipped over top, slowing seepage.

I operated without anaesthetic and Heady was a patient patient. Her tunic opened easily, however my selection of parts for her innards was limited to what was in stock. I stuffed her with liver, spleen, an eyeball and something that was either a big thumb or small penis. Yards of old tape held everything inside. Heady looked like a poster girl for reconstructive surgery.

"Brains," she pleaded and, feeling fatherly, my fingers found some cranial slop at the bottom of my bag. I slapped it onto her hand. Hand-eye coordination needed rehab: Heady splatted the grey mush against her cheek. I pushed it across to her mouth, being careful not to lose fingers. Her eyes twitched, her body trembled, an indistinct murmur emerged from her mouth and a trace of a smile wisped across her face. I wondered if eating brain, albeit dead brain, gave her the same wonderful experience I had. Her pleasure pleased me, but I was disappointed because I had hoped to give her speech by fitting her with a brain. I yearned for words, not moans and groans. I yearned to discuss my kids, the meaning of rebirth and reruns of the Kardashians. I could form thoughts, but words were still reluctant to follow.

 Sunlight reached upper branches as Heady and I trod downhill. She shielded her eyes and grimaced as though her head had been struck by a tire iron. The sun felt like firecrackers exploding between my ears, but it was small price to pay for freedom from the danger of being hunted down in the night like an animal.

 Far ahead three others lurched towards us in the morning glow. I regarded them as suspicious. Could they be decoys? I worried about that while I worried that worrying wasn't good for health. Concerns oozed from my mind like warm tar on a cold day.

 Cautiously I shuffled towards the figures and just as cautiously they lurched towards me; a few clumsy steps at a time. The male, who appeared to be leading, looked like a shrunken whale. A grey, bloated body supported puffy appendages that stuck out like fat fins. A tiny head sank low on his shoulders. Within 10 yards I saw that the whale used a lot of grey duct tape that matched his skin color. He and his accomplices all sported trendy sunglasses. I hadn't thought of that. I hadn't thought of much.

 "Doo yooo talk?" the whale asked and the words startled me. I didn't know the correct answer as my only conversing, since arising, had been a few stunted words tossed towards my wife and a similar unrequited amount aimed at Heady.

 "Yeth," I sputtered.
 "Wonderfoool, I been loooking for talker."
 "Yeth," I repeated.
 "We walk loong time. Doofficult too doo." The voice had some kind of British accent plus a bubbling sound, as if under water.
 I thought deeply then replied, "Yeth."
 "Yoo talk pooor: sooon yoo improove."

Sentences formed in my head, but I knew that when I forced them past broken lips and heavy tongue the result would sound strange, so I kept it simple.

"Yeth."

The man opposite me gave no reaction so I dared a question, "Whoo yoo?"

I asked without the intention of mocking the whale's speech. He sounded like a hungry cow on its way to the barn.

"Oo am I, yoo ask? Doogie Hooper. I need loootenant. I knoow I woooold find yooo."

Doogie pointed to Heady and then to his own two companions. "Soldiers of misfortoon in army of gloom. More in wooods. Must find them. Uoonite them. Are yoo twoo with us?"

Except for *shoulder of misfortoon* I understood the words that came from the birthing bovine. The big picture, however had no clarity. What did he mean by *with us?* Who was in the woods? Carefully and ponderously I posed a second question, "Wha happen to you?"

"I droowned. On froozen lake. Throo the ice before I know it. Doo I loook it?"

"Yeth," I said.

"Retained water. Skin drooping off. Doo yoo have tape? I'm oot."

"Yeth," I whispered and tipped over my pack. A spool of silver tape rolled across the forest floor and disappeared down a hillside. Another roll, one a truck had driven over, landed flat. Doogie picked it up and unwound dirty, thin strips that he put around his shoulder.

Dirt-colored curls clustered on top of Doogie's head. Those, plus skin that must once have been extremely white, made me think Doogie must be of Scandinavian extraction, probably from Tokyo or Oslo.

"Goood to talk tooo yoo," Doogie said, interrupting my meandering mind. "Want the fooll stoory? Coourse yoo doo. Electricity mooves in ground from radio toowers. That wooke us. What a hooot! Alive. And goood foood. Doon't yoo love joocy finger foood?"

Red stains down Doogie's front showed the kind of meal he referred to. My eyes followed the red and then I realized Doogie was naked. The way his breasts puffed out and grey flab sagged to his knees, he could pass for an obese woman. Perhaps he was an obese woman: I didn't want to know.

"Remoove yoor shoos," Doogie commanded. "Current gets in throo yoor fooots. Yoo'll talk more; feel goooder." Doogie held up his foot and bare bone showed on his sole. Flaps of worn, dirty skin hung over the sides.

"Noo pain and much tooo gain," he continued. I admired the way words flowed from his banana lips. "Yoo want to knoow more?"

"Yeth."

"Sooon we moove to oor destiny. Take oover land and harvest former roolers."

I pried off my heavy hiking boots, the ones that pulled me to ocean's bottom, and a trickle of energy flowed into my body as I padded on pine needles and maple leafs. Rather than being an instant jolt, energy arrived as if from an AAA battery connected to my toes.

"Yoo'll need these," Doogie said, opening his sack and offering something.

After fingering the item I realized I had been handed sunglasses and put them to my head, jabbing the arms into my eyes. The ruby-studded frames didn't fit and did nothing for me style-wise so I put them on Heady's head after poking her eyes. She had been bent over, shielding her yellow orbs, but immediately came to life and strutted around the glade as if demonstrating new eyewear on a fashion runway.

Doogie handed me a heavy brown pair and the moment the dark lenses cloaked my eyes I felt relief from the irritation of light. Why hadn't I thought of that? Why hadn't I thought of a lot of things?

26

Jane and Jesse realized, too late, that they wouldn't be able to go home from the police station without risk of being riddled by bullets from nervous teenage soldiers handling their first guns. The day of zombie wrangling had sped by so fast that neither noticed the arrival of dark. Curfew meant no one would come in to relieve them, which was beside the point because, in all the chaos and deaths, no one had scheduled night duty and none of the new replacements had volunteered to do a graveyard shift.

No matter how much she would like to see the English drug lord eaten, Jane couldn't leave him alone all night in his cell beside three crazed flesh eaters and it wasn't because of his constant whining about the stink and his rights. Her duty was to protect one and all. A zombie feeding would be entertaining, Jesse suggested, and none on the force would shed a tear if someone made a meal of the man who had turned young girls into addicted hookers.

Jane kept a sleeping bag for overnight emergencies while Jesse rounded up standard jail issue sheets, which, despite being washed a hundred times, still showed spots where body fluids he didn't like to think about had spilled. They dragged mattresses from cells three and four and paused to observe the captives, but the stink gagged them and they rushed back to their offices. Two doors separated cells from offices but an aroma the townsfolk called *eau d'zee* permeated all. Thoughts of pizza, hamburger or Chinese were accompanied by thoughts of entrails being downed in a few bites. The ungodly stench had kept food from their thoughts for the entire day, a busy day. Media reps pounded on their doors and the parade of scientists taking a look at the captives didn't stop until nightfall.

"Coffee and muffins is all I can handle at the moment," Jane suggested.

"I was thinking steak, rare, with beets, carrots and a glass of red wine," Jesse answered. "Ugh, I can't even joke about it. I'm with you on this one. What's *your* dining pleasure?"

Before Jane could say "blueberry" a howl came over the intercom. Jesse, closest to the door, took the lead and when they got to the cells a captive lay on the floor awkwardly biting into duct tape that bound its legs.

"They're gonna break outta here," screeched the hysterical Englishman. The scream was similar to the cries of drug-addled pimps as he broke their fingers when they didn't pay.

"No worry mate," Jesse replied, "They're just getting ready. Every night, here in the cells, we have *meet your neighbor* social hour."

"Don't get funny, you sarcastic shit. I'm saving your life by warning you."

"We gotta re-cuff 'em," Jane sternly ordered and pulled out three stainless steel pair from a locker. "How do we do it?"

"Carefully," Jesse said.

"Okay. First I open the door, slowly you go in. Cuff the ankle of the one on the floor, drag him to the bed and cuff him to it. The tape should hold on his arms, watch out for teeth. Get the next one on the wrist and cuff him, or her, to the other bed. Cuff inmate three to the door. Two and three have their heads wrapped in tape so they can't bite. Look out for the first one."

"It's a plan. But before I go in there I gotta tell you what I've been thinking. You've watched horror movies. There's always a sidekick, sort of funny, comic relief. That's me. You're the hero-boss. You know what happens to the sidekick?"

"Nothing happens to Robin or Jimmy Olsen: they go along for the ride. Are you worried you're a sacrificial boy toy?"

"I'm thinking horror, not superhero: movies with zombies and crazed killers. The sidekick is second to go. Fifteen minutes in. Right after the wild teens who are drinking and screwing."

"No problem. If you're scared, I'll do it." With that Jane yanked open the door, clamped a shackle on the ankle of the prone zomb and dragged it to a bed. She did the same to the second, possibly a female, and finished the plan by cuffing the loose hand of number three to a bar.

"They don't weigh much," she informed Jesse. "But you can feel their strength, amazing strength."

"Thanks for doing that. My déjà vu gave me a premonition I was just a few steps from my grave."

"We're not finished. You secure loose legs and gnashing teeth." Jane handed a roll of tape and held the cell door open.

Jesse had no choice: he had received an order. The three flesh-crazed monsters terrified him. He had *expendable sidekick* stamped on his forehead. As he entered the cell a latrine of pong made him want to shower with lye.

The nearest creature's head bobbed and its teeth snapped under the layer of silver tape. Loose feet danced and kicked. Jesse got down on his knees, unravelled an arm's span of tape and stuck the end to an ankle that thrust at him. He edged closer and the other foot flew like a karate kick. Despite a delivery that started slowly, it landed on his jaw. It hit hard and rigid and a rivulet of blood seeped from his lip and dribbled down his chin. The zombies frantically twitched and pulled against cuffs and tape while muttering a chorus … *brains.*

"Get outta there," Jane shouted, but he had a job to finish. He swung his feet across the cement floor to knock the zombie's legs from under it, but the creature stood like a bronze statue planted in cement.

"Forget it," Jane shouted and he knew why he was assistant and she boss. She cuffed the enemy with ease and professionalism and he couldn't even knock one over to bind its legs. He fashioned a length of tape into a noose and slid it so it reached the feet of the kicking zombie. When its feet came down inside the circle he pulled and a wad of tape stuck around its feet. Jesse repeated this several times and the more the zombie hopped the more tape stuck and less movement it had. Each time Jesse got a little closer until he reached its ankles and wrapped a dozen layers of tight tape around them.

"Watch for its teeth," Jane yelled as the creature fell forward. Through a tiny opening in the swaddling over its mouth it managed to nip Jesse's neck. Jesse jumped up and mummified its head.

When they got back to the front of the station Jesse slumped into a chair and moaned, "I knew it. I'm a goner."

"What do you mean?"

"I got bit by a zombie. I'm gonna turn into one. And then I'm gonna attack you and eat you. You gotta kill me. You gotta make preparations. I don't wanna be a zombie. I don't wanna eat my friends. Please, put a bullet through my head when I'm not looking. Just do it." Jesse bent his face into hands that filled with tears, sweat and a little blood.

Jane left him to his misery while she went to the bathroom, scrubbed her hands and brought back a first aid kit. Without a word she bandaged his wound then spoke. "Movies don't reflect life, especially horror movies. Has anyone ever arrested a serial killer dressed like a clown or wearing a goalie mask? Have you ever heard of a chainsaw killer? I could go on."

"But you don't know," he said quietly. "We're in new territory. I might turn. I might become Dracula, Frankenstein or Cannibal Lecher. What if it's true? What if I become a zombie? You'd be alone here. What if I wake at 3 a.m. and tear you apart?"

Jane sighed at the unlikelihood of the situation. "The coroner said that doesn't happen. Besides, I've got a backup plan. I bought a Z-D-Capper."

"Cool, I saw them on TV. Tried to get one. Sold out everywhere. How did you get your hands on one?"

"Used some police persuasion and parted with $600."

"Wow, that's gouging. Gotta see it."

Jesse perked up when Jane brought the customized pruner out of a cupboard. He ran his fingers over the curved scythe-like blades and cranked the handle, putting tension on the scissors like an old cross-bow. The blades snapped with the sound of giant shears slicing a tree limb.

"That'll get 'em," he declared proudly, then slumped as he realised the purpose of the sharp, shiny blades was to separate *his* head from *his* body. Again he cranked the handle that armed the blades, put the device to his neck and pulled the trigger. They snapped shut inches in front of his vital corridor.

"We have to test this. Can I try it out in cell two?"

"No, not yet."

"How about cell one?"

"Wish you could. There's a dead tree at the back door, two or three inches thick. See if it will take that down?"

Jesse passed lockup on his way to the back door and saw an undead prisoner stomping relentlessly in front of the bars it was cuffed against. The druggie slept in the middle of his cell, where he had dragged his mattress, out of reach of grasping hands and chomping teeth. Jesse went back, told Jane about the inmates' activities and asked if it would be within the line of duty to try the Z-D-Capper on a zombie that resisted arrest.

"It isn't exactly doing that."

"Sure is. It refuses to sleep."

"Glad you haven't lost your kindergarten humour. You must be feeling better."

Jane grabbed a phone and Jesse headed for the dead tree.

Motion detection lights that normally flooded the parking area behind the police station didn't activate when he opened the back door. Glass littered the laneway. Beside a fence, just three yards away, stood the target tree, its black bark barely visible.

Jesse took one step towards it and heard a shuffling of feet. A mumble he didn't recognize as human rumbled across the parking area. He steadied the de-capper on his forearm and thrust it left then right, peering into blackness. Nothing moved. He resisted snapping the blades. Then he smelled it and heard it, but never saw it.

With trembling hands he blindly thrust the de-capper into the night and pulled the trigger. Blades slid closed but he felt no resistance; no head tumbled. He stepped back. A racoon raced across the lane as he reloaded. A black dog chased and snarled. Something jabbed Jesse's back: the station door's protruding handle prodded him.

Stepping inside, slamming the steel slab and securing both lock and deadbolt made the woes of the dark and dangerous outside world feel detached and distant.

Jesse lumbered into the front office, panting and sweating. He didn't mention his fright outside the back door, but described the racoon and dog. In mid-sentence he paused then continued with a non sequitur, "Since curfew has started does that mean no coffee and muffins? I could reach the deli in a 20 second sprint. But its doors might be locked. Looks like I won't even get a last meal. No lobster. No apple pie. Not even a bran muffin. This sucks."

No reply came so he returned to the previous subject. "You won't be able to decap me if I smash your door and get a piece of you before you wake up."

With measured words Jane responded. "I've been keeping an eye on you. Normal so far. And quit playing with that decapper before you lose a hand. I've got a plan."

"Okay. Share with the class?"

"If I share then you might develop a counter plan."

"Fair enough. But I'll tell you my plan. Should I remain human and zombies attack, our front door is our weakest point. Everything else is solid and barred. First thing we have to do is roll some heavy desks against the door to make sure it can't be opened."

"It swings open to the outside."

"Of course. We tie the handle to desks and if it gets opened the desks will keep them out."

"You forget how strong they are. Is that your entire plan?"

"No. Plan B. I feel like I'm turning so I put one foot behind the other, back into cell four and lock myself in. Nice and safe. Can't be hurt, can't hurt anyone. Win win. You get cell three if there's an attack. No matter what, suite four will be my home for the night. Hide the keys."

"Good idea. My plan arrives in a few minutes. Two soldiers stay in the station tonight. They come with coffee, muffins and a bottle of wine courtesy of May and the winery. The army has an interest in observing you. They want to see you become a zombie. Or not. Cameras will be set up: de-cappers ready."

"Great. But no beheading. I can be a celeb zomb. I'll do talk shows. Get a ghost writer for my bio."

"From what I've seen the undead don't do good interviews. Don't have much to say and can't say it."

Loud thuds from outside suggested an attack on the door. Two soldiers with hands full of coffee and food shouted they were the overnight detail.

The soldiers filmed the captives and set up a camera aimed at the mattress in cell four. Jane and Jesse ate and drank. The army men didn't touch the wine, but joined the police in games of poker and rummy: force vs. force. Police would have won if they hadn't overindulged in wine and got giddy.

During the night the soldiers changed shifts and in early morning a new duo sat in opposite corners playing games on their phones.

Jane woke first and peered at a monitor showing Jesse sleeping. He looked normal and then, as she stared more closely, things didn't appear right. His tight, rigid lips looked like they lacked blood and his forehead frowned forward, more wrinkled and caveman-like than normal. Black curls clung damply to the back of his neck. An hour later Jane impatiently told a soldier to wake him and the uniform clanged on the bars and unlocked the door. Jesse stirred. In the monitor Jane noticed he didn't stand straight as he plodded to his cell door and pushed it open. A soldier stood back with axe ready. Jesse shuffled towards the front room, knuckles near knees, ape-like. Jane held her blades towards him while the second soldier pointed his gun.

Jesse drooled, shuffled another two steps, stuck his arms forward and mumbled, "Jane-brain for breakfast."

"It won't be zombies that get the idiot sidekick killed," she snarled. "It'll be his warped sense of humour."

With a grin that connected his ears, Jesse suggested breakfast and his boss agreed. They thrust open the front door expecting sunlight to blind them. Instead a wall of water and drums of thunder forced them to rethink a run to Tim's. China Cup, directly across, served better breakfast, but had watery coffee. A bolt of lightning lit the street and a gust of cold wind sprayed through the door.

Windbreakers and newspapers atop heads protected them during the sprint to outdistance the lightning that danced above. They plunged through the eatery's front door and headed for a rear booth. Something about being police made them position themselves to observe everything. If a robber pulled a gun and ordered the till emptied they could step into action. They ordered coffee, bacon and eggs then Jesse noticed that the eyes of every man in the restaurant had risen from plates to doorway. His eyes followed to see what caught their interest. If the skirt of the woman walking to a table was any shorter it would have been a belt. If her legs were any longer they would have been grafted from a giraffe. Additional loft from spike heels put her at risk of losing her blonde bouffant to a ceiling fan. From far back in the eatery Jane and Jesse could hear the woman, like a rusty rock crusher, order coffee and French toast as she selected a seat. Jesse stood and signalled Joey to come sit with them. Her heels clacked through a forest of lechers. When she raised her arm to direct the waitress to deliver her food to the new table her hem rose and the men lowered their heads, hoping to catch a glimpse of what she wore, or didn't wear, beneath her skirt. Oblivious to stares, Joey wiggled to a chair and settled into a seat beside Jesse.

"What's new?" Jane asked.

Joey explained, in unsparing detail, that partner Donald had become morose and despondent. "He thinks the demise of his alien theory means the end of our department and loss of our jobs. He's invested so much time doing research and investigating landing sites worldwide that it devastates him to finally face the truth – an invasion by zombies outranks one by aliens. If you ask me …" In mid-sentence she noticed someone standing beside their table and looked up to see Donald.

"How long have you been eavesdropping?" she hawked.

"Long enough to learn how depressed I am. That's such a downer, having someone tell tales behind your back. That could be the last straw that turns me suicidal."

"But it's true. Since your alien bubble burst you've been in a funk and hardly able to converse."

"I've been doing research and thinking. Doing what you should be doing instead of wiggling your ass and watching men drool. I've made discoveries: that's what's depressing. The mass murders and disembowelments in other place have little in common with what's happening here. In other places the killers vanished right after the slaughters. No repercussions, no follow-up, no nothing."

Joey started to squawk about alien obsession when Jane asked if anyone had noticed that there seemed to be a parade of people going out the restaurant's back door. Donald Sinclair said he had been watching and, considering the rainstorm, it did seem peculiar.

"I'll find out." He walked away in his ghostly manner then came back and announced, "I've bought four tickets to the zombie show, $50 each. Courtesy of my department. They have a live zombie in the basement, not locked up. A ticket entitles you to get in the same room with it, talk to it, poke it, prod it. No chains, no cuffs, but safe. Maximum four at a time for five minutes. They'll call when it's our turn."

27

The proprietors of Vladimir's Bar stood and stared at their TV as if rivets attached leather shoes to floor. Hour after hour came one breathtaking announcement after another:
- zombie prisoners in local lock-up
- restaurant displays live zombie
- bite from a zombie doesn't turn you into one
- all civil liberties and rights suspended
- Z-D-Capper sold out, on order at $999 each
- more rewards claimed
- army headquartered at top winery

Vanessa thumped her Bloody Mary mocktail on the counter, paced and said nothing. Victor spoke. "We built The Vault, but haven't used it. Now's the time."

Victor stared at the only customer in the place, Barstool Bob, swaying on his favorite perch. They knew that BB, their best customer, lived alone, had no job, no friends and no family.

Victor and Vanessa conferred while others stared at the TV. Formulating an effective plan and arriving at a group consensus about that plan had the same probability as a Santa Claus knocking on the door with a delivery of fresh blood. Victor ordered fellow vamps to go downstairs and push aside the heavy cooler that blocked the vault. With several buttons undone on her black blouse Vanessa sidled up to Bob and told him she needed someone to sample beer from a new supply they had downstairs. Bob slid off his stool as if it had a Teflon coating and followed like a hungry puppy. At the bottom of the stairs an open door revealed the vault.

"You first," Vanessa said and after the drunken customer stepped inside she slammed the heavy door and slid closed an old deadlock. She assumed her donor yelled for help, but thick walls stopped sound from emerging. Victor led the push to put the cooler back in place and told a henchman to go buy some rollers as the door would now be opened and closed frequently.

Upstairs they huddled and tried to draw up rules for use of their captive. Someone recited an old adage, "Two can stay on a pint a day."

"Who gets the half pints?"

"Who are the two?"

"Who needs it most?"

"How many pints does BB hold?"

Questions outnumbered answers and no one stepped forward to make decisions.

"We need more donors," asserted a man wearing a black tie and black beret. He spoke louder than others, which, given the quiet, was unnecessary. At that moment a familiar customer came in, a 50-year-old woman with a drinking problem who generally got wasted and stayed that way for as long as her money held out.

Victor approached as soon as she entered, "We have a new beer downstairs and I wonder if you would try a free sample and give your opinion."

"Wow. I've come for the cheapest beer in town and you offer it free. Lead the way." She rushed downstairs and got to the vault as vamps pushed aside the cooler and opened the heavy door. Barstool Bob started yelling and tried to get out. Six men pushed them both inside, closed the door and secured it. Insulation deadened their pleas.

As hours passed customers straggled in and, if deemed expendable, Vanessa took them downstairs and added to the collection. With five angry bodies locked in, the vault reached capacity. Adding more became impossible without someone escaping. No one had contemplated the logistics. No one knew how to feed them and no one knew how to suck them.

"We could ask for volunteers," said the black bereted vamp, postulating that prisoners might prefer order over chaos and be willing to offer themselves.

"What about toilets?" another asked, ignoring the previous suggestion. Vampires never needed toilets, but humans had special needs. They created so much waste. Would the vault need a shower? The complexity so overwhelmed Victor and Vanessa that they regretted stocking the vault. Each grabbed a pen and paper and listed necessities. When the last item (battery powered lamp) had been put on Victor's list he headed to Canadian Tire. Vanessa went to Superstore with her list.

Installation of a chain, so the door could be opened a crack to talk to prisoners, came first. With the last screw in place Victor opened the door a few inches and the temporaries surged against it: six screws barely held the clasp that secured the chain. A drunk stuck his arm through the crack and demanded the free beer. Vanessa pulled the appendage as far as it would go and Victor jammed the door against the flabby bicep.

"Who wants it?" she invited.

"I really need some," muttered Vinny as he stepped forward and plunged into the forearm. "Missed," he mumbled. The arm's owner yelled, "Stop, for Christ sake. That hurts like hell, what the fuck are you doing?"

Vinny dipped forward again. "Missed," he repeated and another, expletive laden cry of pain erupted. He tried a third time. "Missed."

Finding a blood vessel in a flabby arm in dim light was like finding a flea in a mattress. Onlookers offered neither criticism nor advice.

"I need a carotid," Vinny declared and stepped back. No one else wanted to bite a purple arm that looked like a dog had gnawed it. The arm lost skin as it was yanked inside.

Frustrated vampires pushed bottled water, toilet paper, soap and hot dogs through the door's gap. The portable toilet wouldn't fit and neither would the lamp. Fearing angry inmates would overwhelm them, the vampires dared not open the door more than a crack.

Five temps thumped weak shoulders and fat hips against the door and the six new screws started to loosen and the gap widened. The size and number of screws required to secure a chain against surging shoulders and smouldering anger was foreign to vamps. When the donors stood back and gathered their forces to make a unified charge, Victor and friends pushed first and got the door bolted.

Victor announced a trip to Wal-Mart was required and he would be back in 20 minutes. "Meanwhile get rollers under the cooler. I'm worn out pushing it back and forth. And place a keg of beer by the door." He returned with a bag under his arm, took out two rubber wedges and placed them beneath the door. "Unlock it," he said and Vanessa turned the handle. Someone on the other side rammed and it jammed against the wedges. Three lengths of rubber tubing came out of Victor's bag. He plunged three tube ends into the keg by the door and shouted, "Here's your free beer."

As soon as the tubes were pushed through the door crack, the sounds of slurping and sucking could be heard.

"Why do we give them free beer?" Vince questioned.

"So they'll drink themselves into a stupor and we can have our way with them. We need more captives. This is brilliant. Once these ones get pickled we'll see who comes into the bar."

After much head scratching about the vault door crushing the drinking tubes when it had to be closed Vanessa spotted a hole where an old skeleton key once turned. Only two tubes squeezed through, but the door shut, the bolt slid and the vamps felt secure.

Victor, Vanessa and others marched upstairs and passed an hour watching TV updates. Little of interest appeared so they headed downstairs, put wedges in place and cracked open the door. No shoulders bashed against it.

"Do you need more beer?" Victor shouted.

"We need a goddam toilet; someone pissed on the floor." The voice had a slur and Vanessa couldn't tell if the slur was faked or if it came from a real drunk. Temps could be tricky.

"We'll open the door and you can come out and use a toilet. We've got food for you and coffee. Just one at a time. There's nothing to worry about. Molson brewery is sponsoring this so all you have to do is drink beer and be happy."

She opened the door an inch and when nothing suspicious happened she opened it wider. Bob came out along with a seepage of urine and a stink of vomit almost as bad as a herd of zombies. Bob zigzagged across the room and stopped at the wall.

"Toilet?" he questioned and started to unzip. Vanessa pushed a porta-potty towards him. "Pwivacy, gotta have some pwivacy."

Vanessa boldly kicked the toilet into the vault and Bob followed it, spraying as he went. She saw that bodies slept or were unconscious on the floor.

What have we done, she wondered? It seemed so simple: lock up a few drunks and take some blood.

Before Bob's fat fingers left his faucet Vinny and Vince pounced. Their weight sank him and as all went down the assailants siphoned noisily from his neck. They didn't take enough to render him dead or unconscious; just enough to satisfy their immediate needs.

Vanessa pushed canines into the thick neck of a thick woman. Never had blood felt so good. All but Victor and Vince joined her and took turns sipping from other bodies and squirting excess into bottles.

Outside the vault they laughed, patted each other's backs, high-fived and joked about captives who could turn beer into blood. Someone shouted they had created a blood factory and Vanessa added, "We should rename our place Vladimir's Blood Bar." Loud laughter erupted. They sat on beer kegs and chuckled about their captives. New blood brought a welcome ecstasy. Never had they been so happy. Angry words from a female within the cell broke the spell.

"Get off me," she shouted, "If you want to play you gotta pay." A slapping noise followed and a man moaned. That spurred another round of laughter.

"That captive woman breaks my heart," mumbled a dour vamp. The poor hooker's personal tragedy would normally have outweighed the humor, but a huge smile cracked across his olive face. The vamp wearing a black beret mockingly strummed air guitar and entertained the coterie around him with a reworked Elvis classic,

"Ever since my baby left me, I found a new place to dwell;
It's down the end of Main Street, at Vladimir's Blood Hotel."

Singing and dancing had never been part of vampire heritage. Victor's downturned mouth and his dark stare showed he despaired of the bizarre behaviour of his comrades. Nevertheless, his bereted buddy continued his impromptu song,

"They all drank at the free-beer well
then got locked in a cell."

A chorus of cheers and giggles followed. Victor recognized the alcohol content of prisoners' blood must be off the charts and his companions were feeling it. Vampires didn't get drunk. Alcohol had never affected them, but never had they sucked so deeply from a tank of drunks.

    Victor slammed the vault door, locked it and stomped upstairs leaving laughter behind. What else, he wondered, could go wrong with the wretched idea of harvesting captives? He no longer cared if temps had toilets, water or anything else. His disgusting hostages laughed last by intoxicating them.

28

As they waited in the restaurant for their turn to visit the zombie captive, Jane and Joey congratulated Sinclair on his good work. Then Jesse burst his bubble by telling him they had zombies in the station and he could look at them for free. Sinclair said he knew about them and would love some observation time, but he was still curious about what went on in the basement.

Before they swallowed the last crust a waitress led them out the back door. Twenty quick paces along a back lane, in the thunderous downpour, took them to a heavy steel doorway and down 13 cement steps.

"Here comes another fart-fest," Jesse quipped as a stench worse than a cabbage-eating skunk drifted up the stairway and took command of their nostrils. The waitress, habituated, shoved aside a garbage can and pulled open a door to an unusually well-lit room with low, beamed ceiling and cement walls. In the far corner a creature huddled, its face covered by its small hands.

According to the waitress the restaurant owner captured it in his yard two nights earlier. She said the people of White Rock deserved a chance to meet the enemy face to face so that they could recognize zombies and learn how to defend against them. It was all for the public good and 10 percent of proceeds went to the fire department.

"And the other $45 covers the electricity bill?" Jesse inquired sarcastically.

"Glad you asked," the waitress responded, like an automaton Disney guide, "The bright light is our defence. We discovered it. Let me demonstrate."

She closed the heavy door. "We are now alone with a genuine flesh-eating zombie." Her hands reached two dimmer switches and cautiously turned them counter-clockwise so the level of lighting diminished and the creature came to life.

The thing stood. It wore a once-white wedding dress that represented purity. Tufts of white patchy hair sprouted from her tiara-topped head. The monster's last wish had been to be buried in her wedding outfit. Her little wrinkled face had an avuncular kindness, although she was undoubtedly a grandmother. The lighting dimmed as the waitress fiddled with controls and the creature snarled, revealing four yellow teeth on top and a matching number on bottom. The light continued to dim, the mouth started snapping, eyes widened and the word *brains* slid out. Quickly the young waitress turned the lights back to full brightness and the zombie cowered and covered its head.

With the floodlights again dimmed to the point that sight became difficult, the mouth snapped open and closed and the agitated monster lumbered forward.

"This is a good demonstration, but too dangerous," Jane asserted. "I'm chief of police and I'm closing this down right now." As she dictated her order a lightning bolt cracked, something crashed above them and the room went black.

"Our generator will kick in," the waitress announced calmly, but nothing happened and *brains* came closer.

"Plan C," the waitress said equally calmly and shone a small, dim flashlight at the approaching ogre.

"We're outta here," shouted Donald, closest to the door. He pushed, but the thick slab wouldn't move. He rammed it with his shoulder and it cracked open only a quarter-inch. The stream of light was insufficient to deter light-sensitive eyes. "Something's fallen behind it."

Illumination from the flashlight weakened.

"Guess we forgot to recharge it," announced the waitress, unperturbed, as the beast moved slowly towards her. "I'll keep my beam on its eyes while someone opens the door."

Donald rammed it again and Jesse whacked it with a piece of wood, making no impression. From his pocket Donald pulled a miniature flashlight and directed the narrow beam at the zombie who stopped moving.

"Let's move on to plan D," Joey croaked and before anyone had a chance to ask about it she danced forward, kicked out her right leg and implanted the heel of her spiked shoe into the zombie's eye socket. "And now plan E."

Before she could deliver another flying kick Jane held her back. "It could go into a blind rage. Without sight the light won't matter. Surly there's another exit."

"No," the waitress replied unemotionally. "For safety's sake we have made sure the captive has no escape route. The generator will run momentarily."

"Your goddam generator has been hit by lightning and when this flashlight battery dies so do you." Donald spoke as calmly as the waitress, although his edgy, clipped words reflected the situation's severity. "Turn off your flashlight and save what's left," he said. "Mine should hold the thing in place. What's above us?"

"Dance studio; doesn't open until late afternoon."

Into her softly glowing phone Jane spoke cryptically, "Need help. Trapped in a basement with enemy. Across from the station, about 50 feet north of the back door of China Cup. Hurry."

She closed the call then took a photo with her phone. The enemy retreated at the flash then raised its arms and blocked the beams from Donald's flashlight. The wilted, yellow ray from the waitress's flashlight continued to arc limply across the room. The other three cell phones combined to put a glow on the monster's good eye. It seemed to juggle pain of light and the gain of meat then shuffled towards the nearest meal, the hostess. Joey's left leg took to the air and her heel landed perfectly in the zombie's other eye. She balanced on one long leg and the blinded beast grabbed her raised ankle and she fell.

The ogre landed on top her and lumpy, yellow puss dribbled from eye sockets into Joey's screaming mouth. Donald hoisted the stick used against the door and laid into the kneeling zombie's head with the fervour of a madman. Cranial fluid sprayed the walls. Jesse grabbed the zombie's left arm and Jane the right and they yanked back, but the beast bent forward, defying their combined strength. It plunged its face into Joey's stomach. She screamed, as a donkey would scream, from both the pain and the horror. Donald decreased the frequency of his blows and increased the force so any one of his swings would have hit the ball out of the park.

Jesse cuffed one wrist but Jane couldn't force the other arm back to link them together. She knew there was no point in asking politely if it would allow itself to be cuffed. A shot from her sidearm whizzed through the old, shrunken head and everyone ducked as it ricocheted off cement walls and ceiling.

Gasping and squirming to get out from under the force that held her in place, Joey thrust her long fingernails into the empty eye holes and gouged the inside of its head.

While the creature dined Jane finally yanked its arm back and Jesse clamped its wrists. The revenant still bent forward and its chomping head vanished inside Joey. A river of coffee flowed and bits of toast floated on top like little islands.

Donald, sweating and gasping, stepped in front and continued cascading blows on the monster's head, rendering it unrecognizable as anything either zombie or human. Its eight yellow teeth hit the walls, too late. Joey's hysteria tapered to pants and groans.

Jane aimed her Taser at the beast's upper region and unloaded. The jolt so energized the thing that it ripped its hands through the tight cuffs and pressed fingers against Joey's skull, trying to break through.

A tsunami of light filled the room as if curtains had been thrown open to a sunny day. The door bounced from its hinges and two police entered at the same time as light. The red-faced beast crawled to a corner. Donald comforted Joey, held her head and pulled together her gaping stomach.

"Get my shoes," Joey hissed, "They're expensive." Those were her last words.

A cop held a polycarbonate riot shield in front of him and a de-capper's blades rested on the bullet-proof edge. He closed in on the creature that had shrunk smaller into its corner. The blades fit around its neck.

As everyone waited for the head to fall the policeman whispered, "That's my Granny. Granny Graham. I know her dress. It's her old wedding dress."

Jane placed her hand over the cop's and together their fingers pressed the trigger. Pruners snapped and Granny Graham's blood-drenched head, with face beaten to mush, thumped to the floor and rolled towards the drain.

"Safety is our first concern," said the waitress.

The next morning a beautifully configured young woman, dressed in black leather, hosted the *A.M. Today* newscast. Vampires knew her as one of their own, but did not regard her fondly because of her penchant for public performance. For a decade she worked part-time at the local station, but her continuing youthful appearance could be attributed to makeup and surgery for only so long.

Straight black hair bounced on her shoulders as she carefully announced, "Colonel Mayhew-Shostakovich …" Off-camera a barely audible voice whispered, *Bless you*. The announcer suppressed a hint of smile and continued, "… has ordered all citizens to keep every light on throughout the night. The Colonel said that the army has discovered that light provides defence against the cannibal killers. A powerful light aimed at an undead will cause it to retreat. The colonel suggested all battery-operated lights be fully charged and ready for use. The army is mounting searchlights on helicopters. Additional floodlights will be installed on city streets. The Colonel said that if the town has sufficient illumination the curfew can be pushed back a few hours and evening business can resume. Bars and restaurants can stay open for dinner and drinks."

29

Where Doogie led, I followed. Through woods and narrow hillside trails we zigzagged; apparently randomly. I didn't question or complain: I had time on my hands and nothing on my mind. If he didn't look like a stewed prune I could have felt some affection for him.

Occasionally Doogie stopped and unearthed hidden, half-buried bodies I could never have found. Using some sixth sense the little leader pulled them from under dirt and gravel and placed dark sunglasses over their squinting eyes. With a shove and a hand gesture they fell in line and marched like obedient soldiers. A few wandered off in search of food and had Doogie not reined them in with yells and slaps they would have become lost. Doogie tried to retain wanderers with a loop of rope around the waist, but had difficulty tying knots with fat, uncoordinated fingers.

When he heard the noise of an army patrol Doogie waved his hands to indicate his followers should disperse and make themselves invisible. Often the army found the fleeing mavericks and the explosion of grenades and mortars indicated their end. Sometimes they found the soldiers first.

Heady and I patrolled the left flank, Doogie took the right and two lieutenants who seemed to understand Doogie kept tabs at the rear.

In his burbling voice Doogie asked me, "Were yoo wed?"

I had been practicing speech and, as Doogie predicted, it improved. After I walked a mile without shoes my mental acuity and energy level took an upswing. Confidently I replied, "Yeth."

"Me tooo," said Doogie. "I droowned in a cool lake. After twoo mooons passed she toook a new grooom."

I asked about his profession. "What dith oo do?" My words sounded right.

"I oopened her nooodle and scoooped. Left blooody body for her pooodle and her new groom. Yoo doo that tooo?"

"I ath Unthle Althert."

"Whoo he?"

"He in bathroom."

"Wooomen! How aboot kids?"

"Dithn't eath kids."

"Nooo. They groow big."

"I hath lithle boy and lithle girl. Wanna see them."

"Woould be good. And yoour wooman?"

"She said for bether or worth. Thith ith juth a bad patch."

"And till death doo yoo part – yoo dead, yoo parted."

"I mith Calculuth, Abacuth, Malady and man friend." The last words shocked me.

"Memories no goood. Boody under this log."

Doogie stumbled to a huge horizontal log, rolled it over, kicked away some leaves and pulled out a full-bodied comrade.

"Welcome to mooonlight army." He pulled sunglasses from his bag and plunked them on the new recruit without jabbing her eyes. The recruit stumbled to where Doogie pointed and disappeared into the shuffling, drooling mob.

30

After saying goodbye to Joey and before spending the evening attacking mundane chores around her house Jane called army headquarters and learned the previous night's death toll. Four lurchers had been killed and three captured alive. Jane wondered about the word *alive*. One soldier had died, but many received wounds from *friendly* fire. Army units had surrounded zombies then panicky soldiers started shooting. Bullets went through the enemy like spoons through pudding then hit fellow privates in the head, chest and privates.

Transferring zombies to jail cells would happen within an hour, announced the Colonel over radio and TV. Jane called him and insisted the drug dealing murderer had to go elsewhere. The Colonel agreed to take him away and lock him in a storage trailer.

It has all happened so quickly, Jane thought. One day she arrested a teenager for tagging a wall and now creatures from horror stories packed her cells, stunk up her office and moaned for brain. No fiction was stranger than White Rock's truth. Now she had no jurisdictional power and the tranquil town where she was born and raised was the source of national hysteria. Helicopters buzzed overhead like bees around a hive and boats, packed with photographers peering through giant lenses hummed up and down bays and rivers. At least they were safe.

Her floor creaked, the wind whistled and pine cones crashed onto a roof that needed new shingles. Carefully and quietly Jane moved from dark room to dark room, turned on every switch and wondered if light was the great white hope. She checked flashlights and put one on the kitchen table, one on top of the TV and one in her pocket. With pale, trembling hands she opened a dark, deep closet in her bedroom. Years ago its bulb burned out and she never replaced it: she knew where everything hung.

She felt for her police belt. Something cold slapped against her wrist and she jumped backwards, falling onto the bed. She rolled off the far side and landed on her feet ready to fight.

The clothes cupboard remained black with sketchy shadows. A thin satin belt rested on the floor where it had fallen after hitting her arm. The flashlight revealed nothing behind the clothing, but its rays couldn't reach the back. Closer she moved, prying left and right with light and ducking down to aim a beam across the floor, fearing it would land on a pair of dirty feet. Sweat beads merged on her back as she poked light into bleak corners, grabbed her police belt and realized she had never experienced fear in her own home. A screaming phone made her jump.

Jesse spoke loudly, as if volume would frighten demons. He said his services had become redundant since the soldiers took over, so he was staying home to work on his sailboat.

For several years he had been crafting it in his basement. Jane suspected he preferred his basement because that's where he had built a *safe room* and stocked it with sufficient supplies to keep him alive through several atomic wars, an apocalypse or two and an earthquake.

After a brief preamble he came to the point. "Since Donald was the boss, then Joey must be the underling, the assistant. Interesting character, funny in a bizarre way, intelligent, but definitely the sidekick. Expendable. I'm like her. All the sidekicks are."

Jane confronted the issue, "You're scared. I'm scared. We're all scared. My clothes closet scares me. I'm wearing my gun and every time I hear a noise I jump. I'm afraid I'm going to put a bullet through the wall and through old Archie who lives next door."

Jane made a suggestion, "The streets are fully lighted and I don't think the army can mistake a cop car for a zombie so I'm going down to the station to help out. The Smiths are on duty and new TV people have been pleading for a chance to film and interview a zombie. New captives should be in the cells. I think the two Smiths are insufficient. You want to be there?"

"For sure. I can hardly wait to shine lights in their eyes. Another night in the clink! I had so much fun last time."

"I'll pick you up. Pack sleeping stuff and some snacks just in case. Be at the door. I'll park as close as I can get."

After her car pulled onto the flat lawn, close to where Jesse sometimes parked his cruiser, Jane got a sinking feeling. Jesse threw his gear onto the back seat and when she slowly pressed the accelerator the tires spun.

"You're ruining my lawn," Jesse protested. "Now I've got sink holes."

The thunderstorm turned the green lawn to mushy mud into which the heavy cruiser's tires sank. Concentrating on gently rocking the car back and forth, Jane took a few seconds before retorting, "At least I've killed some of your weeds."

"We gotta get outta here," Jesse said nervously, "It's too dark for our good." Jane silenced the engine.

"We gotta get into your house. Jeeze, you didn't even leave the lights on."

"Sorry 'bout that. Turning them off is a bad habit."

The car had a full tank of gas so she restarted the engine and turned on the interior lights, spot lights, headlights and emergency flashers then opened her door to leave.

"Did you see that?" Jesse snapped as they stepped out of the sedan.

"Yea, I saw something between the houses. We have to get to your door. Did you lock it?"

"Affirmative. Key's in my hand. Flashlight's ready. Let's go."

"Hold on a sec. Have you got the jagged edge of the key facing the right way? You slip the key in: I turn the handle. Counter clockwise? You realize this is the part where the sidekick drops the key on the porch and it falls through a crack. You won't do that will you?"

"Course not. And don't waste time closing and locking. Leave the engine running. I don't think they drive. Three seconds and we're inside. Three, two, one, go!"

Jesse, closest to the portal of his home, pushed off on the soft lawn and slipped, landing on hands and knees.

"Don't tell me you dropped the key," Jane demanded.

"Course not. No way." Again Jesse slipped in his panicked attempt to get to his feet.

"Just take it easy," she ordered sternly as her own feet slid sideways and she almost went down. The muddy key entered the lock, Jane turned the handle, the door opened, they stepped into the foyer and relief surged over them. Three drooling figures lunged from shadows in the kitchen. The back door hung from one hinge.

A gnarled hand reached for Jane. Jesse flicked a light switch. The zombies raised their hands to shield their eyes, then trundled forward at reduced lurch. The cops backed up a few steps then compounded the creatures' discomfort by aiming flashlights at their faces. When rays of light squeezed between decomposing fingers and reached eyes the lumbering monsters barely moved. Jesse stomped on a floor switch that turned on a reading lamp beside a ratty recliner. A full-figured zombie, wearing a rumpled evening gown, knocked over the floor lamp and stepped on its bulb. She enjoyed the jolt of electricity in her feet and stood atop the broken socket until a breaker snapped and the house went black. Two flashes of blue light accompanied the two bullets that flew from Jane's gun through the closest zombie's head, without effect.

"Can we get to your basement?" she gasped.

"Not with them standing there. We can't go anywhere. Back to the car?"

"No, better off on foot."

They backed out the front door, which Jesse slammed and locked to slow the enemy. Seconds later wood shattered and the door fell. From across the street and from between houses tattered figures moved towards them. Surrounded, the two police scrambled to the safety of their car. Once inside Jane got the army post on her cell while Jesse talked to the station on the cruiser's radio. They locked the doors and aimed spotlights at approaching figures. Jane again tried to rock the cruiser free: spinning tires dug deeper.

Shadowy outlines hesitated 10 feet from the cruiser as if its bright lights presented an impenetrable barrier. Jane looked in the rear-view mirror where objects appeared smaller, but not small enough. An enemy stood within a few feet of the back of the car where lights were fewest. Pushing her foot against the brake pedal turned on a couple of bright reds and moving the gear selector to reverse lit a couple of whites. The added illumination caused the creature to push a hand into a tattered pocket and pull out sunglasses.

A siren broke the Arctic silence as a police cruiser screeched around the corner, skidded across the grass and slid to within inches of Jane's car. Now she couldn't get out her door. Constable Purdy, in the passenger seat of the new arrival, couldn't get out either. The driver of the rescue vehicle exited his car without slipping in the mud. Jane tapped her horn and pointed to approaching zombies. The driver, on seeing the encircling enemy for the first time, looked shocked. His face paled and he turned to get back into his cruiser, but couldn't because Purdy had crawled across the computers and radios and now occupied the driver's spot.

Jane fired an order at Jesse. "Get flares from the trunk."

They discussed his moves and agreed it would be a bad idea to slip, trip or do any other inexplicable thing that expendable characters routinely do. As soon as Jesse got out, the zombie wearing shades strode towards him. Jesse went the other way, keeping the two cruisers between himself and attacker. When the trunk lid went up Jane lost sight of him.

The lid slammed closed and suddenly Jane viewed a creature clamping a hand on Jesse's neck and pulling him backwards. A gunshot severed the stillness and a small hole appeared on the bridge of the predator's nose. Its sunglasses fell in two pieces and its hands went up to block the light. Jesse ran around the side of the car and got in.

"Nice shot," he panted and handed three of six flares to Jane. With a nod she acknowledged her marksmanship and looked to Purdy's cruiser. A zombie pulled the ankles of the cruiser's driver and dragged him away from the car. Purdy held the officer's pleading, outstretched hands, but the tug-of-war went to the strongest.

Jane snapped the top off a flare, handed it to Jesse and he lobbed it over the two cruisers, landing it next to the zombie and the struggling policeman. The bright orange glow halted the beast before it could bite into the constable. The undead thing humped away from the flare, dragging its meal by the ankles, towards darkness. Purdy emptied his gun into the ogre who did not react to the lead in its dead head. The constable on the ground struggled to free his Taser while becoming dazed as his head splashed through puddles and hit rocks.

Jesse lit a second flare and hurled it ahead, causing the zombie to veer from the glow. Hunger outweighed the pain of light. The creature suddenly stopped and sank hard brown teeth into the constable's soft belly. Another undead let a rock drop: the cop's top caved.

Jesse ran ahead, picked up the flares and forced the gaggle of zombies to part like the Red Sea. The beast that bent over the dead constable kept his head buried in the torso and didn't let the new light interrupt his meal. Purdy fled from his car with no apparent plan while Jane scrabbled across the passenger seat and lit a flare. "We're on foot," she quipped.

Just 200 paces ahead, Main Street, brightly lit, welcomed. As it neared, a large-tired army Jeep, sporting searchlight, machine gun and bazooka, sped in from a lane. A woman drove while a man in back attempted to keep his balance, aim the light and fire the gun. Following a flash and a roar the arm and shoulder of a zombie vanished. The bazooka's projectile continued towards Jesse's house and with the disintegration of a supporting pillar the veranda collapsed. That mattered little because the projectile continued into his kitchen which erupted in a blue flame of natural gas. The house vanished in an explosion of smoke and fire.

Jesse's slack mouth managed a few words. "I just read the insurance policy. It doesn't count under martial law, war etc. I'm homeless."

"After what you just did, trying to save that constable, we'll find a way. You went beyond the call of duty. What's in the budget will at least get you a new foundation."

The searchlight on the Jeep ceased projecting light when its glass shattered. A zombie slowly hopped from foot to foot as an apparent display of satisfaction with his marksmanship. Other zombies surged from dark corners.

The dead-eyed marksman on the Jeep turned to his machine gun, swung it from side to side, hit zombies by the score and stopped not a single one. Bullets whizzed through the air and Jane, Jesse and Purdy took cover behind trees. Jane lobbed a flare towards the fray, but it fell short.

The Jeep's driver strategized by going in ever smaller circles as zombs closed in. One creature lunged and got a hand on the door handle, which swung open, but the shooter in camo attire fired his bazooka and removed the lunger's head. His skill with the big gun impressed Jane, but that impression didn't last long because the shell that so cleanly removed the zombie's head exploded near the front wheel, creating a crater into which the vehicle's tire plunged, bringing it to a halt. Undead swarmed, ate and then stumbled off, dragging the empty gunman and the driver by their ankles.

With flares held in front like spelunkers exploring a bat-infested cave the cop trio made their way to Main Street. Their fear level and their pace eased when the lights of town shone on them. At the far end of White Rock their den of security, the police station, waited. Halfway there a woman in a nightgown came out of her house holding a candle.

"Can I join you?" she asked. "What church are you going to?"

At the station the two constables named Smith had everything under control and had mummified the new inmates with two large rolls of fiberglass-reinforced tape per captive. An additional roll held the beasts upright against the bars that formed cell walls. Cuffs completed the job. It took two coffees and two stale donuts before Jane recovered from her close encounter. She called Donald Sinclair at Holiday Inn. Without Joey to keep him on track his theories would likely expand into the twilight zone.

Donald confessed to being depressed and admitted alcohol had touched his lips for the first time in a year. He said he stopped at two drinks. Since saying goodbye to Joey he kept occupied by calling contacts all over the world. Exploring local forests at night gave him something to do when he couldn't sleep. Sprinting from the denizens of the deep woods gave him exercise. He had no difficulty evading slow zombies: looking for hidden ones kept him tense.

"Let's talk in person." Jane said she'd drive over and meet him in the hotel's coffee shop. He countered that since army searchlights, streetlights and extra lights on roofs illuminated all 300 yards between them he would walk over and visit her at the station. "I'll be there in 10 minutes."

Jane overruled him, insisting foot travel was dangerous and she would drive. She first had to introduce zombies to the media.

Jesse loosened a few inches of tape on a prisoner's feet and Constable Smith pushed it out to the sidewalk in front of the station. Flashes popped, microphones thrust, cameras rolled and reporters scribbled. The bloody zombie, despite suffering from the bright lights, put on a good show, mumbling indecipherably and shuffling back and forth until it tripped over an electrical cable. On its way down its fingers grabbed the skirt of an attractive lady holding a microphone inches from its taped mouth. Together they fell. The reporter's skirt ripped off and the zomb landed atop her. Newswoman and attacker squirmed on the ground. Cameras rolled as a flash of silver from Jesse's hands left the attacker beheaded. The media clips set internet records and sent tremors of horror across the planet. Zombie rape and the application of justice with an instant beheading couldn't be topped.

The cool reporter casually pulled up her skirt and turned the microphone to Jesse who was an interviewers dream: a handsome, animated man born to talk.

Jane didn't want a mike in her face so she walked out the station's back door with an ignition key in hand. The two cruisers abandoned on Jesse's lawn constituted the last of her force's fleet. A tow truck would be needed to pull them off the muddy grass: so much for a mobile police presence.

She dropped two blue bubble-lights into a bag and went out the front door to her 10-year-old Dodge Caravan where she popped the lights on the roof and turned on their strobes. After squeezing through a mob of reporters she was happy to be away.

Down the middle of Main Street she drove confidently, stopping to tell a pair of brave but foolish pedestrians to either get off the street or stay in the brightest path of searchlights. Two army patrols took no notice of her and they didn't seem concerned about the pedestrians either. In the distance black smoke twirled skywards: Jesse's house smouldered on the ground. The spiralling plumes made her think the flames did more than blister the paint of her two cars mired on the lawn: rubber burned. Firemen, for good reason, refused to answer calls. The army claimed it had its own fire brigade, but she had seen no evidence of it.

Donald Sinclair sat alone in a booth designed to seat four, reading a newspaper in the midst of a busy restaurant. No beer glasses adorned the table. His strong handshake welcomed Jane. The table stood in the way of a comforting hug. They talked about Joey and how her bubbling personality would be missed. When he rubbed his eyes and his voice quivered Jane turned the subject to new findings. Donald said he had learned so much it frightened him more than an alien invasion. The scariest part had to do with bodies. The army ordered that the dead must be cremated or shipped out of town, but zombies now hauled away their victims.

"I know what you mean," Jane added. "We just lost a new recruit I didn't even get to know, plus two army personnel that got disembowelled. The undead dragged their bodies off. What do they do with them?"

"I don't know for certain, but I think they rebury them."

"But why?"

"Because they become reanimated and rise again. Whatever originally happened to reanimate the dead still happens. It has to do with an electrical charge in the earth. Scientists are conducting measurements, but they started too late, they have no base numbers. Every day we get more living dead. Every time someone gets killed it's not just one fewer player on the home team, it's one more for the opposition. A mathematician could tell how long we have on earth if 25 citizens switch sides today and that number increases to 33 tomorrow, and 44 the next day. It's exponential."

"That's scary."

"Scary and getting scarier. Some wear sunglasses. They come out in daylight. Although many appear brainless, some kind of thought process goes on somewhere with some. A few throw rocks and some hit with sticks. It's like apes using tools."

A waiter took Jane's order of coffees and biscuits. She commented on the activity in the restaurant and the waiter explained, "Zombie tourism is great for business. Every room booked. Most are scared to walk the streets so they hang around the restaurant and leave huge tips."

"Is that a hint?" Donald asked.

"No, you guys are locals. You're exempt. Coffee's on the house."

"I'm not local. I'm from Ottawa," Donald contradicted.

"You sure?"

"I should know."

"I swear I've seen you around town," the waiter insisted. "Don't you work in the drug store?"

"Not that I know of."

"Maybe you're in real estate. I've been looking for a house."

"No, I'm from Ottawa."

"Weren't you at an open house in Richmond last month?"

"No, I was in Ottawa."

"You sure? You're a ringer for the condo salesman there."

Jane ended the circular conversation. "Put the food on my tab. Police policy. No freebies allowed."

The waiter walked away scratching his head and Jane asked about updates on aliens. Donald said those speculations ended when he saw what had happened to the dead.

"I kept up some of that crazy patter to get to Joey. We always joked although she thought I was serious when I extended my theory to fit conditions."

Following a contemplative pause Donald asked Jane what she knew about Vladimir's Bar. It took her a second to put a place to the name. "Pretty tame. Hardly even notice it. Never had a brawl. Don't think they even employ a bouncer. What's your interest?"

"I've been into every business in town. Just snooping around. Vlad's is the strangest bar I've ever seen and I've frequented plenty. How does it stay in business? No clients. No druggies, hookers or bikers. Just an occasional drunk. And a bunch of weird customers who stand around watching TV and don't order drinks or food. All perfectly groomed, all about age 30, all dressed in dark colors. What does that add up to?"

"A gay bar?"

"That's what I thought. The women, good-looking and shapely, show no romantic interest in anyone: no emotions. They just hang with the men watching a big TV."

"I don't think you'd be telling me this unless you had a theory."

"Vampires."

Jane started to laugh but Donald interrupted, "A couple of weeks ago you would have laughed if I said zombies had invaded your town."

"Good point. I've seen the remains of dried out dogs. I've seen people being eaten. I only think it's funny, ironic, in the sense of … this is the last straw. Vampires? What's next?"

"They've got something going on in their basement. Maybe a lab or workshop. We need to find out."

"What the hell?" Jane said with a sigh. "Vampires with a lab in the basement of a pub? Are they building Frankenstein?"

The waiter plunked down coffee and informed Donald he had seen him in a play a year ago. Donald answered he had never acted. The waiter shrugged and walked off, not understanding why an actor would deny a stage career.

Jane said judges respected army control and no longer recognized the RCMP so wouldn't issue a search warrant. "You should tell Mayhew about the basement lab. Soldiers can barge in anytime without warrant or warning."

"Everything the Colonel does ends in disaster. He battles as if fighting rebels in Syria, not reanimated in White Rock. His bullets and shells keep going until they strike something and that something is often house, car or civilian. He should build a wall, moat and electric fence around the town: something to contain them. Soldiers chase them at night - zombie advantage - and then rest during the day when the enemy is weakest."

Jane changed the subject as she didn't want to undercut Mayhew's strategy: he was a fellow law enforcer. "We should go to Vlad's and have a drink. At least I'll have a drink. You can have water. We'll take Jesse. Sometimes he sees things I don't. He could use a drink. Mayhew's men blew up his house."

Donald gulped coffee and cleared his throat. "Before we go, here's something to know. There is no Vlad: no Vladimir. A numbered company made up of 18 people owns the place. They've owned it for 10 years. And for 10 years before that it was owned by some company headed by a guy named Valiant. And for 10 years before that a woman named Victoria owned it. And a decade before that a dude by the name of Velletto had ownership. It goes back to 1923. Every 10 years it changes hands."

Jane sipped coffee as she pushed a biscuit around her plate. She recalled the outpouring of floating islands of toast from Joey's split stomach. The snack stayed on her plate.

"Is the V for Vampire?" she asked. "Do we wear garlic and put wooden stakes through their hearts?"

"Beats me. The myth says a bullet through the brain kills zombs, but that sure doesn't work. Some don't have brains. Why a wooden stake? Why wouldn't a steel pole work? Or aluminum: to give them aluminum poisoning. Or lead for lead poisoning. Or a cobalt pole to radiate them to death. Maybe silver bullets work. Does Wal-Mart stock them? But why kill vampires? They don't do any harm. They've been running their bar for decades and no one has even noticed."

They picked up Jesse at the station then parked in front of Vladimir's Bar. The backlit sign above the window - black script on white - hinted at nothing except lack of creativity. No open or closed sign adorned the door nor did a posting of hours of operation. Many local businesses featured an outside sandwich board advertising the day's specials, but not Vladimir's.

The three in the car agreed about Vlad's lack of business sense and lack of desire to attract customers, but no crime had been committed, no law or bylaw violated. They cautiously entered, avoided the black bar stools with chrome trim, and selected wooden seats at a round table. An oyster-eyed bartender displaying the personality of cardboard glanced their way and showed neither pleasure nor displeasure at the appearance of three new customers. He stepped towards them with a melting glare and said nothing, as his purpose was obvious. Jane ordered wine, Jesse a draught beer and Donald said he would have a bottle of Bud.

"Don't do it," Jane cautioned. "You said you've been good for a year. Don't ruin it now."

"I had one before and I stopped. I can control it." Donald confirmed his order with a nod and the bartender committed it to memory.

They scanned the dim interior. Aged oak trim complemented walls painted flat-black and pod lights threw illumination here and there with neither focus nor pattern. The wooden floor appeared original: untreated fir with gaps between slats. Plastic flowers circa 1996 and framed photos of jungle animals clipped from National Geographic constituted efforts at decoration. A dusty trout that might have talked if its batteries hadn't died a decade ago constituted pop culture.

The lack of ambient music meant the bartender could hear conversation so the trio talked about weather and compared Ottawa's icy autumn winds to the West Coast's lengthy summer. Indecipherable sounds rolled across the floor from the hushed conversation of a serious six seated at a big table in a distant corner. A man in a business suit slept with face flat on a table for two.

The bartender, a 30-year old with greasy black hair, dark blue sweater, black pants and black shoes, clunked three drinks on their table and didn't demand payment. He walked off to join the group-of-six. Jane, Jesse and Donald looked at each other and took turns saying, *Weird, Eerie, Scary.*

"There's no way this place makes money," Jane whispered.

"It's a front," Jesse said. "It's here to launder money or provide cover for something. No wonder we hardly notice it?"

"It's designed not to be noticed," Donald said. "If you search Vladimir's Bar on the web I'll bet a picture of this place won't come up. It has no nightlife, nothing."

After finishing her wine, Jane suggested they leave because they were not going to get to visit the basement. The washrooms had been explored and a door that could lead to a cellar, or to a closet, remained closed and appeared locked. The tab of less than $10 amazed Jesse who told the bartender he would return another day. A slight nod of his perfect head indicated the barkeep didn't care one way or the other. He muttered "thanks," and sauntered away with Donald's ten and no intention of giving the few cents change.

Donald said he wanted to stay, have another drink and study the place some more. Jane pleaded with him to leave, but he only walked half-way to the door with them. She told him to call when he wanted to go back to his hotel, but Donald insisted he would find a ride or just sprint the distance, keeping in the light.

Donald ordered a beer and when he emptied that glass he ordered another. A man in a black beret seated himself beside Donald and asked where he was from. Ottawa was home, he said and studying zombies was why he was in White Rock. The man in black bought two beers and continued questioning him about friends, family and other connections. Donald told him he had bought a drink for the two strangers he came in with as thanks for driving him from his hotel.

The man got up from the table and offered his untouched beer to Donald. After he conferred with fellow dark ones the barman returned to invite Donald downstairs to sample rare imported ale on which he wanted an opinion. Despite fears of ending up in a den of gay depravity Donald said yes.

The man wearing the beret lithely bounded down the steps and Donald wobbled after him, trying to adjust his eyes to the dim cellar. Five men, similarly dressed, looking serious and sinister, waited at the bottom. They didn't offer a welcoming smile. Before Donald could retreat up the stairs the man who led him turned and lunged, affirming fears of a gay vampire gang bang.

The attack did not catch Donald by surprise. His elbow landed between the attacker's eyes and the vamp went down like a drunk who missed his stool. Others lunged. A foot to the knee knocked the next attacker aside and a chop to the neck dissuaded the third. Although the attackers had no appetite for a fight, the combined weight of them took Donald to the cement floor. His elbows, knees and fists shot out in defence but he was overwhelmed.

The unrelenting barrage of blows caused the attackers to abandon bloodletting. They dragged Donald into the dark room that reeked of piss and vomit. A heavy door slammed shut and a lock closed. In the black silence Donald heard labored breathing, reached out and felt sleeping and unconscious bodies around him. His hand dug to where he kept his phone but his pocket had been deftly emptied. His miniature flashlight remained and its thin beam put a glow to bodies flat on the floor or slouched against walls. A woman with pants around her ankles giggled, "Reduced price if you come quickly."

Donald directed his light to her neck and the necks of captives. All had puncture holes as did arms and ankles. Through the heavy door a voice shouted, "Here's the free beer. Let us know if you're hungry." Nothing appeared amiss when Donald rubbed his hand over his own thick neck. He had put up too much resistance. The end of a tube sticking through a big keyhole wiggled. He put it to his mouth and tasted beer.

31

The situation at lock-up exceeded ludicrous. Inside three cells 36 undead, double cuffed and bound in tape, compulsively shuffled using tiny steps that covered inches. A bounty of adhesive prevented arms and heads from moving and made them look like vertical mummies. Like a thick fog with globules of moisture, a wall of stink surrounded them.

Constables worked overtime keeping tape tight and making the undead as immobile as possible. Even with mouths layered the creepy corpses mumbled. The police chief figured six more cannibal cadavers could be taped to cell walls then the *No Vacancy* sign would go up.

Jane phoned the Colonel to learn about incoming bodies and as soon as she said the Z-word he started a rant. He shouted that a judge had just ordered the monsters out of the town's cells. Missing Hill Winery, with high walls, big gate and lots of space would be, according to the judge, a more humane place to pen captives.

"Dog gamn it, excuse my language, but that means headquarters will be compromised; we have to move. We can't operate next to a bunch of reekin' freakin' flesh-eaters. Excuse me, it's going to take a day for us to move. Where do we go? Gull's Gait's a fine winery, but it doesn't have the high walls or view. Anyway, that's not your mucking, excuse me, business. A transporter should be there within a half-hour to rid you of your stinking charges. Have you been following the plucking judicial process?"

Jane admitted she had no time to follow any process, judicial or otherwise. "I thought you guys were in charge. I thought you were above the court system and civil law?"

Silence followed so Jane asked, "Are you still there?" Silence indicated the Colonel had moved on.

Jane turned to the office TV and it showed video of her town taken from a plane. A gravely-voiced comedian, whose ratings had plummeted following accusations of sexual misconduct, said White Rock had little hope of a future unless fenced off, trenched off and promoted as a tourist attraction – the world's only Zombie Zoo. The performer continued as if doing a tourism ad.

"At Zombieville an affordable $30 covers parking and a walk atop our glass viewing platform above the streets. You will see real zombies living in town and dining on child molesters and repeat offenders. Visitors will be lowered in a bite-proof cage to the feeding zone for the experience of a lifetime. You can reach out and touch them, but watch your fingers. In our gift shop, pick up Zeddy, our cuddly doll - a battery-operated biter the kids won't forget. Our snack bar features finger foods with grave-ee. Visit the world's first Z-zoo where security is our first concern. Maps and dead-crumbs for feeding included."

Jane wondered how anyone dared spoof a tragedy in which families had been devastated by unspeakable deaths. She picked up her still-folded newspaper and read that a zombie rights issue unfolded in the courtrooms. Liberals complained about zombies being wrongfully imprisoned as, individually, they may not have broken any laws.

"There are good undead and bad undead, just like people and dogs, and it is extremely prejudicial to lump them all together and convict without due process of law." The quote came from a civil liberties lawyer.

Officials searched past legislation for hints about zombies, undead, resurrected, reanimated, revenants and any other they could think of and came up empty. Religious leaders pointed to retribution for the sins of mankind. Hindus argued that zombies represented the reincarnation of lost souls. Catholics related the risings to the resurrection of Jesus Christ and others. Buddhists said life is suffering and zombie karma makes it worse. Jehovah's Witnesses said, "The end is nigh." Jews said, "This too will pass." Atheists said, "Kill the bastards."

Headlines screamed the essential question, *"Are the reanimated human?"* All agreed they once were human, but beyond that no consensus seemed possible. New territory had opened and waited to be explained and explored. If the deceased had been interred with pockets full of cash, lawyers would have represented them and the matter would have been resolved in court. In one case a captured zomb's wallet reached the hands of an ambitious lawyer. The ambulance-chaser got excited preparing injunctions and writs and demanding his client's freedom. A judge released the zombie into the lawyer's custody, the public defender took it home and it ate his wife. When the lawyer's office processed the credit card it didn't go through as its holder had been dead for a week. The case was dropped.

Violations of habeas corpus rights and wrongful imprisonment charges could have tied up the legal system for years had there been money to be made. No one offered pro bono work on behalf of a decomposing corpse that stank up the court and tried to eat its lawyer.

In crowded jail cells several zombies had collapsed from malnutrition or suffocation and that brought about the creation of the SPCZ. The organization inspired stockholding of undead in outdoor pens so they could be treated with respect and humanity. The new Society to Prevent Cruelty purchased pets and tossed the little animals to zombies. The rabbits, dogs, cats, iguanas and other creatures did little to ease zombie hunger. When they were a few calories short of dropping from starvation zombies bit off the legs off hamsters, hares and hedgehogs. One zomb took a particular liking to rabbits' feet and left several unlucky bunnies bumping around on bloody stumps.

Jane's news update ended when an army transporter arrived to clear her cells. One at a time mumbling mummies were pushed to the dull green vehicle where they were placed flat and stacked one atop the other. As the last passed, Jane wondered about rising from the grave. Did they have awareness of their miserable state or were they numb as a worm? What hell could be worse than being trapped in a cognitive body driven to eating the living?

Jane ordered her men to scrub the cells with lye solution and buy air fresheners in bulk.

32

Crashing through backyards was the most fun I had since meeting Uncle Albert. It wasn't really *that* much fun ... not like bowling, fishing or eating brain, but it passed the time. Despite not producing belly laughs, smashing wooden fences gave me a sense of purpose. Someone wrote that good fences make good neighbors, but that made no sense. No fences made good meals.

Sunglasses dulled the sun that sat low on the horizon: they allowed painless sight. Doogie gets credit for that. Good eyes helped me keep a lookout for posse, soldiers and tarp-covered pits while I tried to turn my lurch into a swagger. My hips were stiff and my arms wouldn't swing in time with feet that slowly inched forward.

My exact location was unknown, but I felt that I headed in the direction of Abacus, Calculus and Malady. The ache in my heart hurt more than I could stand and if I had to shatter 1,000 fences to fall down at their feet I would do so. I tried to hum a Scottish tune but *brains* got in the way.

After shuffling along a deserted lane I arrived at the back of a corner store I had seen before. Once I had considered putting a rock through its window so I could get cigarettes. Now I knew smokes offered no pleasure. A comb and skin care products would help me woo Malady and regain the love of my kids. The store's back door tilted on its hinges: I was not the only one after free hair gel. Looters had knocked asunder shelves laden with boxes and bottles. How could I find what I wanted in this chaos?

Kicking through the litter I came across toothpaste and toothbrushes: a good start. My fingers made no headway in extracting a toothbrush from surrounding plastic, but the toothpaste tube easily came out of the box and a squeeze sent blue paste squirting against a picture of a digestive system. Most landed on a part labeled *duodenum*, which looked delicious, but some hit my toothbrush package. I rubbed the hard plastic against my brown teeth. The taste was horrific and I didn't think decay was being prevented although my breath could surely use freshening.

I wished I had a need for the adult diapers strewn across the floor. I would love to pee and poo. Taking a long and satisfying leak would make my day, but I had no urge to purge. A small box had a picture of a leathery stomach: it must contain laxatives. The bottle of pills came out of the box, but the lid refused to come free from the slippery container. I twisted, dug fingernails in, banged it against a shelf, stomped on it and finally gave up and said, *shit*. It sounded like *thith*.

Locating mouthwash and hair gel proved impossible so I fled the confining shelves and maze-like aisles without so much as a comb. Shopping had never been a favorite pastime. How would I fare with Christmas coming?

Fencing with backyard fencing was necessary because I had to keep out of sight and cutting a swath through backyards served that purpose. People wanted to kill me. The roads were not safe.

My extraordinary strength amazed and amused me as fence after fence fell until I pounded on something solid that did not give way. *Cementh*, I thought in my single-track way, *Built by an idiot*. Then I recognized it as a wall I had built. The neighbor kept two menacing Rhodesian ridgebacks that snapped and growled whenever children went near his old wooden fence. The block wall kept the hounds from hell isolated.

Familiar guttural growls seeped from the darkest corner of the next yard. I could see over the wall and I snarled back at two broad-shouldered, salivating canines that lunged forward. A light breeze carried the reek of decomposing cat from my stuffed stomach to the sensitive noses of the dogs. The larger of the two weakened and lay down. Never had I known a dog to faint.

A rusty gate at the rear of my yard fell to the ground and I passed through. For the second time in my new life I gazed at the windows of my home. A gap in drawn curtains allowed my eyes to scan the family room. Melody, wearing only a push-up bra and very small red panties, watched television. The big screen showed naked couples interacting in odd ways and I recalled something about *adult* shows that fascinated my wife, but didn't interest me. She held a big carrot in her lap.

It annoyed me, as best I could be annoyed, that she put the children at risk with so little defence of her home. She must have expected an attack would come from the front which was lit and patrolled. A cement block wall and metal gate might appear to secure the back, but how little she knew about the strength of the renewed. A light bulb dangling from a tree illuminated the yard. I reached up and crushed it: the charge of electricity surging through my body felt good.

I watched as my wife played with her carrot and I longed to sit beside her. I would watch naked people if that's what she wanted, just so long as I could put an arm around her and hold her close. My mind strayed to other things we used to do together and how exhausted it made me. Would she want to do that again, I wondered and looked down at baggy pants. The initials E D popped into my head and I recalled blue pills that were supposed to cure whatever the initials were. Like an insecure baseball player I tugged at my withered peanut and recalled a man who did the same when we lay on a bed together.

Tapping on the glass and surprising Melody seemed the right thing to do, but would she hold some resentment after our last encounter? I slid along the wall and around the corner to the kids' bedroom. Metal bars had been added to their window and for that I was thankful. Between rusty rods I could see angelic faces sleeping among stuffed toys. I longed to hold them, hug them, protect them and tell them no harm would come.

Daddy's home, I whispered softly.

Returning to the family room window I tapped lightly and grinned. Melody jumped and the carrot fell. From beneath the couch she pulled a device with two shiny blades and pointed it directly at me. Her twisted face didn't spell love. Care and compassion were as far from her as birth from death.

Melody quickly switched off the television and the lights and I liked that. She might not notice my skin condition when she invited me in. The door didn't open. Was she reaching out to a new Uncle Albert so she could make introductions? Was she calling for the kids to tell them daddy was home? I pushed at the door: it didn't open. I ran forward, put my shoulder into it and bounced back: nothing gave. I needed a rock.

The backyard had accumulated a lot of debris since my departure and there was no shortage of weighty objects. A siren splintered the air and flashing lights reflected off rooftops.

Not again, I thought, surely Malady had not turned me in again. Where were her priorities? Who did she love?

I pressed my disfigured visage against the glass and looked directly at my wife. Her mouth opened wide and I thought her lips twisted into *I love you*. Then her scream blasted through windows and doors and into the backyard. She was heartbroken. If she opened the door and let me in I could comfort her. I raised a brick.

The intensity of flashing lights and sirens increased and I knew my foes were on my street. I waved goodbye, blew a kiss, dropped the projectile and made my exit. A protective forest and a rendezvous with Doogie, the only one I could trust, waited just beyond the backyard.

So many questions danced in my head I didn't know how to begin getting answers. Asking Doogie a question took thought and a lot of preparation and sometimes, when I got to the end of that process, I lost sight of where I began. My questions had no end. How long would I live, why did I eat people, why did I feel no pain, why did I not have bowel movements? Why did Doogie collect bodies?

I kept a phone that had fallen from the hand of a victim and I longed to call Melody. What was her number, my number? My pudgy fingers jabbed the only numbers that stayed in my head – 911. A concerned operator figured I was lost in the woods and in danger of being found by zombies. She told me to stay on the line and the army would locate me although this might take an hour since help calls flooded in every minute. She said to check the phone's battery, but in looking for it I broke the case and the battery fell out and rolled away.

I didn't have to find Doogie: he found me as I sat on a rock waiting for something to happen in my pointless life. My 911 call brought two camo-clad privates on an ATV. Before the army men realized they were responding to a distress call from a zombie, several accomplices, directed by Doogie, ambushed them and relished them.

I was glad to see Heady push forward and chew violently: she dined like a pro. I considered her digestive system and figured an hour should be time enough for her stomach to process the new meat and brain. After an uncounted while and some wandering in the woods I unwound the tape that bound her midriff. Bite-size pieces of liver and kidney fell out. So did her own organs, the ones from another that I had stuffed into her. The smell was not good: I feared gangrene.

No digestive action had taken place within Heady so I rebound her without innards. The idea of taking a look at her brains tempted me, but I decided they too had probably been rejected and sat like orphans in her cranium. My imitation of Dr. Frankenstein had failed.

The ATV rescuers were buried in soft soil near a crooked pine then Doogie led his army of misfortune in retracing a rural route from the previous 24 hours, exhuming revitalized bodies from shallow graves.

I pulled together some courage and asked, "Wat with bodies?"

"Noow recroots."

My stiff frown indicated no satisfaction so Doogie elaborated, "In few days all be understoood. Mooonlight Army of Misfortoon will oovercome."

Given the state of my intellect, any answer would have been unclear. However, things upstairs seemed to be on a bit of an upswing. Memories flowed more easily and images of children playing, perhaps my children, flitted through consciousness. I even tried to think about my lifespan, but such thoughts proved too difficult, too depressing.

"More inthormathion," I requested confidently.

"Keep yoor coool," Doogie answered. "The zompire will roole."

The grey whale appeared to be getting shorter as he shuffled barefoot to a pile of rocks then rolled the heaviest ones aside and helped a day-old corpse wake to second life, perhaps half-life. The victim of gastro-intellectual consumption received a pair of sunglasses and directions to a spot on the left flank where dozens of other soldiers stood at attention, or something resembling it. Another 20 waited on the right side and a similar number stooped in front and behind. The motley group ranged from a fresh kill in a fine suit who died of a heart attack just days before the uprising to a decade-dead grandmother with crawly things falling from festering eyes and nose. A snake worked in and out of various body openings.

Doogie helped a soldier out of a shallow grave then led his land armada to a hillside above new housing. We patiently waited and then carefree children came out of a brick building to play in the large yard.

I was shocked. At the school's main entrance, and inside each of the four corners of the unfenced schoolyard, army Jeeps, with four soldiers each, provided protection. That comforted me.

Doogie stared until the school bell rang and simultaneously his bell apparently rang. Children went inside, two Jeeps drove off and Doogie pointed to one of the remaining Jeeps and its four soldiers and said to me, "Trees give yoo cover. Yoo doo that one. Take with yoo 20. I doo others."

Like Napoleon preparing for Waterloo, Doogie scuffled among his troops, his head barely visible. He lifted sunglasses, stood on what remained of his toes and looked up into each pair of yellow eyes and said, clearly and firmly, "Doo not eat children."

Thinking of my own preschoolers, I felt relief. Despite imagining how delicious they might taste, I couldn't abide the thought of eating toddlers. I had guilt about the cat.

Doogie waved his left flank forward and I lumbered to the front of mine. I had led math class outings to study numbers in nature and had coached soccer, but never had I led a squad of anthropophagi in an assault. I couldn't count 20, yet many warriors under my charge clumped down the hillside slipping and falling, but not making a sound, other than the requisite hum of *brains*. Why not *lungs, liver* or *lymph*? Or a vegan chant ...*grains*. I was dumbstruck then felt an unaccountable *brains* trickle from my own lips.

Alert soldiers fired weapons before the first of us emerged from the forest. Propelled by a light breeze, our odor gave us away. Two machine guns, a bazooka and a mortar let loose. Then another Jeep raced up and the armament doubled. I had no idea what to do. To continue would be suicide and to disobey Doogie's orders, whatever they were, would be treason to the zombie nation. I froze behind a tree and from Doogie's end of the school gunfire roared. The recently arrived Jeep turned around and raced back in that direction.

While I contemplated the daunting task of leading my soldiers forward a decrepit reborn nurse, dressed in pale blue, stepped from behind a tree and showed the way. An expert sniper put so many bullets through her head it became a ripe squash falling apart in the field. That's why I didn't step forward. My men interpreted the destruction of the nurse as a sign to advance and moved from behind trees. They could smell living flesh on the yard below and that was all they needed.

A mortar landed at the feet of a dead mechanic and he vanished for all time. A bazooka removed the left half torso of a middle-aged man who dressed as hunter and now was hunted. His Desert Storm camo outfit stood out among the greenness. Repeated shots cut a grandmother in quarters and her twitching arms and legs decorated grass. My battalion of dimness had barely advanced to the school yard and already it was being blown asunder.

Military manoeuvres appeared not to be one of my strengths and as I stood beneath a willow, bewildered, I tried to count my leadership assets and came up empty. My warriors pushed forward and pieces of shattered heads fell to the dirt. I left the tree's shadow to follow the mock-army and a bullet knocked a chunk of puffy flesh from my thigh. Another went through my chest. No pain resulted and I didn't fall dead. The holes in my clothing angered me and I wanted to shout, *I am Mort the Immortal* and charge like a crazed Viking, but restrained myself although anger, a new emotion, felt good. The safety of a tree felt better. A machine gun that never stopped firing made Swiss cheese of lurchers who steadfastly and fearlessly shuffled towards the schoolyard. I was happy not to be among them. Happiness felt good.

Yells, screams and gunfire continued from the far end of the yard where Doogie launched his attack. I had no idea how that siege progressed, but suspected it had no more success than mine. I shrugged my shoulders, uncertain of what the shrug meant; uncertain of what anything meant. Another of my soldiers, so punctured by gunfire that she became transparent, made a slow-motion descent to the earth from which she came.

The army must have stationed its best marksmen at the school. Protecting children with the top shooters was a plan I approved of although I wasn't warm to having my own head vented. I stood with just eight compatriots, including Heady who, despite her military heritage, was more reluctant than me to step into battle. Perhaps she knew a lost cause when she saw it.

A familiar *ratta-tat-tat* erupted from afar and I looked down expecting to find holes in my body. Instead, the army men in front of me – gunner, driver, mortar operator and bazooka holder – all tumbled to the sod beside their Jeep. Down the field Doogie stood behind a smoking machine gun on a tripod and signaled I should join him. It seemed so unfair that a few little bullets could so easily end the reign of the living: they were delicate, they bled. One hole, well-placed and life was over. I looked about my own body: new holes disfigured me but didn't cause pain, stain or drain.

Doogie and squad, making use of tree cover, had overpowered two Jeeps while my group suffered defeat at the hands of one Jeep and four soldiers. A career as military strategist did not lurk in my past or my future.

A lawn covered in carnal decrepitude had to be crossed to get down the field to reach Doogie. Soldiers' bodies had been ripped by the hyenas under his command. My meek men lunched lightly on leftovers.

In shallow troughs etched into soft schoolyard soil the bodies of fallen soldiers found peaceful rest, courtesy of Doogie's men. Hungry buzzards circled the graves and wanted to devour the fresh kill that still contained edible parts. Doogie kept them at bay with stern glances and hands pressed to chests. When one came forward, rock in hand, intent on cracking a dead soldier's skull, Doogie yanked off its sunglasses. The creature doubled over, dropped its rock and hid eyes in hands. Doogie let it suffer then threw the glasses onto the dirt. In stumbling to find them it stepped on them.

The sky came to life when two helicopters, ablaze with machine guns and fragmentation bombs, roared above the school yard. They felled trees, set brush ablaze and disintegrated a couple of laggards, but we had already smashed the school's front door and gained entry.

About 15 staff and a couple of classrooms worth of children cowered at the back of a big gymnasium. Doogie shoved teachers and children in separate directions creating two confused mobs, both crying and cowering. A muscular teacher punched Doogie in the head and was eaten in front of screaming kids and horrified teachers. Doogie wiped his mouth with the victim's shirt, herded the children into a separate classroom then disappeared. Perhaps he needed a bowel movement.

Members of the Army of Misfortune guarded every exit from the school, their teeth their weapons. Sirens wailed as fire trucks, ambulances and army vehicles jerked to a halt in front of the school

Doogie's unique voice came over the school's inside and outside speakers, "Noo child hurt if yoo obey. Noo guns, noo gasses, noo bangs. Yoo light schoolyard and schoool. Point flooodlights away from schoool. Twenty minutes too doo it. In mooorning we talk."

Standing tall, on the bed of a green pick-up truck, a military man with the little black moustache put a hailer to his mouth and responded, "Release the children and your safety will be guaranteed. If you ..."

Doogie boomed, "Yoo have 19 minutes."

33

Mayhew-Shostakovich stood outside the school and fired orders as fast as he could think. "Privates Gudat, Cheadle and Armstrong, take three men each and set up enough lighting to flood the yard. Corporal Dylan, your job is to get everyone except military, Red Cross, fire and police out of here: set up a no go zone: 50 yards for authorized, one mile for everyone else. Get media outta here. Listen up Sergeant Florence: parents will arrive. Set up a compound for them and brief them. Free coffee and muffins. And Corporal Hemstead, I don't care if you have to plant land mines: nobody gets into the no-go zone. Specially the school lawn and drive. Work fast. Everyone else kiss off, excuse me."

Within minutes the military had cleared the unauthorized from schoolyard and surrounding streets.

Sergeant Jane Dougherty arrived in time to hear Mayhew's orders and it reminded her of the time she restored order to the front of her police station. His ability to think clearly and quickly under pressure impressed her even it was all reactive, after the fact. She shuddered to think of children in the hands of undead killers.

Arriving parents learned that rumors and news reports had minimized the situation: no parent's most horrid night terror compared to the reality of having its child held hostage by creatures from the grave. A pedophile could be tracked down. A kidnapper could be paid off. Only one thing could appease a revenant and that was beyond dread.

The school's front door opened and four creatures shuffled into the afternoon's lazy light. Each held a crying child, like a sack of potatoes, over its shoulder. The four shuffled to the Jeep where Mort's men had failed, grabbed the four soldiers shot down by Doogie and dragged them by the heels towards the front door. Jane could hear the helpless children, on zombies' shoulders, screaming and pleading for help. A little girl struggled to get free and her captor smacked her bottom.

After dead soldiers had been dumped on the grass near the door the four zombs, each shouldering a child as a shield, stumbled to the Jeep and gathered shovels, picks and other tools. A green Jaguar sedan shredded sod as it tore across the grass. A young woman wearing a green bicycle helmet drove while a slightly older woman sporting bright red hair waved a rifle out the passenger window. The car appeared destined to fell all four creatures and all four children until brake lights lit and it skidded sideways, thumping zombies' knees and knocking them over. The aim was perfect as zombies took the hit and children fell gently. Both mothers leapt out, grabbed the two nearest children from fallen zombies and pushed them into the back seat. The first revenant to get to its feet received a barrage of bullets from the rifle aimed low by the passenger with red hair flowing. Its right kneecap shattered, bone sprayed and it sank to starboard. While the passenger fired, the driver, who sported an early pregnancy bulge, whacked zombie legs with a metal pole. The women had a plan: they targeted knees.

The two zombies hit hardest by the car tried to rise on mangled limbs. One toppled because its left leg had no more rigidity than a handful of jelly. The other bumped along on knees and grabbed the car's back door handle: two children inside hollered for help. The redhead sailed through the passenger doorway and hit the lock button. Her friend assaulted the zombie that held onto the door. Shots from afar zinged through soft bodies. A zomb, riddled with holes, grabbed the driver from behind and bared its teeth. The passenger swung a shovel with such force the clang against the zombie's head reverberated through the schoolyard and knocked the thing off its feet. The little girl on its shoulder slipped free and ran to the redhead who put her in the car and relocked its doors.

While the redhead took care of the children's safety two zombies got hold of her companion's ankle, took her down and ripped into the warm bun in her oven. They tried to get her brains but couldn't undo her bicycle helmet.

A voice over the speakers boomed, "Doo not shooot. We hold yooor children."

Sergeant Jane felt sick and helpless. Emotions urged her to race across the huge schoolyard and battle beside the warriors. Her rational side knew zombies held 50 children hostage. How would they interpret the assault from two women plus a cop? Those who watched remained frozen with the same dilemma; nauseated by the sight. No one had any idea how a zombie thought or retaliated. No one even imagined a zombie could speak.

The creature with leg reduced to jelly crawled under the car and grabbed the riflewoman's ankle. Jane abandoned rationality, drew her gun and ran. The woman with red locks raised a shovel and in one mighty stroke plunged it into the attacker's arm and chopped off the hand that latched onto her ankle. The woman could have jumped into the car and saved herself and three children. But she was a mother: to leave one child in the hands of an undead stretched beyond contemplation.

Three cannibals staggered and crawled towards her and each faced a shovel swung with accuracy and ferocity. One blow removed a white-haired scalp and another took off most of the meat from a leg. Sunglasses had been smashed and the attackers were nearly blind. Red hair swayed in the afternoon sun as she moved with the majesty of a trained ninja. Two zombies backed her against a fence. She slipped between them and exchanged her shovel for a steel pole and continued beating their knees. She risked everything to save the one child that remained in a zombie's grasp.

Jane ran faster than her slightly short legs had ever propelled her. Soft, slippery grass made her feel mired in bad-dream quicksand.

Flushed and sweating, with pole in hand, the woman warrior kept a safe distance from her hobbling, groping attackers and now thrust at eyes rather than knees. One was blinded by constant poking and loss of glasses. Another stubbornly held the last child on its shoulder.

It was a beautiful thing to watch the woman in action, strategically backing up, thrusting forward, but always remaining close to the car to protect the children. She moved as if choreographed by a Japanese animator as she leapt across the hood to deal blows to the one-eyed assaulter and then circled back to club the other from behind.

Jane sprinted, breath searing, crying that the distance between them diminished so slowly.

While fighting, the woman kept a mental tab on the whereabouts of each zomb, never letting one get behind her or catch her unawares. The beast with a missing hand and one working leg crawled and tried to get behind her, but at the last moment she evaded and landed more hits on a pulpy head. She neglected her discarded shovel and as she backed she tripped and her battle against the forces of evil neared its final chapter.

Jane dropped to a knee, braced herself and aimed at the attacker's eyes. The little bullets hit nothing of significance: she wasn't good enough to sharpshoot an eye from 30 yards. As she closed the final yards the warrior with red hair screamed in defeat.

A shovel smashed a rear window and zombies pulled out three hysterical children. Other reborn arrived to help. On broken rubbery legs the kidnappers crawled and shambled towards the school with crying captives under arms. Jane fired into their lower bodies. They turned, snarled and drooled. The school door opened and they finally dropped their loads. From the entry snarling creatures looked at Jane as a homeless person looks at a picnic. Fresh ones gave chase, but when she kept a safe distance ahead they gave up.

Three revenants grabbed shovels, picks and other tools and scratched trenches into the ground and dragged the dead women to their new graves.

Jane stood alone with no option but to stifle tears and loathing: she trudged back, gun empty. Her efforts were appreciated by all but Col. Mayhew who shouted, "You did more harm. The enemy will make us pay. What were you thinking?"

"I was thinking two women, now dead, and four children, now prisoners, needed help." She turned her back, didn't listen to his reply and behind parked cars she her tears flowed.

34

Prisoners at Missing Hill Winery refused to eat. Soldiers called it a zombie hunger strike and said the monsters were spoiled by always getting the meals they wanted whenever they wanted.

Dog treats, tuna steaks and hamburger rotted in the mid-day sun while lab rats went down in a gulp and came up with a retch. Putrid puddles that captives stepped on and tracked around pathways soiled the grassy yard. Brains from cows, pigs, chickens and horses were offered, but the hungry turned up their noses and refused farm fare. Live goats and sheep did not meet dietary requirements.

Imprisoned zombs shuffled, stumbled and mumbled. Court orders ordained they be kept alive until a higher court determined if they had a right to a trial. Citizens affiliated with the NRA and survivalist groups protested with signs that read *Dead to Rights*, *Bomb the Zomb*, *Give Pieces a Chance*.

When they heard about the schoolyard disaster soldiers on guard-duty at the winery became crueler than their default state and experimented with captives.

"They always have some weakness," a busty young soldier of small stature told her beefy comrade at arms. "It might be silver or fire or vinegar or water ... it's always something obvious that everyone overlooks. I've seen all the movies. Believe me, I know."

She stepped in front of a double-shackled zombie, shook a can of Coke, opened the tab and let it spray in the face of a drop-dead-gorgeous female who might have been able to continue her career in modeling if not for severe eczema and dark fluid running from ear holes.

"Guess that's not the real thing," the soldier said with disappointment as the zombie blinked a few times and continued to shuffle, inches at a time, as shackles restricted her. Next the soldier sprayed the zombie's skirt and silk blouse with WD-40 then threw a match. Clothes and matted blonde hair tuned to ashes and fell on spiked blue shoes. Scorched and naked, she continued her shuffle.

"That's an improvement," a thin male private declared as he leered at the hairless, naked, actress who died after her Mexican boob-job became infected.

The female replied, "Yea, just the way you like women: naked, no brains and barely alive. We need to try something different."

"Just a sec," shouted the muscular male as he stepped through a doorway. He returned with a glass of amber liquid that he threw on the zombie who didn't so much as blink.

"What was that?" asked his cohort.

"Piss on her, I say."

"That's disgusting man."

"We have to try everything."

The soldiers amused themselves by inventing tortures in the guise of looking for a weakness. They exploded firecrackers in the captive's nostrils and ear canals, blowing away chunks of soft skin. They pushed a flare into her anus, watched it burn down and then squirted toilet cleaner into the gaping hole. The charred near-skeleton struggled to maintain a quasi-shuffle in front of a circle of laughing soldiers. Skin had burned from most of her and holes had been created by various small explosives. A wooden stake jutted from her chest, a cross had burned between the remains of lumpy breasts and cloves of garlic filled body openings. Still, her jaw vibrated whenever a soldier neared her. Orange juice, kerosene, gasoline, beer, oven cleaner and every other liquid at hand landed on the reborn in an attempt to stop her in her tracks. She shuffled on.

The busty soldier suggested a grenade in her mouth, but her co-worker argued that was not something found in the average household. He separated the wires of a 220 volt electric cable and led them to damp patches of ground where the zombie trod.

The live leads snapped and sizzled when her feet landed on them and for a split-second she danced. Then the amperage shot up to her eyeballs and they glowed like hot coals melting the skin around them. As if trying to take flight, her arms flapped at her sides – and then vaporized. Two slender legs turned to mushy pedestals that refused to support her body and she sank into an electrified puddle. Her lower jaw skidded across the grass and the limbless torso lay like jelly on the lawn.

Soldiers circled the larva-like mess and the muscled man turned off an electric switch and kicked at the dead head. Its upper jaw tried to grip his boot, but got no support from the absent lower half.

"That thing ain't dead," he declared and found an axe. He chopped through her thin spine and severed what remained of her small head: the jaw quit quivering. Atop a spiked pole, hammered into the ground, he planted the head. The burned face, with black eye-holes, faced shuffling zombies, warning what might happen if they got out of line.

35

Skirting puddles of rejected body fluids, Donald zigzagged, on hands and knees, between beer-soaked somnolent bodies. His flashlight searched corners and crevices for ways out of the vampire's vault, but the door through which he had been dragged proved to be the sole point of egress. The floor didn't even have a drain.

Among drunken and blood-sucked bodies he could recruit neither accomplice nor assistant. Captives couldn't complete a sentence let alone abet an escape. Lack of blood, surplus alcohol or a combination of both did them in. Two knelt at the door, sucking from tubes, while others slept as only the drunk can sleep.

"Who wants to eat? We've got hot dogs." The words came from outside. The response – moans and grunts – could have been in favor or against. Donald added a slurred, "Wat ya got on the dogs? Mustard?"

The instant the door cracked open he barged against it and snapped it back. A tray of hot dogs and condiments sailed from the hands of a vampire and hit other vamps who backed off in astonishment and fear. Such determined strength from the drunk tank hadn't been anticipated. The vamps recognized the combatant who had bloodied them previously. With backs against the wall they watched him squeeze through the vault door and pass in front of them.

Three steps at a time Donald raced upstairs and sped to the police station. The ease of his escape surprised him. He expected to fight his way out. He felt like an action hero who had overcome the insurmountable forces of evil because their guns always missed the target.

Jesse brought Donald up to date with information about the hostage-taking at the school and said he was headed there as soon as he could find some flashing blue strobes for his car. Donald's request to come along got an affirmative and within minutes Jesse had two blue bubbles in his hands. They ran outside, Jesse put the lights on his roof and snapped the shifter of his classic Mustang convertible into drive. Both strobes crashed on the pavement. He repositioned the cracked bulbs on the metal hood although they no longer lit up.

Jane paced near a compound set up to counsel parents. She told the horror story of the mothers who fought and lost then asked Donald, "What happened to you? I thought you succumbed to the allure of alcohol."

Donald related how he had spent his time as a captive in the basement of a vampire stronghold. "The drunk part was a ruse. I loathe beer and poured most of it on the floor between wood slats. A mugful or two got dumped into a toilet. Some had to be swallowed when eyes were on me. Sorry for dragging you in on the act. It had to appear real."

Donald told more about the vampire stronghold then "Hellooo," came over speakers.

Donald asked, "Who's talking?"

Jane told him the odd voice came from the head of the dead.

"Fantastic. Maybe we can learn what this is all about, where they come from, what it's like to be reanimated." The speakers again came to life.

"Oor pact broken. Stoopid too doo. Oor friends got injoored; twoo woomen for oor foood. Thank yooo."

Colonel Mayhew-Shostakovich interrupted by hollering so loudly into his hailer that his voice out-decibelled the amplifier. "Those women were rebels, out of control. We would not put children at risk. Do you understand that?"

"We dooo."

A collective sigh emerged from the crowd's uncanny silence then Doogie finished, "In moorning, more talk."

The planet rotated, mountains shuttered the sun, a cast of darkness fell across the valley and with it came helplessness. Military leaders huddled and discussed plans of action: Emergency Response Team, helicopters, tear gas, a surprise siege ... all arrived at the same juncture: they subjected the children to risk.

From a perch atop a spruce tree Jesse spent 30 minutes observing. He descended like a lumberjack and told Jane about a dark area between rows of lights. If he wore black coveralls and blackened his skin he could sneak up to the school and at least have a look to see if the kids were alright.

"That's what the lights are for," Jane said forcefully. "To see us if we get close to the school. Not worth it. What if you get caught?"

"I'd say I was a father; another rebel."

"They might not buy it a second time. What if ..." She cut off her sentence as she spied the light-colored soles of a soldier's shoes as he crawled in shadows between the lights, exactly as they had discussed. Another soldier wearing an audio headset climbed the tree Jesse had abandoned.

"This is a disgrace," Jane shouted in despair to those around her. No one with authority listened.

"You're right," Donald interjected. "Zombs can see better in the dark than we think. They were reborn in the black: bright light bothers them. It's so obvious they have good night vision. They can probably see that soldier we think is hidden in the shadows. I'll find Mayhew and tell him to stop this madness."

Jane turned to Jesse and barked at him with uncharacteristic abruptness, "Get up that tree and stop that guy from giving directions."

Jesse raced to the tree without a thought of how he was going to carry out an order against the military. Quickly and deftly he scrambled upwards, through long, straight limbs. Thirty seconds later loud, but undecipherable, words come down from the tree along with a small branch, spruce needles and a headset. Jane grabbed the earphones and mike and shouted, "Pull back; abort mission."

No voice came back and she saw a dangling wire that should have led to a battery pack. Jane shouted at Jesse to throw down the battery. Heated words and a flurry of needles and twigs fell.

"He won't give it up," Jesse shouted. "Says he'll die with it."

Jane wanted to tell Jesse, *Let him die*, but little could be gained from two men fighting like monkeys in a tree.

Donald reported that Colonel Mayhew had his ears closed to everything from outside. Jane didn't have time to listen, saying she had to climb a tree to persuade a soldier to relinquish batteries.

"By the time you get up there," Donald insisted, "and throw them down and someone figures out how to connect them and then you order that crawling guy back he will be at the school."

"You're right." Her night binoculars followed light patches of shoe soles. The soldier stretched his fingers to a window ledge and pulled himself up. Donald nudged Jane and pointed to two barely visible outlines shuffling in the unmistakeable style of reanimates.

Silently, with no mumblings of *brains,* two zombies closed on the crawling soldier. Doogie had ordered a fast among his followers: he didn't want anyone eating children and he didn't trust a famished zomb to discern child from adult. Children were the meals of tomorrow. Despite that, salivating hunger proved too much for the flesh-eaters who fell on the crawling soldier. Orders from their boss swirled in the black-holes of echoing craniums like yellow smog.

Before the soldier knew what landed on him his viscera felt the vice-like teeth. Darkness prevented the crowd at the edge of the pavement from viewing the unzipping. Those peering through heat-sensing binoculars didn't see cold zombies, but saw warm pieces glow before they vanished into mouths. With classrooms behind, no shots were fired.

Sideline soldiers became disheartened: a simple recon mission ended in death. Creatures no smarter than the slugs that crawled on them had outfought and outthought trained soldiers. What had gone wrong? Why hadn't the soldier been warned of the approaching menace? As questions were asked, Donald and Jane gazed about with innocent looks until the soldier in the tree pointed to them and shouted, "Sabotage."

A heated row ensued and accusations flew. Both forces had the best of intentions, both worked for the greater good, both were employed by government. There would be no resolution.

Night provided an opportunity to stretch out on car seats or grass and sleep intermittently, roused by gunfire or exploding grenades in the distance. In hills afar good and evil clashed and reports of casualties filtered in. The enemy did not die when shot, stabbed, burned, concussed, shocked, suffocated or gassed. One platoon attacked with roaring chainsaws, but the noise gave them away and allowed the enemy to ambush.

The day's first rays squeezed between the peaks of ancient mountains and reanimates wearing sunglasses lurched from school to schoolyard with shovels. The shaded soldiers of misfortune aided those buried the previous night to rise unsteadily from shallow graves. The arisen commenced their second go-round as living dead. One of the vacated shallow graves found use as home for the crawling soldier who would rise after R&R in the dark.

    A half-hour passed and then a female thing with no hair and no ears shuffled from the school's main door. She walked hand-in-hand with a six-year-old girl dressed in a classic frilly white dress. Her long blonde curls hung in disarray, partially hiding swollen eyes: she had not had a good night. Fingers of the hand the zombie didn't clasp squeezed closed her nostrils.

    Doogie's wet voice wakened loudspeakers, "Yoo broke trust. If yoo doo more bad, yoor chooldren die. Yoo must sooper-size us. Trade half kids for foool-grown adults in twoo hours. Now, yoor penalty."

    As those words were spoken the zombie raised the little girl's arm, put the tiny folded fist to her black mouth and bit off half her hand, leaving a thumb sticking out. The child's scream reverberated through the schoolyard and every parent leaned forward on toes and ran to rescue her. Soldiers pushed them back. The zombie changed hands and the girl instinctively stuck her mitt into her dress, which turned red. Little fingernails and bones were spat from the monster's mouth.

    Colonel Mayhew-Shostakovich's voice boomed, "That was despicable and cowardly. She will bleed to death. A doctor must help her."

    "Yoo have 10 minoots."

    Mayhew commanded that a doctor be sent and designated men to find the right one. He then ordered that delegations be sent to hospitals, to senior citizens' residences, to heart and cancer clinics and to other places where the elderly and the ill resided, in an effort to find volunteers who would give up their few remaining months in exchange for the lives of children.

    A young GP in a pin-stripe suit volunteered to attend to the injured child then ran to his car to get his black bag. Jesse intercepted him in the parking area and flashed his police badge. He told the doctor he knew first aid and had been ordered to attend to the girl. "We need a trained fighter to help her. There's a good chance that whoever goes will be eaten."

The doctor cringed at the idea of becoming a meal and handed his medical bag to Jesse who said he needed brief instructions on where to find the materials needed to treat the girl's injuries.

The doctor replied, "Here's anaesthetic to stop the pain, then antiseptic to clean the wound. There's a good case for infection, but a tetanus shot can wait. Stop the bleeding with this tourniquet then stitch the wound. Here's what you need to …"

"Thanks, I'm good to go," Jesse said impatiently.

"Give her this pill first. You'll be dealing with a screaming six-year-old so you'll need to sedate her."

"Got it." Jesse rushed between cars with black bag at his side. Without a word he darted towards the sobbing girl held tight by the zombie.

"Who's that?" asked those watching. By the time word spread to Mayhew, Jesse had sprinted across the grass and slid to a stop in front of girl and captor.

"I've got a magic pill that will make you feel better," he said calmly and popped it between her parted lips. "What's your name?"

"Liberty," she squealed.

"OK, Libby, here's the plan. First I'm going to put a strap around your wrist to stop it from bleeding and then I'm going to wrap a bandage around your hand. Then you're gonna run. You're gonna run to your mommy and daddy as fast your little legs will take you. I'll make sure no one chases you. Do you understand?"

"I'm Liberty, not Libby. I want my fingers."

"Your mommy and daddy will take care of that, now put out your hand."

Liberty kept her fist pressed against her dress as Jesse tightened a rubber strap around her thin forearm. Blood, screams and tears burst forth when he pulled her hand away and poured antiseptic over it. He looked for signs that the zombie had relaxed its grip on her other hand while positioning himself to evade sudden lunges. The last thing he needed was another zombie bite. Liberty screamed louder when Jesse clumsily wrapped bandages around her hand. The sight of a little white thumb sticking out the side of the red stump churned his stomach and vomit positioned itself at the back of his throat.

Liberty had turned as white as a florescent bulb and Jesse knew he had the same complexion. Both might topple and that would spell their ends. He thought about his car, focused on the grass at his feet and saw red drops paint the green. From his stomach a dry heave rippled upwards. A loose shoe lace caught his attention and he spent precious seconds retying while his nerves and nausea settled.

Plan A could not be executed unless the girl could run. Plan B involved negotiating with zombies. Jesse tugged lightly on Liberty's good hand and could feel resistance from the ghoul's grip.

"You must have been a mother," Jesse said to the creature with no hair. "You can help save the kids."

A slow snarl from a drooling lipless mouth came back at him.

Jesse stood tall and shouted towards the school, "I want to talk to your leader, to the person who speaks. I have an offer."

36

Donald's escape from the blood bank initiated new worries among vampires who thought they had exceeded capacity for mental torment. They feared the escapee would reveal what he had found and alert the town to their presence. On the other hand, thought the vamps, the town had much bigger problems on its collective hands and perhaps the presence of a passel of bloodsuckers would be overshadowed. If there was a good time to be found out, this might be it.

The mental fatigue of juggling possibilities caused the bar owners' heads to throb. Headaches also resulted from hangovers following intake of blood spiked with alcohol. No one saw that coming. Limiting the amount of beer given to captives would reduce the blood-alcohol count, but donors would be less manageable. Without beer the alcoholics would plan escapes. Complex problems didn't present simple solutions. Life was easy for zombies: they ate their problems.

Vanessa looked at Victor and neither showed joy. Night business was normally nil as regulars had pickled themselves by 7 p.m. and staggered home to sleep until morning. The soldiers and newsgatherers who flooded the town did their drinking elsewhere. Word spread. The bar stayed open in the evenings because that's what bars did.

Victor shook his dark head. "It's bad enough no one walks around outdoors anymore. Those floodlights add to our migraines. Every one of us has thirst: reserves consist of two bottles for an emergency. Humans, bursting with blood, decrease in number and these dead creatures, with kitty litter in their veins, increase in number. Hookers don't answer the call. Dentist and hairdresser appointments get cancelled. People shouldn't neglect their teeth and hair just because of zombies."

"Be patient," said Vince and several nodded. But patience fluttered when television showed blood wells drying up as temps died, streets closed and citizens trembled behind barred doors. Now a school fell under undead control. Vampires had never sipped children's blood. The thought of children as pedovats disgusted them and represented poor resource management

Coverage on the tavern's bigger than life TV induced a moan of despair when a news camera followed an RCMP officer running towards a schoolgirl who cradled a bleeding hand. A zombie clamped onto her other hand.

"He's a goner," pronounced Vince confidently. "What a waste. That cop has enough blood for eight of us."

Vince turned down the TV's volume. "Our number one problem is the clot in our blood supply chain, excuse the pun. It's not an escapee telling what he found. How long can we keep drunks locked in our basement anyway? Do we kill them so they won't talk? Eventually they will walk and talk. We need three times the number of donors we have. Hookers have vanished and curfew keeps us indoors. Look at me. I'm white as snow. And look at Vaughn and Vicky. Would you know they're Jamaican? They're pale as the rest of us. It's out of control and we have to do something. We have to get rid of flesh eaters: we have to do it now."

Vince stopped and took a breath: talking loudly took energy. His eyes jittered from face to face as he judged the reaction and frowned. He could think of nothing more to say.

"You're stating the obvious," said Vaughn, stating the obvious. "Do we go to the school and tell them they're diluting our blood bank and they should go back to where they came from? I'm sure co-operation is part of the zombie code of ethics."

"No need to get sarcastic," Vince cautioned. "Sarcasm is the lowest form of humor."

"A low form of humor is better than no form of humor."

"I think irony is lower than sarcasm," a third voice added.

"Get back on subject," shouted Vanessa, "Some sort of electric charge keeps them going and that charge has got many of us going too. Without the early awakenings, we might, with rationing, get by. But that's not the way it is. You might recall how police Tasers got us dancing. That was fun, man. It's all related to electricity and the resolution comes from that direction. Cutting off electricity will accomplish nothing because the extra charge comes through the ground, not through wires. Adding electricity might yield better results. If we get them dancing then some sort of ion implosion might fry them. Also, to finish, I think mockery is the lowest form of humor."

"And how do we do that?" questioned a mirthless voice from the back who had no interest in determining the lowest form of humor.

"No idea. Velo is the electrician. Someone call him and get him over here."

"He hasn't had much work since the fire in the seniors' home," the dour voice added. Six hands withdrew six phones from six pockets and dialled the same number. The fastest spoke to a morose Velo, who said he would come if they promised a sip of blood.

The wait for Velo allowed the congregation to recover from the dizzying talk. No one could recall so many words.

Following several minutes of quiet Vince cleared his throat and stood, "You have a point. But if teasing and bantering are part of that wide category of mockery then I don't think, strictly speaking, we are talking about humor. And back to puns, they …"

Velo walked in, sat down and gulped the thinnest bloody Mary ever concocted. After licking every trace from his lips he edged forward on a wooden chair, ready to answer questions he no longer wanted to hear.

Vanessa briefed him about the electrical theory and explained that zombies must be stopped if vampires wished to continue living contentedly in White Rock. If not, relocation would come up for consideration. It would be quick, with little time to pack electronic toys. That concerned Velo who had an addiction to internet gaming and played League of Legends on a 75 inch screen.

Velo pondered for a long time. "We can *borrow* one of the generators placed around town that power the new lighting. I could stick 220 volt wires into the schoolyard, into the school or even into an undead. Eliminating a single zombie would have little impact although *One less zombie* makes a good bumper sticker."

"Should be one fewer zombie," Vince said.

"I think not," Velo replied. "The number of zombies is indeterminate."

"Just because they haven't been counted…"

Vanessa hollered, "We're at the apocalypse of vamkind and you argue about grammar, about less versus fewer? One fewer brain cell and you'd have less than a potato. No wonder we're mired in this mess. Does anyone have anything worthwhile to contribute?"

"We could disguise ourselves as zombies," suggested a vamp sporting a black beret. "The army wouldn't harm us because of the kids held hostage. This is an opportunity to get close and do some damage."

"What kind of damage?"

"We could incapacitate them with electricity and then bring out our Z-D-Cappers. We're faster than them so there should be no danger. And here's our biggest advantage over army and police: they don't want to eat us. They don't like our taste, we're immune. We can get close. If we look like zombies we have free rein to do anything and go anywhere."

The cabal slowly nodded. Due to a lack of dissention they seemed to have a consensus. Vaughn took over and told everyone to line up in front of the bar, facing the door. "The plan depends on us passing for zombies. Everyone come slowly forward. Stoop, hunch, lurch. You have no brains, no thoughts. You just want to eat people."

After two steps he shouted, *Stop*, and then addressed them individually.

"Victoria – you look like a kid going for candy. Get rid of the grin and slow down. Velo, quit thinking about your TV. No thoughts allowed. Lower your shoulders. Your posture's too good. Veronica, your cleavage is distracting. Sex doesn't sell with zombies. Val, put a stone in your shoe so you hump along more slowly."

One by one Vaughn went through the ranks and then backed everyone to the bar and started over. They took six steps before he halted the second walk and graded them.

"Much better. No Oscars, but nominations for supporting roles. Facial expression is poor. You look like you're thinking about life insurance. Remember, your brains don't work. Drool. Eyes unfocused. Back to the bar, let's do it again."

On the third try they didn't even get in a first step. "Too much. Half your tongues dangle like dogs and half drool like taps. Spread it around. Men drool, women look cruel, oldest do tongue, everyone else focus on unfocusing eyes. You can mumble, but not loudly. Once more."

By the sixth try they shambled and stumbled across the wooden floor like demented imbeciles who had lost their way from the asylum.

"Great work," Vince announced gleefully. "George Romero would be proud. This afternoon at 2 o'clock we reconvene for costume design and makeup. Create some rotting, ragged clothes and wear them under your usual garb. Bring dirt, dye and any filth you can find that will make you look like you crawled out from under a rock."

"I did crawl out from behind a rock," announced a woman in the midst of the room. She was ignored.

As the clock hit 2 p.m. a dozen vamps returned to the bar and shed their dark outerwear, revealing ripped and filthy clothing. They rubbed muck in their black hair, smeared dirt on their faces and shuffled about the bar humming *brains*. The first customer of the day, a regular, walked in, screamed and made a U-turn. Vanessa jumped in front and explained, "We're rehearsing a play. And, by the way, we've opened a new room downstairs and have free beer samples."

The customer, an out-of-town TV reporter, became part of the stock of blood letters even though they had not vetted her and knew nothing about her.

"Step one is to commandeer a generator," said Vince confidently. "Second is to tow said generator to the school. Third is to start said generator and plug it into the school's electrical system or into the ground; whatever works for Velo. Fourth is to infiltrate zombies while they are under the electric charge and free the children and other hostages. A quick sip would be in order. We'll then clip the mother-eaters' heads and send them to zombie hell. Is everyone clear on this?"

"What if the army de-caps us?" The questioner stood defiantly with hands on hips.

"You weren't listening. They fear retaliation against the kids if they harm a zombie. If in danger you just speak slowly and clearly and say, 'Wait soldier, I'm a citizen trying to free children so back off'."

Since no one challenged Vince continued, "We wear regular clothing underneath in case we have to change. So let's switch up then go get a generator."

Without inhibition she vamps revealed their perfect bodies and switched clothing so soiled zombie wear cloaked the outside.

Victoria walked out the door and as she passed Vince ladled a scoop of yellowy-brown liquid from a pail and anointed her.

"What the hell is that shit?" Victoria demanded. "It stinks to high heaven. I'm gonna be sick."

"You have to smell like a zombie," Vince explained.

"But what is it?" Victoria demanded. "I know that bucket. Is that the toilet from downstairs?"

Vaughn flung scoops of the lumpy liquid at his cohorts who tried to duck and cover as they rushed to get out the door.

A generator on wheels throbbed next to a steel lamp post just a few yards from their front door. It was chained to the post. No one had bolt cutters. Victoria recalled another generator had been placed behind their bar to light the alley so they made a U-turn and stomped out the back door. A locked chain secured the throbbing machine to a wooden lamp post. The zomb/vamps stared at the pole with hands on hips.

"Bloody hell," Victoria exclaimed. "Who's going to steal from the army? Talk about paranoia." She pulled keys from her pocket and jumped into her black Hummer in the bar's parking lot. Without a moment's hesitation she backed up at full speed and splintered the base of the wooden lamp post, knocking it from its mooring. The tall post pivoted on six electrical wires about two-thirds of the way up and swayed back and forth, top-heavy with insulators and a light fixture.

A breath of wind tipped the delicate balance and the upper end dipped forward and smashed onto the roof of Vladimir's Bar. Electric sparks jumped, a swirl of smoke rose and a flicker of fire ignited ancient shingles.

Twelve hands took out 12 phones and several got through to 911. By the time a hesitant fire truck reached the bar its roof crackled with leaping flames. Hoses from the truck and a hydrant spewed tons of water and in 20 minutes they quelled the blaze. Another 10 minutes of hosing eliminated the last wisp of smoke.

During the commotion the gaggle of vampires stood back, wanting to sigh and to cry. A youth in the growing crowd of onlookers crowed, "I got one."

The teenage boy with blue hair stood smiling beside his bloody Z-D-Capper. In his hand a head dangled by the hair and his foot perched atop Velo's chest.

"You're next," the boy snarled. He had a demented look in his eyes and pointed giant scissors at Victoria. Her zombie make-up was inferior to Velo's and dribbled down her face with mist from firefighters' hoses.

37

With the simple pointing of a finger Doogie sent me outside and I shuffle-stepped from behind the school door.

"Are you the leader?" a tall policeman asked.

"No, juth shoulder of mithfortune."

"How many of you can talk?"

"Juth two."

"Can I speak to the leader?"

"No, juth me."

"Fine. Listen up. My name is Jesse and I'm a cop and this little girl needs help. See how pale she is. Her good hand is hurting too because that zombie dame holds her too tight. I offer myself in exchange for her."

"Ith not my choith," I said. Then I stepped forward, took the fingers of the girl's captor and pried them looser. I stepped back, not knowing what more to do. It was up to the policeman to do something. We stood and stared. He asked, "Do you accept my offer?"

"What offer?"

"Me for the girl."

I asserted myself and confidently answered, "Yeth." Doogie would be pleased with my negotiating skills.

"OK. Tell that thing to release the girl and I'll go with you."

A crackling sound came as I unwound the fingers of my fellow undead and in a flurry of short legs the girl fled across the lawn and ran until she disappeared into loving arms. Before she had taken her first fleeing steps my hand clamped on the cop's wrist. Doogie wouldn't be happy if he ran away.

"I told you my name's Jesse, what's yours?"

"Morth."

"Moth is a strange name."

"Not Moth! Morth."

"That's what I said. What's it like to be a zombie?"

"Ith hell."

"Why do you eat people?"

"Taste good. Give orgathms."

"Do you have a choice?"

"Doogie order no more eathing."

"Who is Doogie?"

"He ith light shines on mithfortunes."

"You and Doogie are the only ones that talk? How ith that, I mean how *is* that?"

"We drowned. Brains got oxthygen from wather. Doogie said so."

"If you free the children we could help you with your eating disorder. We have drugs, therapies, councillors. You could be enjoying your second life and have a good future. Everyone wins. What do you say?"

The wall of words sounded like a cement mixer. Behind the big gymnasium door teachers, secretaries and caretakers milled about and that's where I took Jesse.

"Do you expect me to go in there?" he asked when I opened the door and removed my hand from his wrist.

"You hath no choith."

"Of course I hath a choice. I'm human. You could have choices too if you'd let us help you. You could decide to eat or not to eat. Things like that. Do you like movies?"

"Go in room."

"Why should I? I can run down that hallway, past that guard and be free."

"Doogie would eat child." I gave a slight push that made Jesse stumble forward into the big room. The door slammed, the room shuddered.

38

For his first five minutes of captivity Jesse studied the school gym and came up with at least one escape plan per minute. The easiest involved using athletic climbing ropes that dangled from above. Anyone with strong arms could climb them and reach the high ceiling. Then they could unscrew the screens that protected glass from wayward balls, open the glass, toss the ropes outside, slide down and run to freedom. This plan was based on the assumption zombies could not climb ropes and teachers could, although some were rotund and out of shape. Exiting via similar high windows on the inside walls of the gym meant landing in a hallway that had a gaggle of hungry zombs wandering about.

Another escape plan involved distracting zombie guards and then barging through the doors. Jesse debated surrounding them with volleyball nets and tangling them together, but he never saw more than two next to each other. Escaping did not help the children and likely it put them in greater danger of being eaten or disfigured.

Teachers milled in the big gymnasium while reanimates guarded each exit. Jesse kicked open a cupboard, put screwdriver, hammer and pliers under his belt, then wired together coat hooks to make a grappling device that he attached to the end of a rope. Zombies ignored him until he threw the grapple and it caught the screen that protected a window. Snapping teeth missed his shoes as he hoisted himself aloft.

Jesse thought it unwise to undo the screening while clinging to it so after removing a couple of screws he swung over to the next screen and leaned across to finish the job. When the last screw came out he dropped the heavy metal so it landed on the head of a zombie who hardly noticed. Teachers applauded. After cranking open the window Jesse leaned out and saw three zombies waiting in the hall below.

Voices shouted warnings. A cringe-worthy creature clinched its hands around the rope and inched upward without difficulty. Tremendous strength allowed it to use only arms, but co-ordination seemed to be a problem. Sometimes it missed the rope and grasped air with one hand while hanging on with the other. Jesse waited for it to grasp air with both hands, but that didn't happen so his Swiss Army knife started into the thick sisal. The climbing zombie grabbed for Jesse's ankle as the last strands parted and the thing plummeted to the hardwood. Teachers moved a trampoline that might have facilitated a soft landing and stood back to watch an appropriate thud and the snapping of bones. Again they applauded.

Clinging to mesh screens Jesse scuttled around the perimeter of the gym, exploring options like an obsessive-compulsive monkey. He moved from window to window and peered through, scanning for children. Empty offices, vacant classrooms and halls filled with mumbling, stumbling undead were all he found. At the last corner he glimpsed the short fat one talking to the tall dumb one.

39

"Sooon I tell yoo plan." Doogie was speaking to me.

I responded, "Yeth."

"Yoo fill poool."

Between us stood an inflated plastic wading pool. I turned on the water and aimed a hose into the double ring, hitting it half the time.

"Don't wanth to swim," I said. "Scared of wather."

"Just twoo fooot deep. We sink twoo schoool temps. Electricity charge water. In moorning they rise, like us, droowned, but talking."
With that Doogie waddled away and left me holding the hose.

I saw the friendly cop looking down at us from a window above the gym. He turned to the teachers on his side of the wall and I heard him tell the teachers to prepare to fight. Zombies would be looking for two to drown.

"What are *you* doing?" the cop shouted down to me.

I thought about it then raised my head towards his voice and said, "Put wather in pool."

"But why?"

"Forget."

"I can't believe I'm talking to a dead man. Tell me, where did you live?"

"My name ith Morth." I couldn't remember where I lived and I couldn't remember his name. It might have been Jessica.

"I *know* your name is Morth, we met ..."

"I forgeth quethion."

"OK, I'll make it simple. What's death like?"

"Dark. Quiet."

Doogie entered the gym and told everyone to remove their clothes and put them in a wheeled hamper that he kicked towards them. I didn't know why he wanted to look at naked people. My wife Melania liked to look at naked people on TV. Was Doogie like that too? Three women shouted they wouldn't do it and Doogie said, "Children die."

A minute later staff stripped to underwear and less. They were not pretty.

Doogie dragged away the hamper and I helped myself to a blue jacket and dangling tie that belonged to a teacher. Putting on a shirt proved impossible and I couldn't button the jacket. Doogie ordered others to change and it looked like a sale at a thrift shop.

I pushed the reeking hamper of our rotting vestments towards the teachers. My bloody hockey sweater sat near the top.

40

Clinging to the metal window protector, Jesse located a vent that expelled warm air: it looked big enough for an undernourished child. He thrust his arms into the tunnel and his broad shoulders pushed the duct's sides. The stream of warm air had him popping raindrop perspiration within seconds. Writhing, snake-like he moved slowly forward clutching his tools. Inspired by the faint sound of cries and laughter Jesse oozed forward like a worm in a straw. Jagged ends of screws gave him the look of someone who had fought with a cat and lost.

With the screwdriver he pried open a crack between metal sections and used pliers to bend back a thin flap of metal. A waft of cool air splashed his steaming face and four glazed eyes gazed up. He spat hot saliva on them, but they were beyond humiliation, beyond understanding his gesture. The flow of warm air stopped. Some thoughtful person had turned down the thermostat.

The fresh air refueled his determination. After kicking through thin tin he descended from the metal chamber and clambered onto the top of a tall wall between rooms. No children came into sight, but young voices, whose laughter contradicted their situation, sailed from beyond the wall. The enemy guarded the floor and two salivating sacks of puss looked up.

A false ceiling, similar to a drop-ceiling he had installed in the attic of his now burned-to-the-ground home, hung below an older, original ceiling. He doubted the thin metal rails, which held 2 by 4-foot tiles, could bear his weight. Frail wires attached the corner junctions of each rail to the original ceiling. It looked to be a union job as each four-foot rail section had an optional wire half way along, also secured to the ceiling. Jesse stared at the slight twists in the wire ends that acted as knots. He studied the short screws that snugged wires against ceiling. When he installed his ceiling he never thought about hanging from the wires or standing on the rails to test their strength. Bats, cats and rats had crossed them and nothing failed, but he had a few pounds on the featherweight mammals.

With hands on the first rail Jesse pushed down. The insulating panel fell out and now six well-dressed zombies looked up. Dirt and debris landed in their eyes and they didn't blink. An avalanche of hot anvils wouldn't perturb them. The first wires held: 12 bony hands reached up, but fell short. They jumped up but their feet didn't leave the floor: basketball was not their sport.

Each panel had six wires. Dividing 210 pounds by six meant each wire had to support 35 pounds – if he kept his weight evenly distributed. He slid forward so his hands rested on a far junction. Then he pulled his knees forward, moving like an inchworm.

Nearby, children laughed and cried.

With maximum caution he eased his way towards the kids until a wire snapped and his feet fell to the hands of cannibals whose drool output doubled. One grabbed his shoe, but Jesse jerked his foot from the runner and swung both feet forward and onto the next section of ceiling. Another wire snapped and he hung upside-down like a bat. Dirty fingernails brushed the back of his dangling shirt: he wished he had tucked it in: neatness had rewards.

Jesse saw a gap between a dim pair, swung like an acrobat on a trapeze and landed on top of a partition wall. He flung his remaining shoe and hit a zombie in the neck doing the damage of a flying marshmallow.

Children in the room played zomb-tag. A gaggle of kids lurched around like zombies while the others evaded. When one of the *it* kids got caught they shouted, *you're diner* and that kid joined the pack. Last one alive won.

Doogie, dressed in an unbuttoned suit, staggered into the classroom as if to give a lecture on healthy eating. Jesse feared for the youngsters' safety as looked through the broken ceiling.

In full burble Doogie announced that most kids would go back to their parents. He singled out a small group and said they must stay. That brought a chorus of tears and cries. Doogie threatened a *time out*.

41

"We're not zombies." Victoria pleaded as the teenage boy aimed his Z-D-Capper, dripping Velo's dark blood, at her neck. "We're just dressed like them. We're trying to help out. Believe me, we're normal people."

"You stink like them," the teen snarled menacingly.

"That's our disguise. Listen, we talk normally. You just killed an innocent man."

"You go around looking an' reekin' like a zombie you gonna die." He stepped within snapping distance.

"She's right," Victor interceded. "We live here. That's our bar. You can have a free beer. I'm just like you."

Victor jumped up and down and waved his arms. "Look at me. I'm fast and I can walk, talk and jump."

"Yea, maybe. But that guy got what he deserved. That's just stupid to dress like a zombie. What are you thinking?"

"We were infiltrating, we …" started Victoria.

Victor butted in, "You should be ashamed. Velo was an outstanding member of this community. You can't mend a broken head." Victor started laughing: he had gulped too much captive blood.

The vamps stripped off their zombie garb so they could look as much like temps as possible. With Velo's head under his arm the boy strutted off, expecting to collect his reward.

Vanessa unlocked the back door and entered the water-soaked tavern. Before she could slam the heavy slab behind her four firemen followed. Three firefighters climbed into the attic and extinguished embers. The fourth said he had to go to the basement and inspect for fire damage and electrical problems. Victor had turned on a battery-operated radio to cover cries for help that might emerge from below. He told the fireman the damp basement had been sealed for years and no one ever went down. Several vampires stood in front of the cellar door, which was hard to see as it was painted the same flat black as the rest of the room. Victor announced he was an electrician and would do an inspection as soon as he found a way into the substructure. He showed the fire-chief Velo's wallet with his electrician's photo ID and that satisfied him. With neatly trimmed black hair and pale complexions they looked alike.

    When the last spark doused the firemen finally departed. Vaughn swung open the door to the basement and water lapped within inches of the top step: no sounds emerged. A flashlight scanned the black liquid and its beam lit the back of a head. In the corner a pair of woman's legs floated, heels up. Another still body was doing a dead man's float. Vamps who had received blood supplements from the captives giggled at the mess. Flooding from firefighters' hoses meant they lost captives, the last blood supply and future blood supply. They had no idea why that was funny.

42

Cancer patients, terminally ill and others who loved children more than they loved themselves mingled with tearful parents who couldn't stop thanking them for sacrifices to be made.

I knew I would volunteer if Abacus and Calculus were threatened. But a rotting zombie had no value either as hostage or ransom. *Rotting zombie*, that what's I was. With regret, I accepted my place in the order. The horrors that surrounded me made we think I was better off dead. I had had no worries when I floated beneath the briny waves.

Army personnel had dressed the volunteers in trendy clothes, dyed their hair and generally made them look as young and fit as possible. Doogie had not specified who we wanted in exchange for children and the army must have feared that if we recognized fodder from hospices the prisoner exchange would go south. A gaggle of rail-thin 90-year-olds, leaning on walkers, shuffled towards us. Soup dribbles dotted their chests.

The fittest volunteers walked slowly at the front of the group. Infirm huddled at the back and helped each other. Video cameras and mikes attached to volunteers were monitored by an army crew. Was a new reality show in the making, I wondered.

The boss man of the temps hoisted his hailer and announced they were ready to swap. Doogie's voice immediately asked, "How many yoo give?"

The Colonel answered, "We have 53." I couldn't count that high but remembered that five plus three were ate. Doogie could count. He amazed me. Why did I get the short end of the stick? How long was the stick?

Fifty-three volunteers funeral-marched across the school's yard. Armed soldiers walked at their side. From the other direction came 53 children accompanied by well-dressed comrades who stooped as they plodded.

With whoops of joy the children took off towards parents who rushed forward and entombed them in their arms. The forlorn group of sacrificial lambs continued into the school.

Doogie pointed at a plump school librarian and a pudgy, older teacher. Custodians, clerks and teachers armed with brooms and sports equipment mounted a pathetic defence as six comrades hauled away the selected two. They threw the pair of guinea pigs into the inflated pool and held them underwater until they stopped floundering.

Doogie's fear of water kept his hands clean while assistants did the dirty work. Wires from flashlights, cell phones and low-voltage devices led to the water. Cautiously Doogie immersed their live ends and walked away as if leaving a buffet while hungry.

I ushered the troop of ailing volunteers into the same room as the school's staff. Doogie arrived and singled out a jaundiced man, a lady who could barely walk and a cancer patient with no hair and shoved them into a corner of the gym.

"Foood," he bellowed.

The trio hardly had time to recite the first line of a prayer before being swarmed. Doogie held back those without brains and stomachs, warning them they were wasting their time. The words meant nothing yet they held their instincts in check while fellow eaters tore like ravenous raptors, slurping, spitting, slobbering and pushing. Hunger was so great they even gnawed on hearts too tough to chew. I wanted some but Doogie glared at me. Heady also wanted a share, but was pushed back.

Tire irons and rocks were not available so my friends swung bodies by the ankles and whacked heads against a brick wall. Teachers turned from the thumping and cracking and avoided looking at the river of blood that pooled at the center of the room.

The volunteers went down with dignity: without whimper, protest, plea or tear. No dignity was bestowed upon their lifeless bodies which, after feeding time, were dragged outside and buried in a trench. Thus it went for the next few hours as Doogie singled out trio after trio and the place of learning became an abattoir.

The man known as Jessica must have heard the coconuts cracking. He looked sad. Even as a cop it was unlikely he had ever seen the worst drunken, tattooed motorcycle gang act so ruthlessly.

The school throbbed with undead and from both sides of the wall we stared at him, waiting for a false move when we could get the slightest grip on arm or leg.

Swapping clothes was brilliant strategy. Only by looking for rotting flesh on faces and hands could one distinguish reanimated from temp. Although we stooped, lurched and shuffled we blended sufficiently in fresh suits and dresses that had gained stains.

Children continued to act as children, oblivious to danger, playing, crying and quickly forgetting.

The gulping and chewing sounds of volunteers going down the hatch make me think hunger levels must be exceptional, but what did I know? Maybe that's how the uncouth always ate, even when alive, at KFC or Olive Garden. What is zombie etiquette? Don't pick your teeth! Wipe your chin! Chew 20 times before swallowing! Elbows off the corpse! I walked a few paces behind Doogie, pleased with my ability to think, to figure things out.

He handed me a notebook and pen. "Yoo shoold keep diary. Histoory being made."

The pen in my fist made a diagonal line across the page. I had written *I*, a good start. *M* looked like a mountain range covering the entire white rectangle. There were not enough pages if I were to continue at a letter a page. Notes would have to wait. *I Mort* would be today's entry in the diary. I remembered a teacher telling my mother, "Mortimer can do better."

43

Jane and Donald paced the marge of the schoolyard as if on the sidelines of a high school football game: score lopsided, sixty seconds left in the fourth quarter. Visitors dominated Home Team. A comeback? Only if they recovered a fumble, intercepted a pass and completed a couple of Hail Marys in the remaining minute. The Home Team quarterback threw interceptions and incompletions.

Loving arms enveloped the 53 lucky children who had run to the end-zone. Parents who didn't see their offspring searched frantically then wept hysterically. Kids who watched TV, ate junk food and led sedentary lives were the missing ones. Parents of the plump paid the price. Zombies kept those that would feed most.

Cameras attached to hats and lapels of volunteers broadcast shaky, unsettling video of senior citizens being eaten alive. Particularly galling were close ups of an elderly woman mouthing the words *I love you* while zombies undid her. Like the others, she retained her dignity and didn't scream for help, beg for mercy or pray to god. She could have knitted socks while the beasts followed their instincts.

Thoughts of volunteering crossed Jane's mind and she hoped that she too would go down honourably with a smile and a thanks for all the wonderful years above ground. Would her lonely life flash before her: a too-short life without children or partner? She had specified cremation in her will, but had made no arrangements. Zombies weren't likely to read her will and carry out her wishes.

She wondered what went on in demented heads, especially the heads of those who talked. Did they know what they were doing? Why waste a second life by eating people, by taking children captive? They could be on host shows telling audiences what death was like, what rising was like. With all that strength they could be sports heroes batting balls out of the park. Their indestructible nature could serve them well in the octagon although a propensity for biting would lead to disqualification.

Donald asked, "Do you know how much dignity you'd have in that situation? I'd scream like a baby and fight like a madman if zombies were on me."

Before Jane could offer a response her phone rang and her fingers fumbled. Jesse spoke and she breathed again. His words came quickly and quietly without a trace of trademark humor.

"I can see the remaining children. For the moment they're safe. I've got a plan you should hear before I call the Colonel. I need a driver to ram a hole in the wall of the room where the children are held. We should be able to get them out. At exactly the same time another truck must break through the gym wall and free the staff and maybe some remaining volunteers. There will be adult casualties. Once the hostages are out we can bomb the shit outta the school and annihilate the bastards. More than 100 monsters are milling about in here. There can't be many more. Just a few at the winery waiting for some idiot to decide on a trial. And a few wandering in the woods. I'm working on how to co-ordinate everything, but you've got the general idea."

"You've got a plan," Jane replied. "That's more than we have. That's way more than Mayhew has."

"The zombies have swapped clothes with volunteers," Jesse warned. "So when the army breaks down the wall they won't know good guys from bad. They can't just open fire."

There was a pause while Jane took in this additional information and realized the enemy had the capability to plot. "That's important, I'll pass it on. We noticed some well-dressed ones."

"While soldiers try to figure who is who, the zombs will start eating," Jesse continued. "They might do kids, don't know. The beasts will be able to see the battering trucks 10 seconds before they hit the school. Have to act fast."

Jane said she admired his planning and courage, but it was definitely a Plan B. "We need a Plan A. I wish Mayhew would voice a strategy. How's your phone battery?"

"Good, I keep it charged. I have doubts too, that's why I wanted to run it around the track. I'm on a wall overlooking the most northerly classroom in the school, next to the side entrance. The sacks of shit know I'm here. They'd love to get me. Ring if you think of anything."

Jane jogged 50 yards to Mayhew-Shostakovich's station. He seemed single-mindedly occupied with receiving gratitudes and platitudes from the parents of rescued children. Parents of those still in captivity barraged him with questions and demanded a rescue. Everything stopped as a familiar voice blasted over the speakers.

"Thank yoo for yoor cooperation. Yoo saved yoor babies. Yoo obey rooles, no harm. Yoor man is snoooping. We want him. Yoo have 15 minutes or baby foood."

The voice stopped as abruptly as it started. Jane phoned and told Jesse he had a five minute deadline to come up with Plan A, otherwise he would have no choice to turn himself in. Three minutes later her phone rang.

"Look at the big picture," Jesse explained hurriedly. "Adult hostages are doomed. One by one they will be eaten. I'm doomed: we knew that from the start. Plan A. Three zombs guard the door from kids' room to outside. Three more stand guard on the outside. No guards on door to hallway, but hall swarms with zombs. I have access to air vents. I start a fire in vent that leads to kids' room. Burn rubber, tar paper, whatever. Heavy black smoke descends and reaches zombs' heads and they can't see. Before smoke surrounds the kids' heads I jump down and lure the eaters to me, away from the outside wall. That's when Mayhew's men smash through the wall and door. They blast every maggot-faced, puss-head they see. Aim for well-dressed ones. I have a white, loose T-shirt, grey slacks, no shoes. I'll bend low, near the floor, herding kids out the hole knocked in wall. At the same time Mayhew's men drive another armoured car, or a tank, through gym wall and save as many adults as possible. That's plan A. Ten minutes to implement. Hit the two target walls at the exact moment you see smoke through the low windows of the room at the north end. You'll see smoke in the upper windows first, but wait for it to drop. Over and out."

Jane, with Donald a step behind, barged in on the Colonel's conversation with a mother and explained the plan as quickly as possible. She told him she would ride in the first vehicle in order to coordinate the assault. Donald sprinted to an armoured personnel carrier and told the crew to prepare to knock a hole in the wall on the north side of the school the moment they saw smoke through the bottom windows. He told them to prepare a second vehicle to blast through the wall of the gym at exactly the same time. He climbed aboard vehicle two.

Colonel Mayhew-Shostakovich nodded to the strategy that unfolded before him whether he liked it or not. Parents surrounding him backed away and gave him space. He declared that acting immediately had elements of logic and surprise. The Emergency Response Team received his orders. They would weaken the walls with bazooka fire and seconds later drive through. Jane and Donald exhibited such authority when they climbed aboard that no one questioned them.

The heavy vehicles drove along the town's back roads and positioned themselves, just out of sight, on streets facing the targeted walls.

Jesse unfolded his wallet and found that his flammables consisted of a few receipts plus paper money in denominations of fives and twenties. *This is going to be an expensive fire,* he deduced.

He pried open a junction of heating duct and bent it to shield his fire so cool furnace air would fan it rather than extinguish it. Assorted receipts, business cards and $125 in crumpled bills acted as kindling. On top of that he placed crumpled strips of tar paper torn from an open section of roof. It caught fire on the first strike of the first match from a flattened pack he secreted in the corner of his wallet next to his *hot tickler* condom. A small fire flared and he ripped off more tar paper and dropped it on top. When the flames reached 12 inches he dumped his wallet, minus MasterCard and driver's license, on top. The loss of his Costco card and condom caused no sorrow, but seeing his Hooters membership melting brought a moment of regret even though there were no establishments within 50 miles.

Smoke billowed black, but hardly enough to fill a closet, let alone a classroom. He tossed in the matches and an insignificant flare ensued. Larger tarpaper strips from the ceiling quickly flared and finally wisps of dark smoke blew into the space below. In frenzied action he gathered bigger chunks of black paper, a section of discarded newspaper and dusty wood leftovers. A rusty tray holding thick black gook sat alongside some creosote impregnated wood and he tossed all onto the growing blaze. They flared beautifully.

The fire alarm sounded and the sprinkler system spewed water. Within the protective duct his dark flames blazed. The screaming alarm and spraying water could only help the cause by adding confusion. A call to Jane confirmed he had a good start on his childhood dream – a burning schoolhouse – and the plan looked good. Everything was in order.

"You should see smoke in the lower windows within two minutes," he said as he found more waste to fuel the fire. "Get ready to hit the wall." It pleased him Jane was aboard the armoured truck. Another armload of debris grew his campfire to bonfire proportions.

Doogie experimented with the buoyancy of two bodies face-down in his pool. He added a cup of salt and stirred: the problem might be the solution. The fire alarm sounded. He ordered six full-bodied zombs to the children's room and shouted, "If they try to escape, eat them," but doubted they understood, given the annoyance of the incessant alarm. Then the ceiling exploded with rain.

44

I had not liked holding kids hostage, but it worked out. The exchange meant our army of misfortune now had a meat locker full of bodies, ripe and ready. We might get even more meals in exchange for the remaining kids. Doogie did good planning. I looked forward to the time my mind reached such levels as I could make a plan and carry it out. Now, to comb my hair, I put toothpaste on a fork and ran it across my forehead.

Despite my respect for our leader, I hated the idea of using children, no matter how nourishing. It hurt to think of little Liberty's missing fingers. I tried to think what I would do if my children were in the classroom, but couldn't get beyond standing in front and protecting them with shouts of *Not for Eathing*. I got out the notebook Doogie had given me and made a big circle with a bite out of it. Then a little circle with a little stick. Then two telephone poles. After a space I created a small mountain range then a squiggly thing and then a big mountain range and a little circle and something like a crutch. I couldn't figure out what to do next so I read *Call me Mor...* It spread over two pages.

Six cohorts passed me, at top zomb speed, heading for the kids' room. They were the executioners, I feared. The wailing siren and water spraying on floors added panic. I lurched sideways, blocked the doorway and grabbed each cohort by the shoulders the way Doogie did, and stared into their vacant eyes. Loudly and clearly I ordered, "Do not eath children." The same void gaze would have returned to me if I had told them they had won a Caribbean cruise.

45

Jesse threw a final load of tar-impregnated paper onto the blaze that reached the roof and started it burning. He swung down from the ceiling and landed a short lunge from the grasping hands of ghoul guards. In the grey air he danced backwards, a few feet ahead of them, taunting and leading them to the corner farthest from children. Thicker smoke descended around their heads. Water from the ceiling gathered soot as it fell. The smoggy spray trickled from their mottled hair into their eyes, half blinding them, but not hindering them.

The air trembled with the boom of bazookas and staccato rattling of machine guns. The crash into the wall came on cue.

"Don't shoot till you see the yellow of their eyes," screamed a female voice. Jane jumped off the carrier, ran through the broken wall, pulled a child to safety and then gathered up another.

Jesse ducked under the smoke's black pall and pushed kids towards daylight. As children scrambled to freedom he did a head count and one could not be accounted for. He rose above the smoke to look for the missing kid. A bullet cracked his temple and exploded out the back of his head. He never heard the shot that ended his life in one example of perfect marksmanship. He never heard a sergeant scream, "Hold your fire," at the same time as a terrified teen pulled the trigger. His heart continued beating after the shot killed him and 10 grimy nails pulled at his torso.

In hand-to-hand combat the soldiers did not fare well and their shooting skills did not match the standards of the private who felled Jesse with one shot. More zombies filled the room and refused to die unless hit directly with a bazooka or spray of bullets that beheaded them. Only two such shots found their marks amidst the wet, smoky, noisy chaos.

Children scrambled to where Jesse had directed them and raced out the door to freedom. Two lumbering zombs tried to catch them, but turned to mush as a dozen machine guns got them in their sights and opened fire. Soldiers grabbed escaped children and ushered them to safety.

The *ram and shoot* tactic proved less effective in the gymnasium full of teachers due to the indistinguishable mix of zombies and civilians. Had there been smoke in that room the military would have known to behead the ones that didn't possess enough sense to duck under the black blanket. Zombies swarmed soldiers who paused to discern differences before firing. Yellow bleary eyes, rotting skin, patchy scalp and the presence of flies were what they looked for. Trigger fingers paused because they had been warned the sneaky creatures might change clothes once more.

In Darwinian accord the strongest, fittest and fastest teachers broke from the school and raced to safety. Many teachers and soldiers fell to teeth and nails. Zombies were having a field day eating captives and soldiers faster than they themselves were being killed. Someone screamed *retreat!*

46

Eaters never got to the brains of the nice man who had talked to me. I chased them away after they consumed below his neck. In the room where children had been held I felt a strange satisfaction with their escape. From a cupboard a muffled whimpering sound emerged and I opened its door. A pudgy boy huddled under a blanket, cowering and crying. He looked delicious. I put out my hand and said, "Won't hurth you, I hath two kids."

The boy put out his shaky hand and I helped him step forward. I could taste the lad's buttery lard melting in my mouth. I could see him with bulging pink belly, on a platter, apple in mouth. My new and improved imagination impressed me.

Daylight rushed through the wall's gaping hole. Freedom for the boy was a sprint away, but Doogie had posted new guards, three inside and three out.

"Stay in cuthboard," I told the cowering lad in my clearest, slowest words. The boy returned a puzzled stare. Using two walking fingers to indicate going away and returning I conveyed that I would be back in a few minutes.

"I geth you food," I said. It was my duty to keep the kid fat.

47

Parents jubilantly celebrated the return of their children. The military congratulated each other on a successful operation and lamented the loss of fellow soldiers, but it came with the job. Despite the fact undead still controlled the school and held a few staff hostage, there was a feeling the war had been fought and won and everything had returned to normal. A little laughter was heard.

A mother's moan shattered the day and word spread that one child remained unaccounted for. Then came calmness, as if a cloud of Dramamine had blown in.

Eyes glanced to a forlorn couple as if it was their fault that everyone could no longer relax and celebrate. Why hadn't they taught their child to follow the crowd, to seek out the light and run to freedom? What kind of parents were they that their child should remain with filthy ogres? Had he gone native? A teacher suggested Stockholm syndrome.

Jane and Donald worried about Jesse, who had dropped out of sight beneath the smoke blanket as soldiers retreated with children. His comical voice, which had become so serious during the crisis, did not respond to phone calls.

48

Chaos, never before known to vamkind, erupted at Vladimir's smoky bar. Veronica, Victor and other Vees argued vehemently in raised voices about what to do with a wine cellar full of bloated floaters. Their plan to overcome the enemy and save the town resulted in them burning their bar and drowning their resources.

Never had a bleak and depressing future hung before them like damp, soiled laundry. No one had the energy to fish out the bodies, take them deep into the woods and make them disappear.

Basement water receded by a fraction of an inch an hour. It would be weeks before they could get to the few remaining vials of blood in the back of the cooler. Who knew if water had diluted them? Who knew the shelf life of a bottle of blood? No one volunteered to snorkel into the dark, among the decaying dead.

The effects of sera deprivation hit everyone in the vampire community and each looked wan and anaemic. Most wanted to walk away from the problem, head for the cemetery, crawl into a crypt, go dormant for a decade and emerge in improved times. To do so they had to be in full health and for that their blood supply had to be replenished. Catch 22. Only those few who drank deeply from drunks felt well, albeit delusional.

Their carefully planned schemes swirled in their heads: an embarrassing disaster on the dock, a cellar full of death, a roofless tavern, a dearth of dead zombies and a continuing blood shortage. Any more botched problem solving and they could slip into the netherworld and end up as bodies on their damp barroom floor. Someone would find them, locate no next of kin and bury them. Then they would rise as blood-sucking cannibals: hybrid zom-pires. What a mess! What a miserable end to a golden era. Never again would they play spider solitaire or Wii bowling.

No solution presented itself and no one had the inclination to search for one. A small, battery-powered television displayed how a properly executed plan had saved the school kids and mowed down a significant number of the enemy. Watchers of the tiny screen wished they could get their teeth into the necks of robust soldiers. They licked their lips: blood-thinning saliva leaked from the corners of mouths.

The vamps couldn't call a construction crew to have their tavern repaired and pumped out for fear workers would uncover waterlogged carcases. Calling an insurance company didn't come up for discussion as they carried no insurance and didn't need it. Paying for repairs was like buying a postage stamp.

At the moment of maximum despair a dripping rat raced past their feet and all eyed it with the same thought, but not one would stoop that low, at least not in front of others.

A damp calendar showed the end of October and Vladimir's Bar, their only meeting place, wouldn't be repaired for months. That meant no heat and no electricity. They could be mushing through slush in the dead of winter before things got close to normal, assuming they lived that long. They hated cold and snow; even the kind that melted before kids could think about a snowman. They also hated extreme summer heat. Their quiet White Rock locale, next to the ocean, in the rain-shadow of mountainous islands, served them well.

The zombie invasion had brought comfort crashing like a glass shelf in a china shop. Nothing inspired them to look at the sunny side of life. Amidst the silence Veronica's small voice quivered with the very words no one wanted to hear, "I have an idea."

She avoided the words *plan* and *proposal*. Nevertheless several moaned. She continued. "I have to think it through. Meet here tomorrow at six in the evening. Meanwhile go home, get warm, get rest." Everyone in attendance silently shuffled off, happy to comply.

49

Colonel Mayhew-Shostakovich almost cursed and then apologized as he stared at the school. One small bomb could vaporize all the zombies within. He blamed the stupid kid who hadn't fled with the others. Were it not for him the mission would have been perfect and he would be a hero. Just one retarded kid.

The Colonel knew not all adults had escaped, but certain lives could be sacrificed. Teachers who hadn't run as fast as the others and some ailing seniors would die in the bomb blast but the horror would end. It would be for the greater good. Mayhew could count the loss of one idiot boy as collateral damage, but explaining to his parents and the public that the army had bombed the little bugger into oblivion would require some serious spin.

The commander grabbed his hailer, aimed at the school and shouted, "You have one child. We would like to offer an adult in exchange."

50

I didn't want anyone to know about the hidden boy: I wanted to get him out. Doogie would never allow the boy to go if he knew about him and now he knew. I was mortified when I heard the words penetrate the school.

Although I craved fresh meat I curbed a desire to dig into the turkey roasting in the cupboard. Restraint pleased me. Knowing I was pleased pleased me. On hearing the announcement a trace of smile tried to transform Doogie's stern visage. He had questioned why the army didn't regroup, march through the broken walls, toss grenades and slay them all. Now he knew. One child remained unaccounted for.

"Doo yoo know where kid is?" Doogie stared at me.

I shook my head vigorously. A bit of hairy scalp slid off. The sprinklers, now shut off, had been cruel to me. Doogie fared better, he was smarter: he found an umbrella. Plain grey tape held him together: it matched his skin color and didn't stand out. The patterned green business suit he wore made his head look like a baked potato on top of salad.

Doogie assembled a group of full-bodied zombs plus Heady, who followed any group, welcome or not, and ordered them to find the child. The unthinking creatures had some basic grasp of his loud commands.

"Loook behind dooors, under flooors, in cupboords ... yoo bring me child. Then yoo eat. But not child." Some zombs had taken advantage of dead teachers and soldiers. To Doogie, dining on the dead equalled dumpster diving. It was like eating pizza boxes for the taste of tomato sauce.

I joined the search team and when they reached the room where the boy hid I loudly suggested, "I searth here." Heady followed me and the others moved on. I was very clever.

On opening the cupboard door, the teary-eyed boy proclaimed, "I'm hungry."

I said "thorry" for not bringing food and promised to find some.

"You like liver?" I asked: I knew where to find some. The boy screwed up his face and I remembered that children prefer the bland.

"Thardine sandwith?" He made a vomiting motion and then I suggested "peanuth buther." It sounded like organs in a blender.

I trod back towards the door, pretending to have completed my search of the room. Heady shuffled behind, silent and loyal, then made a U-turn and rushed for the cupboard, salivating and mumbling. I grabbed her and held her as she struggled. I told her not to eat and not to blab about the boy and then realized she couldn't comprehend and couldn't talk.

"Donth eat boy," I shouted at her and pushed her out the door.

The speaker system crackled and Doogie announced, "We not give yoo child. It oor protection."

He waddled down the hall to check his two floating bodies. The batteries still had charge in them and the new solution swirled. Resurrection of talking heads waited.

Doogie's shuffle slowed and his shoulders slumped as he headed to the door. The floor of the school had not conducted amperage from the charge in the ground and everyone drooped. He gathered a group of 25 full-bodies and a half-dozen hollows, including Heady, and showed them how to shed their shoes. They walked outside the school, sliding feet across grass and picking up a weak trickle charge.

After the group dispersed I did the dandelion shuffle with a second group that Heady also joined. It felt good, like an electric blanket on a cold day.

51

Colonel Mayhew-Shostakovich paced among his men, deep in thought. He juggled rumors of who else might be in the school and who was unaccounted for. His right hand clenched a list of teachers, inspectors, students, janitors, teachers' assistants and visiting parents. Most had a red line through them, many had a black line and a few had nothing.

He watched the procession of barefoot zombies and wondered what was going on. Surely they didn't need exercise or fresh air. At any time the military could have blasted them and, but for the sake of one young hostage, would have done so. Adult hostages were expendable.

Jane and Donald approached.

"How much do you think they know?" Jane asked.

The army boss rephrased her question and spat it back, "What do those spit-heads, excuse my language, know?"

"Yes. How much do they know about the missing boy? We never specified boy or girl. The talking zombie said, 'We will not give up child. *It* is' …"

Jane paused for a reaction, but the colonel seemed confused.

She continued, "If I was talking about a kid I was familiar with, I'd say 'We will not give up the boy. He is … Or, we will not give up the girl. She is'…"

"So you think they may not know the whereabouts of said boy," the Colonel deduced.

Donald chipped in, "An hour passed before the talking one replied to our offer of a swap. They may be looking for him. I'd guess they can't find him. Maybe he isn't there. Maybe he skipped school. Are you considering attacking?"

"That's exactly what I'm considering."

"What about the video cameras? Any signals?" Jane asked.

The colonel explained that volunteers who wore cameras were now dead and buried. Cameras had shown zombies feeding, then ceiling, then sky, then black. Before the colonel walked away he said he wouldn't order an attack before morning's first light.

With overcast sky and a hint of drizzle, morning crept in carefully. Most had slept in cars, tents and on the ground.

Doogie hadn't slept, he didn't do that. The time had come for resurrection and he stared at the small swimming pool. The two bodies in the water did not rise of their own accord. They did not do anything. He poked, pushed and prodded. Nothing happened. He plugged in a small radio, turned it on and angrily heaved it into the water. It sizzled, flashed and a breaker tripped. The room darkened: the bodies did not move. Doogie pushed a broom onto the edge of the inflated pool. Water drained onto the tiles and the two bodies lay flat as flounders.

Doogie stomped, as best he could stomp, to the basement door, but before heading downstairs signalled his cohorts, indicating they could dine if they so wished. Innards from distended abdomens of drowned teachers were venomously barfed onto the floor. No one had a stomach for the deceased, even drowned and electrified deceased. Doogie wondered about the *best before* date on bodies. Did the tissue issue concern time of death or time of immersion in water? Henchmen consumed bodies that had been dead for a minute or two, although they did so with less relish than when consuming the living. They spat out anything that had been dead longer than a minute or two. Necrophagy had no place on a zombie menu.

52

My search through drawers, lockers and cupboards uncovered a soft apple, a peanut cookie, half a bottle of soda and an opened bag of vinegar-flavored chips. When Doogie went to the school basement and Heady followed him I sped to the cupboard. The frightened lad, curled on the floor, jumped up when the door opened.

"I brouth food," I said and handed the apple to the pale, chubby child.

"I hate apples," the boy shot back without gratitude. "You eat it."

I took a big, encouraging bite from the red Mac and thought a sick skunk had sprayed my mouth. My cheeks puckered, teeth ached and a bilious nausea rose from the bottom of my oesophagus. I spat out the offending piece that had turned black.

"I told you," the boy mocked.

"Thith ith all I found," I explained as I handed over the rest.

The lad examined the food like it might explode then gave his assessment. "The pop's flat, the chips are stale and I'm allergic to peanuts. I'm going home." He pushed against the door, but I wouldn't let it open.

"If they know you in cuthboard they eath you."

"I gotta pee."

"Drink pop: pee in bothle."

"I gotta poo."

"Eath chips: poo in bag."

"You're disgusting."

"I am zombie."

"You're not eating me."

"I hath children. Love them."

"Zombies reproduce? You've got a weenie?"

"Hath children before I wath zombie."

"Why did you become a zombie?"

"Electhrithity in earth."

"Maybe my gramma's a zombie. She's dead. Her name's Margaret. She's nice. Do you know her?"

"We not talk. Don''t hath names."

"She has white hair, wears glasses and has false teeth."

"No more talk or geth caught and eathen."

"I'm going home." The boy slammed his shoulder against the door and surprised me by pushing it half open. That meant it was half closed. I deduced that. The boy lunged at my forearm and bit. I felt little. He spat out a piece of blue skin the size of a potato chip.

"You taste like yellow, shitty, chicken. You're disgusting."

"Need 10 minuthes to geth you free." I slammed the door on the boy's fingers and stepped towards the hallway. The boy screamed, leapt forwards and ran towards freedom. Three henchmen cut him off. Despite his obesity the lad danced backwards keeping beyond grasping hands. They cornered him and closed in for a meal. I stood horrified; indecisive.

"Why yoo not chasing him?" asked Doogie. My sad eyes followed the doomed lad.

"Juth got here," I quickly lied. It surprised me I could lie with ease. Among the living dishonesty troubled me. Melody had been dishonest, I vaguely recalled, and that had troubled me. She had been unfaithful, but I didn't know what that meant. Perhaps she hadn't gone to church or secretly ate ice cream.

"Doon't eat boy," Doogie bellowed, then waddled towards the lad. Half-heartedly, I followed.

Confused by what they should do if they weren't going to eat, the stalkers stood and stared while streams of dark, lumpy saliva flowed. The pause gave the prey a chance to dive to the floor and squirm past the legs of the numb. Outstretched arms belonging to me and Doogie were the only barrier between boy and the hole in the wall. With three stunned zombies lumbering behind, the boy sprinted, intending to do an end run around Doogie, who looked incapable of throwing a tackle. In anticipation Doogie moved slightly faster than one could foresee from a short-legged corpse. The avenue of escape closed. The boy's only other route led past me.

My fingers, fingers that could empty a torso in seconds, landed on the boy's shoulder, grabbed, and the child slipped past. Three chasing zombies maintained a steady pace as the boy struggled across the lawn. Then obesity stopped him and, with hands on knees, he sucked wind into weak, inedible lungs.

Machine guns fired and patches of skin and hair popped off pursuers. To those who felt no pain this did not act as a deterrent. Bazookas exploded against cars, walls and hillsides.

Doogie and me waddled directly behind the boy so that no shots came in our direction. Pursuit was a lost cause as I lacked enthusiasm and Doogie lacked speed. Our cadaverous compatriots had stamina and gained on the panting, pudgy prey. Despite the warning to refrain from dining, the boy was destined to be catch of the day. Chasers drooled like a flash flood hit their throats.

Anticipating that the order to fast would not be obeyed, Doogie and I retreated towards the school, keeping the boy between us and guns. That was Doogie's idea. As I didn't want to view a HungryMan-boy dinner, my eyes focused on the door ahead.

53

Without a horn honk of warning, a red convertible roared into the spray of angled bullets that slowed the three chasers only slightly. Jane pointed Jesse's powerful Mustang at the zombie about to bend over the gasping boy. From the two women in the Jaguar she had learned how to disable the monsters from hell and hit legs. She hoped she had also learned how not to become their next meal. From the passenger seat Donald swung an axe. A token effort, he knew, but sabres and Z-D-Cappers were not as effective and not at hand.

Jane executed a spinning U-turn and aimed at the second undead, expecting to run over the first on her way back. Undead number one could not be seen: it dragged along beneath the low-slung car. Number two bounced back over the fabric roof and Jane wished Jesse had bought a hardtop. She also wished Jesse was with her. When he phoned from the school and announced his plan to rescue the kids, she knew her hopes for him were realized. He had abandoned his infantile humor and self-serving ways and stepped to the forefront as a peace officer and a man. Desperately she wanted him to survive and fight beside her. His bad jokes would break the tension. She might even give a chuckle from time to time.

Undead cannibal three, wearing an apron, dark glasses and white stockings, bounced sideways when the Mustang rammed her. Dentures flew out and Donald quipped that the beast would be eating pudding for dinner.

Jane gave the puss-filled pestilence another taste of Jesse's deep tread. A permanent Pirelli imprint sank into soft skin. Jane saw number three crawl back, lean over the boy and dig in. Without teeth it could do little more than gum his tummy. Donald jumped out of the car, pulled the beefy boy away from the gummer and tossed him over the passenger seat and into the back. The lad's wimpy, heaving lungs wailed about the rough treatment.

Behind the wheel Jane shared the field with two crippled zombies and a third beneath the car. Tires crunched bones until two beasts crawled across the grass like gelatinous slugs. She parked a rear wheel atop a zombie head and accelerated with spinning tires. Lips, nose and eyes flew out behind.

The time had come, Donald suggested, to get off the field and let the army do some beheading. Jane answered that running down zombies was such vengeful fun she couldn't resist another pass. At 35 mph she headed directly at two creatures crawling on the grass and connected with their chests. In the mirrors she expected to view carnage, but saw an empty field.

"Look at the mess you've got us into," Donald roared above the rattle of beer cans beneath seats and howls from the boy in the back. Mirrors showed bony hands clawing up over the trunk.

"Drive to the edge of the field, but not too close," Donald shouted. "Then go through the gate and onto Lillian St. then right into Tannis Park. But first slow down near the group."

"I bet you're thinking what I think you're thinking." She slightly resented him giving orders, but what he said made sense, so it didn't matter where it came from. "How do you know the streets? This is my town."

"I study maps. My life could depend on knowing how to get in and out of situations."

"Impressive."

Black fingernails clawed through the fabric roof above the back seat.

"Slowing down," Jane shouted and Donald pulled the heavy boy from the rear before gnarled fingers reached him. The passenger door opened and Donald pushed the screaming boy out, feeling relief to be rid of the whining zombie bait. His rotundness helped him roll to a safe stop and no creature followed. Parents rushed to his side.

"Now we need speed," Jane yelled and the pony car raced out of the schoolyard and along a paved road. She hit speed bumps full tilt and envisioned the clinging creatures being flattened and catapulted into ditches, but again no bodies appeared behind. Ignoring a dead end sign, she turned onto a dirt lane that led to a small park that overlooked the ocean.

"Seat belts off, doors open, I'm going left onto that soft grass; we're bailing." Jane described her intentions clearly. "I don't want us to get hurt ... slowing down ... oh shit."

The head of a zombie ripped through the ragtop. Arms grabbed Donald's jacket, pulled him upwards and grey lips curled back to reveal yellow and black incisors readied to bite. A cliff loomed ahead and Donald hoped the car would go over it and he would die before the zombie hoisted him onto the canvass dining platform. Drowning would be quicker if he could keep teeth from his flesh for another few seconds. Death as hero wasn't the worst fate, he thought, and then considered, that might be his last ever thought. Shouldn't life flash before him? A boy had been saved. Perhaps tubby would grow up to be a great leader and find the path to world peace. That was the least he could do.

A second pair of creeping hands reached Jane. She calmly took the unlatched end of her seat belt, extended it to its full length and pushed the tongue-end through a metal stay in the convertible top. She snapped in the end so the seatbelt secured the roof rather than her. A jab of the brake forced Donald down into his seat and out of zombie hands. He twisted his seatbelt through the metal roof truss as she had and snapped it in. A rooftop zombie pulled Jane's hair. She released a J-hook above the windshield then pushed a silver button marked *Top Down*. An electric motor strained against seatbelts that held the canvass. Scabby fingers pulled driver and passenger upwards, out of their seats. On her way up Jane grabbed the emergency brake lever and the sudden deceleration pushed the creatures forward. A twist of the wheel sent the car skidding backwards towards cliff edge.

"Three, two, one," she shouted and Donald and Jane pressed their seatbelt release buttons and the top sprung backwards. Two zombies sling-shotted over the trunk, over the cliff and into salt water. With gear shift in neutral Jane and Donald bailed and the car continued over the edge. Like a parachute the roof billowed and the Mustang fell in slow motion, landing on top of the two jettisoned monsters that flapped their arms in a futile attempt to stay afloat. The third creature, wearing an apron, clung to the car's greasy bottom and went down with the ship.

Jane peered over the edge and smiled as car and zombies sank into clear ocean water. "Jesse has lost his house and his beloved car. The department is going to go bankrupt paying him back."

"We've got budget," Donald added with a smile. "Might even be able to salvage. Had a soft landing. Can still see it, settling on the bottom. Thought I was a goner back there. Had my last thoughts."

"About loved ones?"

"No. Thinking about my last thoughts. My life didn't flash before my eyes."

Hugs and kisses from adoring parents almost suffocated the pair after a jeep drove them back to the school. The colonel congratulated them and said he had lined up his mortars to blast the school and everything in it. Most staff had escaped, but a few remained captive.

Jane and Donald wondered why the Colonel's plan to destroy the school had not been carried out although Jane was relieved. Jesse might be alive: his survival skills would surely cover that possibility. On the other hand, if the enemy could be eradicated with one simple bombing, the sacrifice of a few lives did not amount to much, certainly not in the cold, calculating eyes of the army.

At the military station Jane caught the end of a conversation. One missing hostage was the assistant superintendent of education who was making a surprise inspection of the school at the time of the invasion. With two children at home and one on the way, she elicited maximum empathy. Pregnancy limited her mobility and were it not for Doogie's fasting order she would have been done like dinner and desert. A teacher, near retirement age, had stayed behind to help her.

Sentiment among the military favored a rescue attempt before blasting the school to oblivion. Jane added that one of her officers should be considered missing and probably alive. Civilians' sentiments exasperated the Colonel, "Why is everyone being so difficult? If soldiers were inside I would bomb the bustards, 'scuze me."

54

Doogie visited the school basement a lot. To my question about what went on below, he curtly responded, "Goood prooject." I found no satisfaction in his vagueness, but curiosity was not a major part of my misty mind.

Sentry duty was my assignment and it meant I could do what I wanted since I didn't know how to be a sentry. I got out my notebook and scratched *to be or not*. It seemed appropriate and I could read my wiggly lines. I thought another *to be* should come next, but it would be dumb to repeat the obvious. *Redundant*, they said in school. After scribbling more words I gave up; writing was hard. Numbers had always worked better than words: *two plus two makes more*. I wandered the halls, came upon a steel door, opened it, and without over-thinking, descended to a dark, damp environment. Heaps of rock and rubble covered the hard floor. Muted voices came from ahead. Before I could decipher them a hollow one quickly pushed a wheelbarrow full of dirt towards me. I slowly moved aside and then Doogie appeared.

"So yoo come tooo bottom flooor!" His face cracked with a painful smile. "We close tooo oor third coming."

A tunnel large enough for a stooped human penetrated the wall behind Doogie.

"Where thath go?"

"Sooon yoo know."

Doogie left me staring into the tunnel that wheel barrows and buckets of dirt came out of. The empty zombs moved faster than any I had seen and their speed made me envious. They even possessed a degree of dexterity as they swung picks and axes that, for the most part, missed arms and legs. The extra trickle of electricity from beneath the surface worked miracles. After staring at the slaves there was nothing for me to do but go back upstairs and continue sentry duty. Again I tried writing. My autobiography would be a long time coming. *I stink, therefore I am,* should cover it. That took two pages.

Doogie's voice boomed over the address system, "We have hoostages. Talk toomorrow."

The Colonel's voice countered, "We negotiate now. If you do not respond in 15 minutes we will destroy the school and all in it."

No response came in 15 minutes or in one hour or in two hours. No bombs fell. Twenty-four hours passed before Doogie returned to the microphone. "Want three for one. One big man, twoo others. Swap in one hoour."

The colonel's assistants had trouble rounding up volunteers. Sacrificing one's life for children was fine, but no one would step up to the plate with a note pinned to their back that said *eat me* in exchange for an adult, even a pregnant adult. Already there was resentment about educators getting full time pay for a part time job.

At the cancer ward two frail volunteers were willing to save an expectant mother, but large, healthy men were in short supply. A hospice produced a doomed male of middle age who had AIDS. He stood relatively tall but the disease had taken away much of his weight. The Colonel asserted that zombies couldn't distinguish sick from healthy so it didn't matter as long as they got meat. His observations proved to be correct as all three were accepted, but satisfaction turned to disappointment when the zombies released a meek male teacher instead of the pregnant lady they hoped to see.

The first of the three volunteers had barely entered the school when Doogie waved his hand and five droolers, like snorting hyenas, fell into a mindless bloodfest.

Starvation struck me and I lost control. I had been proud of my restraint. I lunged forward, elbowed in and bit into anything red. Lightning bolts of pleasure forked through by body then diminished like fog in a morning breeze. I licked my ragged, split lips, looked at my bloodstained clothes and wanted to weep. What madness had gripped me? What crazy cannibalistic carnage controlled my life? The answer came quickly: I behaved as those from the grave must behave. Recreation went beyond understanding.

Did this second life represent an improvement over the eternal blackness I had previously inhabited? Resurrection's only pleasure came with eating. Otherwise I droned along caring little if I was dead, alive or somewhere between. If only I could hold my children and wrap Melody in my arms there might be a life to live. I wanted to go home; I wanted to go to school and teach addition and subtraction. Two is the square root of four, four is the square root of sixteen, six teens form the hypothesis of a triangle.

I longed to listen to music on my little radio, wash my car, clean the eaves, shampoo my hair, move my bowels, phone my friend. Rarely had I taken a moment to savor life's simplest activities. Now those unappreciated pleasures disappeared like solved equations erased from a whiteboard. What I would give to mow my lawn on an autumn day, deadhead the flowers, smell cut grass and throw clippings onto the compost heap? How could I have considered that a chore? Gladly I would sacrifice my remaining zombiedom, whatever that was, for a day with my family: a day to go to the library, buy groceries, change a diaper, tell a bedtime story, return Malady's beer bottles.

The sound of clashing teeth and slurping fluids emerged from a corner and ended my reverie as Doogie directed dining on an elderly gent who accepted his fate without complaint. Heady shuffled to the front, but Doogie shouted "No," and slapped the back of her head. Grey matter dribbled from the sock restraining her borrowed brains. I didn't like the unnecessary violence, but did nothing, said nothing.

55

Despite the loss of lives and the never ending standoff at the school, the populace of White Rock desperately wanted to celebrate a victory. Valiant volunteers had given their lives and now it seemed just one woman remained hostage and one policeman remained unaccounted for. Hungry zombies would make another exchange and, with that done, the school could be razed and the invasion from hell would be over.

No one had recently vanished in the night. It appeared the enemy had made the strategic error of gathering all its forces in the same place at the same time. Before month's end the townsfolk could get back to raking leaves, preparing their pools for winter and watching television without fear of breaking news forcing young ones from the room.

Crime had come to a standstill. Not so much as a looter, drunk driver or shoplifter dotted Jane's blotter. Introducing new officers to routines, standing guard at the school, patrolling a few streets and forwarding calls about suspected prowlers kept her busy. She heard she would receive a citation for bravery and dreaded having to make a speech. In theory, patrolling was army work, but as long as she kept busy she had less time to think about Jesse and suffer the pain that accompanied such thoughts.

Again she tried his phone and decided there was no point in leaving the same "Me Jane, you call," message over and over. Worrying about him kept her awake; worrying about everything kept her awake. The playing field of worry covered thousands of acres and there was nowhere to hide. Her mind moved from office to home to school and found no comfort.

Dozens of plans to invade the school and free Jesse bounced through her head until ultimately they hit the same brick wall: his phone worked. Even if he lost it he would find a way to communicate or run from the school. Tears streamed over her emotional brick wall, etching the soft sandstone of her face. She prayed the enemy had tied him up and locked him in a room, holding him for future negotiation. The hope was slight; unrealistic.

In a motel room Donald slept restlessly. He heard bulldozers clearing the remains of Jesse's house and contemplated the survival of Jane's best friend.

As the last of daylight sifted through the window of Jane's car, where she dozed, Doogie's voice bellowed that a hostage would be released in exchange for three large volunteers. The Colonel countered that he had exhausted the supply of large volunteers and only thin and aged could be found and even those were in short supply. Doogie said the Colonel was big enough to volunteer. The Colonel responded that if Doogie would accept one elderly volunteer plus himself, he would go.

A gasp followed by a murmur spread through the ranks like a large rock tossed into a placid pond.

Doogie agreed and the Colonel muttered a near-profanity then apologized. The exchange went smoothly and the army boss plus a senior citizen got what they expected. One died a hero rather than as a disease-wracked invalid fading away on a hospital bed. The other entered the annals of warfare as an example of action far beyond the call of duty. Colonel Mayhew-Shostakovich died with a dignified salute and lips muttering "muck you, sorry."

As soon as the superintendent of education's plodding steps took her from lawn to the hands of medics, Mayhew's last order was executed. Fragmentation mortars and high explosive mortars struck 22 different parts of the school. For a minute bricks and mortar blew sky-high and for 10 minutes smoke clung to the still air. Soldiers, teachers, police and other officials rubbed their eyes at the memory of lost comrades and then reigned in emotions. A light wind pushed away smoke and eyes stared at rubble. Applause and cheers broke out, slowly at first and then a cascade of joy. Backs were slapped, high-fives exchanged and hugs given. Never did they think that anyone but students would celebrate the destruction of a school. The worst in Canadian homicide history ended as quickly as it started.

Jane questioned the new commander about why the enemy would release the last hostage, knowing they would be defenceless and would be annihilated. The new chief, a young man with a positive attitude, replied that zombies had probably reached their best-before date and were going to die anyway. Perhaps painfully slowly.

A tidal wave of sorrow for the loss of Jesse hit Jane and forced her to drop the argument. Donald took her place, questioning the new leader about how he knew so much about the undead's life expectancy and where he learned it.

"What would you do?" the commander challenged with a deadpan stare.

"I'd at least check for zombie parts in the ashes."

"What do you think those muckers are doing?" The new boss pointed to three soldiers half-heartedly poking hoes, rakes and the barrels of rifles into damp, smouldering ashes. Donald grabbed a rake and a hoe that naïve citizens had intended to use to fight zombies. He shouted to Jane, "Take one of these, we've got to investigate."

The uninspired probing by the soldiers didn't satisfy him and he thought that giving Jane something to do might help her deal with her sorrow. He led her to his approximation of where kids had been held and dragged his rake through the ashes. They pulled at broken bricks and dislodged cracked concrete.

"What exactly are we looking for?" she asked.

"Zombie remains: bones, skulls, bits of clothes … something to show they died when the mortars hit."

"Maybe they dug graves in the school basement and they're waiting to rise again."

"That's what we need to know."

For 30 minutes Jane and Donald poked through ashes. They found charred lumber, bits of desks, broken glass and a few bits of bones, but not nearly enough to account for the annihilation of a horde of undead. At a spot where a chimney had fallen Jane sighted a patch of dull cloth beneath charred bricks and shouted to Donald, "I see something."

They pulled at bricks and rubble. Bits of a charred leg appeared, covered with fragments of burned and shredded pants material.

"Let's try the other end," Jane suggested and they moved to where an upper torso should be. More clearing unveiled a black, mutilated chest from which chunks of flesh had been blown. The body sat upright and a mouthful of gleaming teeth snapped.

Jane's chin quivered and her face paled: she couldn't voice emotions, couldn't move. Her heart ceased beating.

"Brains," hissed Jesse. The thick ash handle of a rake snapped as Donald whacked it over the burned head that had lost its curly hair. A cold hand grabbed Jane's wrist. She recoiled as much as she could with her hand in a bear trap. Bricks from the fallen chimney held the bottom half of Jesse in place. Jane yanked, but mouth-snapping Jesse's hand held tight. Donald hugged her waist and pulled. The body came out of the ground like last season's carrot tugged upwards in autumn. Everything below the navel stayed behind.

"Get over here," Jane shouted to soldiers as she squirmed to keep teeth from reaching her. One brought a shovel, the right tool for the job at hand. Donald grabbed it, swung it and severed Jesse's arm. Jane jumped back. A head and torso clawed itself towards her using one arm. Donald went at the handsome head like he was splitting firewood. It took 20 ferocious blows to break the spine, trachea, oesophagus and assorted vessels and muscles that kept Jesse's head bobbing atop his neck.

Jane's body trembled to throw up and pass out. She buried her face in Donald's chest, shivering. When her deep sobs abated Donald stepped back and she stood alone, surrounded by wreckage, ashes and the body of her fellow warrior. An alien in a lost land would feel more at home.

"It's not over," said Donald.

"Take care of that body," Jane feebly ordered a soldier, voice quivering, barely audible, "That man's a hero."

"That's a zombie. I'm not going near it," the soldier answered.

Jane summoned volume, "That's Corporal Jesse Nesterinko. You'll treat him with the utmost respect. He's a hero." She could speak no more.

Donald finished for her, "Bring two bags, one for head and one for body. Tell your new commander to arrange a proper funeral for this brave man. He'll get medals."

"Do you want to keep that arm?" the private asked with the slightest touch of sarcasm. Jane looked puzzled until she followed his eyes. Donald carefully unwound Jesse's five digits and respectfully placed the appendage next to the body.

Exploding mortars had rattled the basement of the school. The cement roof caved in as Doogie led undead followers through the tunnel they had dug. The passage led gradually upwards and emerged inside an old wooden double garage located on a slight hummock close to the school. A large brick house and a grove of wild, thorny trees hid it. Within, zombies stood shoulder to shoulder. If anyone had walked past, the stench and the mob of angry flies would have alerted them to the presence of an outlandish force.

The chilly, dank interior of Vladimir's Bar reeked of smoke. Never had they allowed customers to light up and now they would never be able to get rid of the stink. Vamps' sensitive nostrils despised unpleasant odors. Taking down the *No Smoking* signs could have improved business, but would have offended good taste. An odor far worse than stale smoke oozed up from the cellar.

At exactly 6 p.m. Veronica, dressed in her usual leather skirt and low blouse that revealed a tsunami of quivering cleavage, stepped into the bleak tavern. Without preamble she spoke, "We can no longer waste away. Tonight the streets are awash with blood donors. In these troubled times discretion and secretiveness go out the window. Tonight we drink. We drink till we are sated, till we overflow, till the cows come home. That's my plan. I have no plan. Drink or die. Don't be cowards; don't be afraid of the future because without blood the future does not arrive. We are vampires, we dress as vampires, we act as vampires. We take a pint from every person we meet. They won't know what hit them and won't remember a thing and we don't care. It's all or nothing. Do or die. We will be flush with the red badge of courage. In 30 minutes, when darkness sets in, we drink. Phone those not present and tell them to get into town and fill up."

56

Doogie cracked open the heavy wooden doors of the garage, looked out then ordered, "Eat yoor hearts oot then bury bodies. Kids we eat in footure, foood for toomorrow."

Pushing, shoving and bumping into each other, we oozed through the doors and, on the street, met a couple of drably dressed adults accompanying a pair of kids with scarred, scabby faces and bloody clothes who moved with the unmistakable gait of junior zombies.

I wondered if some newly-arisen had been added to our tribe, but the parents had no zombie characteristics: no smell that indicated origins beneath the earth. We stumbled towards them. The parents showed no fear and the children's faces lit with glee. That lasted until the first lurchers knocked the adults to the ground and fell upon them. For dessert they lunged at the terrorized children, but I stood stiffly in their way. Propelled by terror, the kids ran off at the speed of fright.

My heart ached as I imagined children being ripped to shadows of their selves. A mouthful would surely make my day, but I couldn't. The idea of baby brain intrigued, but it would horrify and shame me to break the rules. Would Doogie take my sunglasses?

Never again would I eat like a zombie, I vowed, and then wondered what control I had. How could I stop myself from digging in if instinct took over? At least I should use knife, fork and white napkin. I should act civilized. If I could resist children I could resist adults. A trace of smile smudged my macabre visage. This new ability to imagine and speculate intrigued me. I could make pictures in my head, could imagine a future. A picture is worth a thousand turds, I thought, a stitch in time stops on a dime. I could rhyme. I could create poetry.

57

Veronica eyed an adult couple that herded a gaggle of oddly-dressed children clutching bags. She moved quietly behind them and, without a care about who might be watching, spiked the woman's neck. The mother quivered then sagged like a potato sac emptied of spuds. Victor did the same to the man and after the draining he felt young, restless and full of life. Nothing compared to a river of fresh blood rushing through the body, sweeping away logjams of plaque and fat.

Other vamps turned to the children whose bodies had half the blood of adults and started sucking. Draining children was a long-standing verboten, but these were difficult times and vamp bodies had not been properly nourished for weeks. Veronica had told them to go forth and drink. Within minutes six children with painted faces and bright clothing lay on the sidewalk, limp but not lifeless. In the future they could donate again, but they had become orphans. Their parents gave to the greater good.

Groups of kids cried "Shell out, shell out, the witches are out." Their cry should have been "Look out, look out the vampires are out… Look out, look out the zombies are out."

A disguise as a zombie claimed a top 10 spot on the Halloween fashion list, preceded by super-heroes, Disney cartoon characters and cowboys. Vampires, whose fame had waned like twilight, didn't make the list.

58

My role as assistant leader seemed to have ended. To Doogie I must have been a disappointment. I lagged 10 yards behind, feeling sorry for victims; feeling sorry for White Rock; feeling sorry for myself. Feeling sorry was good, even bad feelings were good.

On the sidewalk ahead marched a pair of tots dressed as ballerina and airplane pilot. A short, pretty woman and a hairy, tattooed man, who swigged from a bottle in a brown paper bag, chaperoned them. Dark drool dripped from the mouth of the zomb near me when it spotted the targets. The zomb set sights on the mature, ink-stained meat: tiny kids might follow. I yelled in the loudest voice I had used since rising, "Don't eath them."

The woman's downcast eyes suddenly looked up and she gasped, "Oh my God, not you again."

"Yeth," I gleefully shouted and walked closer. "I talkth bether. We are family."

"You're a fuckin' zombie," Melody shrieked and our children heard. "Don't come near me you sack of shit." Her eyes glazed over and she fainted to the pavement against which her head thumped. The hairy man offered no support.

"I got deothorant and mouthwath," I muttered as she fell. "And don't use bad words with kids."

I stooped to Melody's side and lifted her head. Blood trickled from near her ear and red droplets stained the sidewalk: I licked them up. Then I wanted brains and organs – memories of ovaries from dinners past danced in my head. Just a few nibbles. She would survive and we could live as husband and wife. But I shouldn't devour my wife, the woman of my dreams, the mother of my children. We should mate first and then, like a praying mantis, I'd consume her. Or was it the other way round?

Who ate who? Was it playing manatees did that? Like a doomed insect I would gladly give myself to Melody. I was probably not to everyone's taste, but if it floated her boat, I would offer myself.

The inky lowlife drinking from the brown bag rolled his sleeves over muscular arms and planted punch after punch on the expressionless faces that surrounded him. He loosened some teeth and moved several noses closer to ears, but the recipients of the blows made no howls of objection or cries of pain. They surged, hungry.

Calculus and Abacus patted their mother's limp hand. Abacus shouted, "Daddy still stinks."

I bent over to kiss Calculus, but she recoiled, screaming.

"Are you going to eat Uncle Walter?" Abacus asked.

"No," I mumbled, unsure of the truth and unsure of parental guidelines. Should you always tell children the truth?

"On new diet," I lied, "Only eath peaths, carroths and spinath."

Four zombs surrounded Uncle Walter, got hands on him, pulled him down and the best went to the fittest. Heady, who had not fared well in the fight for organs, hovered over the remains of Uncle Walter. She appeared to be making a decision and then bent over and pulled down his pants. I looked away. She stood, chewed vigorously, swallowed and parts thumped against the tape wrapped around her midriff.

Melony sat up in time to see what remained of Walter and fell back again. Two zombs bent over her, dribbling onto her face. Another grabbed Abacus.

I bellowed "No" and grubby hands let my child go. I smacked the backs of the heads of the two closing in on Melody and again shouted "No." They backed away. I felt powerful. Melody lifted her head and pulled her children into her. No words of thanks came from her mouth so I spoke. "I take you home. Cook dinner. Wath TV. I promith not eat Abacuth and Calculuth."

With a hatred that started at the bottom of her soul and permeated every atom of her existence Melody glared at me then wobbled to her feet with a child in each arm. The foulest of her curses were insufficient to poison my ears, but she tried. I reached for her hand. She shrieked like a burning witch then secured our children and ran. Her legs took her in the direction of the family home and I presumed she wanted me to follow. I hobbled along and kept up, which was not difficult as she carried two children and never did much in the way exercise.

A yellow car pulled up and she got in and pointed to me. Perhaps the taxi would give me a lift too, although I had concerns about my ability to pay the fare, let alone add a tip. The cab's tires screeched. When two wheels mounted the sidewalk I understood its aim was for a fatality rather than a fare. A rock garden offered protection and I scrambled to the far side of a row of boulders. When the car slewed into a U-turn I grabbed the door handle to get in beside my life-long love. The cab sped away taking Melody, my children and two of my fingers. Longingly I gazed after it, my heart heavy with the loss of loved ones and digits. Luckily it was my left so I could still write my diary. So much to say: so little time. Or so much time: so little to say. I knew nothing.

Long ago I had forgiven Melody for her indiscretions. I understood why so many men would love her and how could she resist? Surely she could forgive me for what I had become. Bad diet and body odor were not traits I had taken on of my own choosing. The children could adapt and if they didn't we could adopt.

59

A borrowed squad car started with a race-car roar and Jane began an early sweep of White Rock's hilly streets exactly as she and Jesse had done every Halloween. She recognized Donald walking alone and stopped to ask if he needed a lift. He said that with the school bombed, he had little on his agenda except to locate lost zombies. He asked to ride along and she *agreed*, hoping it would keep her mind off Jesse and help her focus on police business.

Plants and pumpkins dumped on sidewalks constituted the only evidence that local kids carried out pranks on the day of the dead. Tipping an outhouse never entered their thoughts despite the fact, with the army in town, temptation sat at every street corner.

Rural roads and lanes received a quick scan and, as usual, no activities required investigation or intervention. Gaggles of kids did not straggle from suburban house to house as the focus of *trick or treat* shifted to the safety of downtown. Locals, with the enemy annihilated, didn't want kids to miss the annual dress-up and free candy. They saw the leveled school on newscasts and knew no creature survived.

Jane chatted about getting back to normal, locking up the town drunk, giving parking tickets and filing a weekly report in which the most serious crime was an NSF cheque passed at the grocery store. It would be so dull and so welcome. Donald remained quiet as she nervously rattled on.

With the police radio not yet hooked up Jane selected an FM station. Donald thrummed and hummed along with popular songs and she tapped time on the steering wheel. He asked, "What did the zombie eat after his teeth were pulled?"

Jane glanced at him blankly, "Is that the opening for a joke?"

"Yes, zombie jokes got bantered about at the coffee shop. I thought it might amuse you if it's not in too bad taste."

"It's in terrible taste. We've both lost our partners. But if Jesse sat in the back seat right now he'd say 'tell the damn joke.' So what did the zombie eat?"

"The dentist."

"Ooh that's bad."

"Do zombies eat popcorn with their fingers?"

This time Jane was more alert and had a response. "No, they eat them separately."

"You're sharp. OK, one more. What did the zombie professor say to the doctoral candidate?"

"I've no idea."

"Brains."

"Of course. That was obvious."

"Speaking of brains," Donald said, "I'm not 100 percent convinced that's their mantra. Their diction isn't good, it could be *pains* they are saying: they are in pain. To the casual ear the bilabial plosives sound similar."

Jane understood the concept, but didn't want to get involved in a discussion about labia, bi or otherwise. "They deserve to be in pain. I hope they hurt like hell and if there is everlasting damnation they deserve it. Is that it for zombie jokes?"

Before Donald could think of another they approached the town's main crossroads and their eyes locked onto a pair of black boots sticking out from a hedge. Mirth crashed like a racist joke. Attached to the boots was a body bearing all the signs of a zombie feast.

"There's a zombie loose," Jane said dejectedly. She excavated her phone from the depths of her purse and called her location into army headquarters. A dispatcher copied directions and said they already had too much to deal with and abruptly ended the call. A turn onto Johnston St. brought a diorama of carnage: bodies of families ravaged beyond recognition; bodies that appeared untouched by zombies, but were pale, thin, dead or unconscious. It was worse than before the bombing, far worse.

Donald said he knew about vampires and had fallen for the fallacy that the bloodsuckers did no harm. Jane's hardened eyes could not remain dry when she saw six-year-old children, dressed as princesses and action heroes, lying on sidewalks with their tiny, pale bodies looking lifeless. Some, ironically, had dressed as zombies, a few as vampires. Amidst a salty sea of tears she said, "We're supposed to protect them."

Donald's hands draped his face. "I know," he whispered and his wet hand reached for hers.

"Where's the army?" she sobbed, squeezing his fingers. "Where were we, the police, when those poor people needed us? Everyone thought it was over; that they were blown to bits. Who, what, could do that to a child?"

They got out and felt the pulse of a Spiderman boy and a Wonder Woman girl and they were alive. After taking them to the overflowing hospital Jane's foot jabbed the gas and a few minutes later she swung into a parking spot in front of the police station. While issuing orders both in person and over the phone she unlocked cupboards and handed weapons to Donald and the duty officers.

Jane and Donald loaded the borrowed car with shotguns, rifles, tear gas, Z-D-Cappers and confiscated knives and baseball bats. Fueled by anger and hatred they drove three blocks and came upon a festering zombie feasting on remains beyond recognition. Two private cars driven by uniformed RCMP pulled up beside their squad car and each driver received new munitions. Jane pointed to the zombie standing over the body in the park and fired her shotgun from 20 feet. Scalp, hair and ear vanished from the left side of its head. The beast, wearing a pale pink dress with crimson stains, didn't flinch. Jane fired again and the same happened on the right side of its head.

Donald closed to six feet and fired point blank. The forehead and nose vanished leaving bare bone stained with brown liquid. One of the police officers shot his handgun and the left eye became an empty socket as the yellow orb splatted through the back of its skull. With one eye blind and little left of a face the zombie bent and groped for giblets on the ground. The creature, which had a broken spinal column that poked out back, stuffed orts into its mouth and strutted defiantly towards the shooters as if to say, "You can't hurt me, but I'm going to eat you."

Jane circled behind, planted the Z-D-Capper on its neck and was shocked that the zombie swung and grabbed Jane's hair as the blades snapped. The decapper lopped off the arm but its grip remained firm and the arm swung on Jane's back in time with her movements as she reloaded. Another officer approached with an axe and swung wildly, landing a blow that glanced off the creature's shoulder, removing a steak-size chunk. The next chop landed atop the head and split the monster in two, leaving it with an eye and a bit of scalp hanging on the left and an eye hole and some jaw on the right. A few teeth moved up and down, attempting to bite. A second Z-D-Capper finished it off.

"Looks like you need a hand once more." Donald pulled away the cold fingers and arm that clung to her hair.

The noise of gunfire and smell of humans attracted other zombies and before the four could congratulate themselves on the elimination of one beast, a fresh mob of fleshmen stumbled towards them.

Disabling the zombie was easy, thought Jane. If four cops could incapacitate one in a minute they could all be dispatched in a few days. The army should fight as ferociously. Reality hit like a slap with an icy mitt when she saw what surrounded them. It was the humans that could be easily eliminated. The cops backed onto grass then stepped onto the broad pedestal of a statue that Mayor Baldwin had erected of himself. Droolers surrounded them.

Veronica's group had not feasted so recklessly since taking serendipitous advantage of a train derailment in the 1980s. Many, for the first time, could say they were sated. Rosy cheeks and renewed energy accompanied their march through town. Disguise and pretension were abandoned: they were gluttons grabbing double dessert after a buffet.

The number of ruined bodies distressed vamps. If zombs continued their anti-ecological and unsustainable rampage a future with far worse consequences that a hangover headache awaited. Among them they possessed six Z-D-Cappers yet no one had the courage to creep up behind and clip a head, although zombs were everywhere.

Veronica received congratulations for her idea of coming out on Halloween and feasting on a populace that did not recognize them for what they were. The vamps swaggered through town as if they owned it. Swagger came cheap as long as lurchers didn't view them as meals on heels.

Doogie and his group struck the widest path of destruction, mercilessly felling all they came across, making no concessions for sex, race or religion. They tore off turbans to get at brains and held true to the maxim, *it's what's inside that counts*. On Halloween they didn't judge a spook by its cover. Fat and thin, black and white, short and tall, army and civilian got equal treatment. Only children and bloodsuckers got a pass. The latter, with organs like kitty litter used by an incontinent cat, earned their exemptions.

60

A few citizens and four police retreated to the base of a statue and fought a ragged and disorganized group of meat eaters that I tried to lead. To Doogie I must have been a terrible lieutenant. His band of 50 ate its way through an army post while my fellows received split heads and spasmed on the ground. A few of my remaining mates closed on the fighting temps like flies in a butcher shop while others walked in circles and scratched their bellies

The soldiers, blasting with flamethrowers, reduced heads to burning marshmallows on a stick. No one blew them out. Then fuel on the fire-spitting weapons ran out. The demise of the poor peacekeepers seemed inevitable and Doogie licked what he had in the way of lips as he and his disciples lumbered from the remains of the army post to the statue. A chunk of his shoulder vanished in shotgun fire. The fresh green suit provided by a teacher was ruined.

61

An armored tank, covered with revenants, rumbled in from a side street and the three remaining cops cheered the arrival of the cavalry. Through the cloak of undead, the tank driver could see nothing and veered through a frame building that came down like toothpicks. The tank continued up a steep incline of shale until it slid sideways, overturned and rolled in the direction of the statue of the mayor. It crushed several eaters. The disoriented crew assumed the human cloak had been shaken loose and opened the hatch. Ghouls, who no longer feared the tread, jumped in.

A gang of ruddy Draculas headed towards gunshots, figuring the wounded could be easily drained. Storage jars waited to be filled. New blood charging through veins and arteries put them in the right frame of mind for action as long as it was action from a safe distance. The vamps came upon three cops, a few soldiers and a gaggle of locals all clinging to a bronze statue, keeping away from reaching arms. Well-dressed reekers surrounded them.

The vamps got the courage to decap an unaware zomb at the back of the pack. Hands slowly went up in subdued high-fives.

Danger instilled a feeling of nausea that vamps took great pains to avoid. They didn't drive with the gas gauge below half, they didn't stand at the edge of a cliff and didn't dislodge smoking toast with a fork. The long-tooths recalled how a mere prick into a zombie's neck sickened them. Sucking from a tube dipped into the mire below an outhouse would be an improvement over the contents of an undead's carotid. By killing zombs the vamps could secure their long term existence, but zombs gained nothing by killing vamps. The fight was motivationally unfair: precisely the type of battle vamps willingly waged.

A recranked Z-D-Capper snapped off the top of a zomb who turned too slowly. Like a coconut from a tree, the head hit the ground and rolled to a ditch. Battling police saw the head fall and gave a wave of welcome to dark allies. Killing zombies was like shooting fish in a barrel, thought Veronica although she had never actually shot a fish in a barrel. She wondered why fish would be in a barrel. If you missed a fish the barrel would drain through the bullet hole anyway and you could lift them out. She puzzled over this then thrust her cutters at a tall zombie. It grabbed the cutters from Veronica and attempted to whack her. Hand-eye coordination disappeared somewhere between cradle, grave and rebirth: the swing missed. Veronica smirked until a second swing landed above her ear and turned her grin to a grave stare of disbelief. She had never been hit in anger and knew nothing of a wound inflicted by another. Purple fluid foamed from the cut like juice from a hot blueberry pie and steamed down her astonished face. She felt some pain, but not a lot.

The battle paused when an armored carrier with screaming siren roared into the midst of the mayhem and knocked reborn bodies left and right. Standing on top, pointing a shoulder-launch missile, the new colonel shouted directions to the driver. The heavy vehicle rumbled up behind a zombie and drove over her. Despite squishing sounds when tires flattened her breasty chest she rose and clambered aboard the vehicle. One soldier Swiss-cheesed her with a barrage of machine gun fire and another landed the pointed end of a pick-axe deep into her skull where it remained when she pulled back her head. The wounds and the weight of the metal and wood atop her head did not hinder her and she wrapped her hand around the calf of the new colonel. He held her at bay by holding the handle of the axe in her head and steered her around the truck's bed. A soldier aimed his bazooka at the zombie's head, but the colonel screamed, "The gas tank is under us." The soldier jumped to the road, aimed his shooter parallel to the ground and severed the attacker's head in a single blast.

"Baaahzoook," the colonel hollered as the slime-covered shell continued into a house that erupted in flames. The shooter paused to admire the destruction then hopped back aboard as the vehicle rumbled to the nucleus of the fight.

Speed and dexterity kept vamps away from the arms of zombies who saw what the vamps did with the de-capper and didn't like it. Now their leader ordered them to kill vamps despite their bad taste.

Arrival of the new colonel and his truck of dead-eyed shooters allowed Jane, Donald and others to descend from the protective base of the bronze statue and take an offensive position. They used an assortment of traditional weapons plus a Z-D-Capper to battle Doogie and horde.

Vees in the background excitedly decapped any Zee that turned a scabby back. Risk assessment protocol determined that attacking from behind minimized vulnerability.

The cacophony of gunfire ended the town's celebration of the end of zombiedom that had come with the bombing of the school. The resumption of sirens, loudspeakers, bazooka fire, news bulletins and the roar of tanks alerted all to the resumption of a war they thought had been won. The town reeled as if plague, earthquake, firestorm and tsunami hit simultaneously. The emotional blow equalled the physical one. Families wept as news bulletins related that the bombing of the school had accomplished nothing. Mothers raced homewards with crying, disappointed children who left behind trails of candy. Angry fathers followed the noise of gunfire: they weren't going to take it any longer. According to the TV, local police had been forced into action by an inept army; an army that had blown up houses and set stores afire. They had bombed a school whose only inhabitants were school staff and sick volunteers.

Armed with sticks, stones, gardening tools and fighting words, local men and a few women angrily marched into town, merging with other like-minded citizens. Had they held lanterns, an apt comic book caption would have read, "Angry villagers surge forward to confront the enemy."

The members of the noisy mob came face to face, for the first time, with the forces of evil. Their offensive contribution constituted a divergence rather than a force to be feared. Baseball bats, rifles, slingshots and hoes were not going to eradicate anything enjoying a second coming. To zombies and vampires alike, the vigilante mob represented a new supply of food and drink.

The house that had been set ablaze by the bazooka alerted a fire brigade that returned to work the moment the school's bricks turned to dust. Their wailing siren added to the chaos of the battle to save the town. Excited to be dousing an inferno, the fire fighters proved easy prey. Doogie's band abandoned the challenging task of overpowering Jane and Donald's determined group, which received reinforcement from the pathetic posse and the new colonel.

The zombs found rain-coated firefighters whose attention was divided and who anticipated protection from the army. Two firefighters devoted to dousing flames lost lives and livers. Their co-workers, standing atop a pumper, used their only weapon on the carnivorous crowd. The force of water expelled from heavy hoses knocked whoever it hit off their feet and the hosers took pleasure in using their unique weaponry to push back waves of attackers.

Army snipers, safely firing from rooftops, exploited a known weakness in zombie attackers. When they shot them between the eyes – not an easy target – sunglasses broke and they were stunned by the battery of floodlights that illuminated the evening. The talking zomb, short and pudgy, carried a bag of shades and quickly stuck them on the faces of those without. The marksmen shot up the bag of glasses forcing the zomb to rummage until he found eye protectors that would stay on a face. While he did this they put useless holes in him.

Another zombie-cloaked tank churned through town, ripping up streets and trying to get the enemy into its slow-moving sights. The ponderous machine manoeuvred too blindly to get a bead on creatures that moved as if quicksand gripped their legs. Tanks did most damage when they rolled over zombies not wise enough to evade the tread. Flat, corrugated creatures sat up like cardboard snakes. With eyes and teeth crushed they had neither bite nor sight and were easy prey for vigilantes who removed their flat heads with axes.

Tank drivers tried to dislodge swarming zombies by swivelling turrets, driving through thickets and running through broken brick structures. Nothing cleared those who gripped like ticks. Ghoul drool slid down the metal, dripped inside and soaked occupants. Blindly the tanks drove and eventually went over cliffs and into the sea or slid on shale and overturned. For the first time clingers who died or were disabled outnumbered crew.

Personnel carriers with a dozen soldiers armed with grenade launchers, flame throwers, mortars, bazookas and machine guns proved to be the best army offence. Unlimited ammunition riddled attackers with so many holes they could no longer stand. Once the monsters went down, a grenade or two separated head from body in an enormous flesh flood. Soldiers' lives ended quickly when Zombies swarmed transporters.

Confident vampires, immune from vivisection, dished out beheadings until someone got hurt, severely hurt. A zombie, annoyed at having a stick jabbed into its eyes, took a chunk out of the neck of a V who dropped to the ground with an explosion of blood. To say the victim had high blood pressure would be to say Old Faithful oozed some warm water.

Seeing their comrade go off like a crate of Roman candles discouraged the bloodsucking gaggle. "We need a new plan," Veronica sadly intoned and everyone held their breath fearing what might come next. A long silence preceded the realization that she had opened the door to suggestions from others and had nothing to offer herself. When the quiet continued most decided to go home and watch the news on larger-than-life screens. It was far safer than being there and you could regulate the volume. On the recliner-sofa they could relax and enjoy the satisfaction of new blood. A few didn't join the retreat. They enjoyed hiding behind trees with their Z-D-Cappers cocked for flesh-eaters who had the misfortune to turn their backs.

Surviving firemen repelled the continuous onslaught with aquatic blasts. They noticed that when a hard stream of water hit a certain squat zombie bits of skin washed off. Other flesh-eaters felt the fury of hard rivers of water, but only the grey, chubby one suffered. For the rest it was water off a duck's back.

As firefighters hosed the hungry little man his shoulders and arms slowly eroded and grey liquid dribbled from beneath sleeve and pant cuffs. He waddled for cover, but his stubby legs moved him too slowly. An umbrella snapped to attention and vanished in the driving mist. Waterlogged pants fell to his ankles and tripped him. He got up, but little flesh remained on white lower limbs. Bone showed on his skull.

"Help me, I'm droowning," he cried, but no help came and little could be done to save him except turn off the water. That had the same likelihood as a snowball surviving Hades in July. A fireman, shooting water from a long hose, pursued Doogie, sensing a kill as he blasted off epidermal layers. Murky liquid ran from sleeves and then the soaked jacket fell off and joined pants on the ground. Doogie tried to evade the spray, but his bare bone legs snagged on his clothing and he fell into a grey puddle that flowed to storm sewer. He put up his hands in surrender and their flesh washed away.

"I'm melting," were his barely audible last words. The spray got harder as the fireman moved closer, ready to put a notch in his hose. A few steps from the chattering skeleton he blasted the bones and, with no flesh binding them, they scattered in all directions. Sewers carried the undead effluent into the ocean not far from where children paddled in summer.

Disappointment for soldiers and citizens came with the realization that the secret, undead-destroying weapon that everyone searched for had not been discovered. Only one creature fell apart under a jetstream of water.

62

I had the same water weakness as Doogie: my outer layer was made of the same mushy stuff. Never had I washed my hands before or after eating the living. The idea of drinking water made me think of unflushed toilets. As one body among many dozens, it seemed unlikely the humans would identify me as a melter unless spray hit me accidentally. That frightened me. Being frightened pleased me. Another old emotion resurfaced. I wrote that down. Now I could get many words on a page although spelling challenged me.

Doogie's undoing gave me a reprieve. My leash had lengthened and I could make decisions on my own. What a pleasure to make a decision, what a joy to have control over one's actions. Inevitably my thoughts wandered to Melody, our children and a reunion. I would bounce Abacus and Calculus on my knees while I told them stories and looked out the window at the sun's rays playing on the water. I would mow the lawn, trim the hedge, go grocery shopping, taste the coffee and smell the roses.

I remembered her harsh words and stern looks at our last encounter. My love had not been reciprocated. She misunderstood me now as she had misunderstood me in the past. But always we patched up leaks in our relationship. Sometimes I cried and sometimes I begged, but always we remained united. The demise of Uncle Albert and Uncle Walter rushed into my thoughts. In the past other uncles lurked. Young men had been hired to do yard work and painting, but I never ate them. Perhaps I should have. They were very muscular and good looking but didn't want to be my friends. They wanted to be Malady's friends.

I had to convince my wife I was a good man with an eating disorder. Skin problems and a touch of halitosis could be remedied. I would get back my job. The teachers' union would support my taking time off because we were allowed emotional leave. Monday would be the right back-to-work day, but I didn't know Monday from doomsday. As well as being a teacher, father, boyfriend and husband I was a zombie. Too many roles: which one to play? Making the right decision had the same likelihood as turning vegan.

    I didn't give orders the way Doogie gave them. They obeyed him when he lifted their sunglasses, looked deep into their eyes and uttered burbling, waterlogged commands and threats. Body language, especially hand gestures, accompanied Doogie's instructions. Zombies liked charades.

    A water bomber flew overhead and dropped fire retardant on flaming buildings. I didn't see it coming, but my station beneath a wide tree protected me from most of the deluge. A stream of red liquid dripped through the branches like a leak in an umbrella. A patch of wet mush fell onto my shoulder. There went my good ear.

63

Jane, Donald, the new Colonel, the disorganized army, malingering vampires, surviving firefighters and remnants of a posse fought into the night. Guns blazed, zombies ate, Z-D-Cappers snapped and teeth gnashed. So many eviscerated temps paved the road that it looked like a mortuary. Flat, dry corpses appeared incapable of returning to life even if inflated with an air compressor. Zombie heads rolled onto the road like a bowling alley without pins.

Whenever the allied forces reached the verge of victory more zombies raged from doorways and alleys and a win, once so close, moved out of range. Whenever the undead approached victory, more soldiers and citizens joined the battle, tossed grenades and swung axes: balance returned. Fire hoses claimed no more victims. Only two, having ascended from Davey Jones's locker, had a body structure that water had preserved and water could destroy. One of them remained under cover and out of range.

Jane and Donald fought at the nucleus and the new Colonel smashed through a sea of stench to join them. He fought recklessly and shouted, "Another zombie to hell," whenever an undead head departed its body. Jane harbored too much fear to make a sound other than the occasional grunt when she put another bullet through a putrid head that refused to go down despite more air passing through it than through a screen door. Donald talked sarcastically to zombies he imagined he knew.

"Good evening Mr. Morrison, aren't you the green grocer? How about a head of cabbage?" He swung his axe. "Hello Mrs. Saunders, enjoy your new split personality. Goodbye Reverend Larkin. Hope you enjoy your stay in hell."

"I didn't know you had a morbid sense of humor," Jane shouted.

"That's fear cracking jokes − a defence mechanism."

Firefighters, trapped by zombs, couldn't put out blazes caused by badly aimed weapons. The town was on fire. Through the night angry citizens joined the melee as did fresh soldiers and police from distant jurisdictions. Some lost lives and others became mentally depleted after hours of battling. Citizens questioned what had possessed them to join a war and tried to sprint homewards through the monster mosh.

Among the quitters were the last vampires who could no longer handle the tension. Despite not being in danger of being eaten, they were in danger of being killed because they had sided with the temps and in so doing became enemy. Just before 3 a.m. the last V's cashed in their chips and dodged homeward to warm, welcoming PosturePerfect mattresses with lifetime warrantees. Their departure did not mark a turning point in the battle. as it mattered little, in the big picture, that none of the dark force remained to behead the occasional stray at the back of the pack. They would not be confused with Green Berets.

Before the brightening sky announced morning the situation worsened in an unforeseen way. Civilian casualties and soldiers who had died in culverts and ditches and had a layer of dirt pushed over them by Doogie's tribe, returned to life as famished zombies and joined the fight. They wanted brains and fought hardest to get them. The playing field tilted.

Jane, Donald and the new Colonel, exhausted and sleepless, continued to battle side-by-side with trigger fingers blistered and arms aching. Only a dozen foot-soldiers, assorted snipers, a plumber, a pharmacist and two firefighters, atop their truck, remained at the core. The zombie horde surrounded and minute by minute came closer. At the perimeter, where it was safer, soldiers fought

"Got a plan?" Jane asked in desperation.

"Fight till I die," Donald shot back.

"To hell, monster." The new Colonel fired a bazooka through the head of a zombie and into a distant car which exploded. The beast's remains collapsed, never to bite again. A closer cannibal got a hand on the new Colonel's leg.

"Zombie grope," he shouted and Jane pounded the hand with her rifle butt. The attacker pulled the leg to its teeth and bit into Achilles tendon. Another zombie, oblivious to a barrage of bullets, stumbled forward and pulled new Colonel's other leg. He went down and Jane knew no hope remained, nothing could save him. Those who went down never came up.

"Don't let me be one of them," the Colonel roared and those were his last words. A bullet from Donald went through the new Colonel's cranium. No one could chop off his head to prevent him rising the next day.

"Any regrets?" Jane shouted to Donald.

"We should have gone on a date," he gasped.

"Dinner and a movie? Pawn of the Dead might still be showing."

"I don't have a car. Do you mind walking?"

"Not at all. We could …" Jane didn't finish her sentence. Grey, bony fingers of a wall-eyed creature pulled her shoulder and she staggered backwards. The plumber fighting beside her swung his axe, missed the attacker's head, but chopped off part of an arm and then lost his balance with the follow-through. Two creatures from the grave got him.

The police chief feared the same fate as putrid faces plunged the plumber. He screamed he had children to look after and he would find plump people for them to eat if they would just spare him. A bullet gave him the same relief as it gave the new Colonel.

64

Pushed to the front of the fight by salivating soldiers of misfortune, who filled gaps left by those who took a fatal hit, I had a prime view of the meat market battling beneath the statue. My soldiers refused to follow the orders I shouted. I didn't stand tall as their new commander. My words did not have the clarity or command of Doogie's even when I pulled off sunglasses and slapped heads.

A small school for tots and toddlers stood within a 20 minute shuffle. In the morning it would burst with jubilant children excited to learn to read, write and understand numbers. I yearned to teach: Cardinal numbers are ordinary and pies have square roots.

I stepped onto a curb and then backed onto a platform supporting another bronze statue of another local hero. A dozen yards away a nucleus of living bodies managed to hold off my soldiers. I eyed the female cop, slightly plump, and imagined she would taste as good as Heady had. As always, Heady stood beside me: silent and faithful. My legs trembled: I think sweat formed on my back. The glazed stares of human fighters made me think of the daze of the weak. There were about seven left.

"There ith more meath, fresh baby meat." I shouted as loud as I could and lot of drool came forth. A scooping motion of hand to mouth indicated that redder pastures lay ahead. Both my hands pointed to a narrow path that led to the pre-school. Despite the saliva surplus I upped the volume and bellowed, "Thith path take uth to more meat, baby brainth. New school."

Heady understood. She pulled bodies from the fight and pointed them to the path I indicated. Her brain transplant must be working.

I randomly pushed up sunglasses, stared into vacant eyes and repeated, "Take thith path." I jabbed in the right direction with all fingers except the missing ones. Zombs with ears that didn't hear and with rains that didn't think slumped in the right direction as if a teacher had given them a detention and they had to go and serve it.

With hand rubbing stomach, I sent the message that ripe children would be served at the end of the path.

65

Jane heard poorly pronounced words come from the mouth of a relatively young zomb who pointed towards a path. It mumbled about a school.

Two of the monsters about to attack her were pulled away by an undead soldier who wore a sock on her head. The private pulled more from the fray then turned and shambled away. Jane surmised the talking dead may have figured out there was no longer sufficient food at the battle site. Starving, newly-risen wanted to eat, but not enough remained to go around. A march to a nearby school could produce new stock; new hostages for an exchange.

KinderKids preschool opened in an hour and a shiver of fear quaked through Jane's tired body at the thought of going through it all again. She prayed the army would get there first. Then she had second thoughts, grabbed her phone and ordered road blocks and extra security at the school.

66

I moved from one agitated, bloodthirsty zomb to another, calming them with a stare and a repeated order. When I turned them around and pushed them towards the path they continued lurching in the right direction. Others followed. Zombies were like sheep, but not as smart. Wading among the carnage, taking shot after shot to head and body, I yelled, "Retreath," and was surprised that they did. The last eaters, fighting the remaining humans, deserted the battle and joined their comrades in the march for more meat.

Along a dirt trail I slowly shuffled with my soldiers. They trudged in disarray while moaning and groaning, possibly in protest, possibly in hunger, possibly in pain. Loud words and hand to mouth motions promised a great feast ahead. Without much cognitive ability they followed, smelling the kindergarten. From her station at the rear Heady kept the horde moving.

The narrow trail twisted upwards, across a hillside and then down to a park and the school. I had walked it a hundred times without revelling in the beauty of nature, without stopping to smell the wild roses, without enjoying butterflies that landed on my shoulder. I had things on my mind: shopping lists, bowling scores and dentist appointments. Now I walked senseless, still blind to nature, fighting the urge to tear apart people and consume them. I had seen so many die! I was hungry; I hadn't eaten lately. I couldn't smell roses and butterflies did not land on my shoulder. The surf broke below and I could hear it and fear it.

I led the sorry parade and Heady trundled behind making sure no one changed whatever mind they had. A herding instinct took hold. The trail wound uphill for 10 minutes then twisted between two boulders and turned sharply left. Heady worked her way to the front.

The lights of town faded and not one of the walkers appreciated the beauty of the land in the thickening morning mist or appreciated the sounds of rolling ocean waves or heard the animated cries of seagulls. I blocked the path at its turn, waved Heady ahead onto a flat gravel spot where hundreds of hikers had stopped to enjoy the view. She stepped forward. Despite the eau d'zombie from her rotting transplants and her limited conversation I was getting to like her. Her feet shuffled on dirt and stones. She stepped into the fog, but didn't stop to enjoy the view. Silence followed.

I tried to think clearly about what should happen next. After a second came her splash.

One by one I directed the lemmings to shuffle ahead onto the gravel and one by one they lumbered into the dull morning mist. One by one came splash after splash. When none remained at the end of the long procession I scribbled a page of sorry words and placed my notebook on a rock. The last I wrote, "You can't know life till you know death." That was profound. I stepped forward and looked down at the ocean I loved and loathed. I felt shame for what I had done, although I knew something beyond my understanding had driven me. The experience made me a better man and a better zombie. Perhaps I would be resurrected and things would go better. Instead of eating I would mow the lawn, wash the dishes and do other things I had once considered work. I understood what it was to be alive.

"It ith a far, far bether thing I do," I said quietly, not remembering how Dick, or was it Charlie, had written it. "Ith a bether rest I go to."

I shuffled two steps forward and fear clenched its steely hand around my throat. I welcomed feelings, even fear of water. I stepped ahead. No one heard the splash and for the second time in my life I was dead in the water.

67

In town a few lone zombies who didn't see the big picture were dealt with. Grenades and rocket launchers could be deployed without worry about hitting or missing their targets as little remained to be destroyed and the smouldering town was nearly deserted.

The new colonel got his wish as Jane and Donald made sure his body was among those thrown onto a flaming fire truck. The survivors didn't wait for a court order: they cremated every dead body, whether vampire, zombie, soldier or citizen. As they worked, the lack of gunfire brought curious citizens from their homes. Some brought coffee and food and others brought weapons that seemed token gestures as they knew the battle had been fought and won. Everyone wanted to celebrate with a big party, but they had made that error before.

Jane and Donald wanted nothing but sleep and that's what they got after the last body burned.

Vamps, mentally depleted, took taxis to cemeteries in towns several miles distant and, full of blood, found quiet security within crypts where others dared not go. They would wait for better times. When they emerged Vladimir's bar would be rebuilt and in new hands. New electronics stores would be open with exciting products.

Jane and Donald slept all day then kept their date. They walked to the theatre and walked out of the movie after 30 minutes. It portrayed the night creatures as pathetic, defenceless things that could be downed with a single shot to the head.

"Were it only that easy," they said, almost simultaneously, upon exit.

At dinner they happily held hands until their medium-rare steaks arrived: they couldn't stomach them. Omelettes were substituted and then they dug into apple pie with vanilla ice cream. After dinner they strolled towards Tim's for coffee. Out of the dusky dark they heard "brains" from behind bushes and quickly turned, terror pounding within hearts that could take no more.

Behind a hedge a girl bent forward with arms in front as she stumbled towards a gaggle of youngsters who screamed, ran a few feet, then stopped.

A boy shouted, "Let's play something else. I'm bored. Zombies are stupid."

Author

Jim Couper lives quietly in the town of White Rock. He has written three travel books and one work of fiction. His travels and writings can be found on Facebook and he can be contacted at okedits@hotmail.com

Homeward I Lurched was first published by an Australian house under the name Zombie Angst. Originally set in Peachland, B.C. the locale has been changed as has much of the content. Excerpts have appeared in books of short stories published in London, England. The Canadian author, born in Scotland, has traveled in close to 100 countries. This book is printed in United States.

CPSIA information can be obtained
at www.ICGtesting.com
Printed in the USA
LVHW010939230821
695886LV00002B/129

"You can't know life until you know death.

She vowed: in sickness and in health, for better or for worse, till death do ... This was just a rough patch.

Like a bloated fish floating up from the depths of a polluted pond my name surfaced.

Why did I lurch along like I carried bags of bowling balls?

She glared at me with a hatred that started at the bottom of her soul and permeated every atom of her existence."

— Mortimer Smithers

"Daddy ate Uncle Albert."

- Mortimer's son

"Rare that book comes along with a perpendicular take on such a well established genre, and succeeds on so many levels. Not your average zombie book!"

-L. Schroeder

Jim Couper is an author in multiple types of media and the founder of several magazines. His take on the zombie genre is a compounded product of decades of enjoying the classic films as well as a contemporary sense of humour and a desire to bring something new to something so well established. Based in British Columbia, Canada, he writes about travel and travels about writing.